LOUISA

Jenn LeBlanc

The Lady's Secret and Her Lover

Dedication

FOR AMANDA

my thanks :

RHONDA MERWARTH :
EDITING

PRODUCTION :

KATI RODRIGUEZ :
ASSISTANT OF ALL THE THINGS

SHELLY DAS :
PRODUCTION

KIMBERLY DISTEL :
MAKE UP / HAIR

CHAOS :
JOHNNY, ADAM, SALTER, AND ALL MY
WEDNESDAY NIGHT PEEPS

credits:

LADY LOUISA ALICE PRESENT
Jess Adams

MAITLAND ALLISON ELIOTT RIGSBY
Katie Phillips

HUGH GARRISON, BARON ENDSLEIGH
Jordan Farris

CHARLES JACKSON, DUKE OF CASTLEBERRY
Dave Collins

AMELIA
Shelly Das

This book is a love letter to my readers...

When The Duke and The Baron came out (under the title Absolute Surrender) you fell in love with Amelia, Charles, and Hugh. You also fell in love with Amelia's ladies maid Louisa, and her love, Maitland. You asked for their story, even though you knew it was a tragedy and to be honest, I'm grateful.

This book took five years to write, for a lot of different reasons, but the biggest one is that it's not an easy story to tell. I've always known Louisa's story. I knew what happened to her when I wrote Amelia's story. I've always known how special Louisa is. But I've never been in the habit of intentionally telling tragedies, and that's how I saw her story. Sure she gets her HEA so it isn't a true tragedy— but what she has to go through to get there is and it broke my heart.

Louisa is one of the sweetest and bravest women I've written. She's very self aware, but quite sheltered in the beginning. Her path to her forever is fraught with introspection and fear. The ending in this case does not make up for the journey, but I do believe I did my best. We can call it mother's guilt.

Does it make the story a bit too sweet? Perhaps. I could have made it much more angsty, I hear I'm good with the angst. But I wanted something beautiful and simple for Louisa. I wanted happiness and I wanted everything taken from her to be restored under no uncertain terms.

Sometimes I think we need a story that is unbelievably sweet so the rest can be savored. I guess this, for me, is that book.

It's also a farewell— for now.

I know there are more stories in the Lords of Time Saga. I know Celeste and Calder have a few things they'd like to say to each other. And I'm sure Gray has found at least three words he'd like to share about his brother's return. For now though, I'll be leaving the world in peace with HEA's all around.

I truly hope you've enjoyed this trip with me and these beautiful souls who've graciously allowed us into their private lives, even if it was—for some— a bit begrudgingly (You know who you are— Grayson)

It has given me an enormous amount of pride bringing these stories to life, and sharing them with the world, and hearing from you that you love these people just as much as—and possibly more than—I do.

Hugs n' smooches,

The illustrations are meant to be a work unto themselves.

They aren't meant to depict the scenes with perfect accuracy in setting, costuming or design. They're meant to accompany the text and evoke the emotions of the scenes in the same way the words do. More of a companion than a direct visual translation.

Certainly you will notice discrepancies between the scene and details in the images, but that's the nature of creation, some things don't work visually when they do work with words.

Thank you for understanding.
I hope you enjoy this illustrated edition of Louisa.

Epigraph:

MERE AIR, THESE WORDS,
BUT DELICIOUS TO HEAR.

~Sappho

Before

London, England

1878

ALL THE WHILE, BELIEVE ME,
I PRAYED OUR NIGHT
WOULD LAST TWICE AS LONG

~Sappho

Louisa

Louisa sailed through the crush that heralded the beginning of the season. She put on quite the show, considering it was her third, but she was well practiced. She staked out the perfect position—on the left wall as you entered, midway down, between the potted palms.

One, so she could see everyone who entered, and two, so she could see everyone who spent entirely too much time off in the gardens. Knowledge was power in society.

Her first season had been nerve-wracking because she'd needed a husband—or so she'd been trained to think. When she hadn't landed a husband by the end of the season and life had continued on as it had for her first seventeen years, she'd begun to wonder what the purpose of marriage would be.

Of course it was for the children and household management and knitting and subjugation, and etcetera, *ad infinitum*. Yes, she understood *that* facet of it. What she failed to see was...to what end? Louisa couldn't see why spending her life as the subject of a man was reasonable, expected, and even—*dare she think it? Oh...she dared*—looked forward to.

There'd been girls in her first year, and girls in her second year as well, who'd spoken volumes on love and enchantment with such desperate longing it had started to sound more like a plague than matrimony. Louisa, for her part, couldn't look at a man and understand why—*why* anyone would want to spend their life tending one. Or tending *to* one...and his cock. And so she didn't pursue any.

Sure she danced, sure she was courted, but she remained aloof and let her mother believe the men were simply not interested no matter how hard she tried—and a few of them did try, more than she wanted them to. She'd had hands in places she wished to never feel hands again. Hard and calloused, soft and mushy, manicured and scratchy, none of them pleasing and one particular set quite the opposite of that. She couldn't figure why anyone would wish for any of that. Not ever.

Perhaps if they were delicate, gentle, searching—

She shook it off and glanced around the ballroom for that particular man—the one who'd attempted liberties—for she refused him the moniker of "gentlemen" even if society bestowed it him. Even if society bestowed him much more than that. She didn't see him so she took a deep breath to calm her nerves. He was probably off playing cards with her father, which was good, because she wouldn't have to keep an eye out for him while attempting to be unattainable as well as available.

Louisa twitched her fan open and returned to watching the room. The new set of girls would be arriving, and she wanted to scout them because most of her friends from the last season were off bearing children. She needed a new set in order to survive, a group of girls who would look out for one another making sure nobody was left behind, or gone too long from the ballroom with any one gentleman.

Louisa knew most of the ladies who'd come out this season... at least, she knew *of* them. She hoped this year she might find at least one other girl who wasn't so determined to marry that they might become friends and remain so for a bit longer than she and the girls from previous years. She'd tried to keep up with them, but once married, it was all *Manage the household! Have the babies! Clean the nappies!*

Disgusting business, even if it was necessary. Though, having the babies was something she understood, for she did want children...just, maybe, some she could perhaps borrow. Some she didn't necessarily have to keep, or clean, or birth, or—for that matter—create. She had no interest in childbearing. Child rearing, perhaps, but the one wasn't possible without the other. Not for a woman.

She watched a group of young ladies milling about the room, shifting from the front of the ballroom toward the gardens and knew they were a green bunch. Placing themselves near the gardens was a new girl's mistake and their matrons weren't paying attention. As the night went on, they would catch a chill, and their wraps would be wrapped tighter—their wares less visible.

Louisa shook her head. She shouldn't be so cold and bitter. Perhaps she should go over and wish them well. Perhaps her new friend would be in this group...perhaps she would find even more than friendship.

She shook the thought off once again and inspected each of the girls individually, judging their hair, their dress, their mannerisms. She closed her eyes, admonishing herself. She refused to become one of *them*, one of the *ton*, one of *those people* who thought of the new year of girls simply as the next year's selection for marriage. As chattel. She wouldn't. She'd been one of the chattel, still was really.

A shudder wracked her spine, and she opened her eyes this time, truly looking at them, knowing how nervous they were, set apart from the rest by their virginal white gowns—a cluster of fluffy soft clouds amidst the hardened jewels of society, so easily damaged. She smoothed the fabric of her own blue gown and realized she didn't want to be counted as one of the hardened jewels either, so she needed to stop the cynicism. She needed to be the woman she'd never had, caught somewhere between matron and innocent, the woman who *knew* but could still walk amongst the lilies.

She glanced back up to the group and tried to see them differently. One girl stood with her back facing the room—the ultimate faux pas. Her gown wasn't quite bright white but more of a blush on a rose, the very hint of flesh trimmed with a pink so subtle even the flower itself wasn't aware of it. Louisa could tell from the dress this girl was money, for a dress of that style would only be attainable at the finest of shops. Louisa's eyes followed the neckline down one arm to a reticule dangling and swaying as she fidgeted with the string that bound it to her. She watched that reticule twist and turn, as a leaf on the wind, then followed the line of buttons on the inside of the girl's wrist up to the edge of the glove near her shoulder. Her skin was so pale, like it wasn't told it should be separate from her gloves, or her dress. She was so awash with pale, so lacking in any true color, it was as though she were hiding in plain sight.

Louisa could see the tension ripple across the girl's back through the shift of muscle and as she turned her head, her chin dropped to her shoulder. Her eyelids fluttered, and Louisa could see from where she stood the only color this subtle wash of a girl carried— and it struck her at the center of her chest like an arrow to the heart. Deepest lavender. Her heart stuttered in her chest as her hand fluttered at her breast, and Louisa attempted to contain her reaction before anyone saw.

This girl was not hiding within reach of the *ton* jewels—she was their crown jewel, and they'd yet to figure that out. Someone should tell them before she was lost to some poor sap who wouldn't worship her as she should be worshipped.

The girl raised her shoulder a touch as if to remind her spine to hold her body straight and tall—and it did. Then she lifted her chin, and the brilliant color of her eyes was lost to Louisa. She felt the loss like a blow, even as she swayed toward her, wishing to run a finger along the edge of her jaw to lift her gaze. The creep of a warm flush traveled Louisa's shoulders, arrowed down her spine, loosening her hips.

The girls' neck —decorated with the silky spun strands of her pale blond hair— elongated, became regal, held her perfectly. Louisa watched those strands as they shifted across her skin, loosed from the perfect chignon at her nape, and Louisa realized she hadn't taken a breath in a very long time.

The girl turned. Looked directly at her. Louisa coughed at the rush of air to her lungs, the lavender gaze held hers curiously, and Louisa fell back between the potted palms, realizing they had one other use Louisa hadn't conceded—they were good for hiding.

Ellie gave up trying to find the woman who'd caught her attention and turned back to her friends—group—set— whatever they were. All that held them together was the fact they'd all come out this year. As if they'd been kept away from all good society. Locked away like so many little mice striving for their chance in the sunlight. And wasn't that the ultimate tease? Such a game...the white dresses announcements as loud as a circus barker: *"Wait until you see what we have for you to choose from this year. Sixpence a stocking! Not to your liking? Wait until next year! Next year will be even better..."*

The problem was convincing a man to offer for you the first year, because the following year, the shine would wear thin. The opening of the *Season* was to put them on display for the gentlemen—one of which would be her husband. Hopefully as quickly as possible so she could be done with it. Her entire life had revolved around this moment—and those that followed—in the service of a husband. She hoped he would be kind.

She felt another chill and turned again hoping to see *her* again, but this time she met the eyes of a striking man. Tall and blond. He smiled perfunctorily at her, then turned away. She filed the memory for later since he seemed interesting, not here for the wares, as it were.

She'd have to find out who he was, if he were worthy, and whether to set her cap for him. For while the cats circled, the mice plotted. They were much more well-trained than any mouse had a right to be, and for the most part were no simpering misses—at least not on the inside. As the pickings for good husbands had waned over the years, the mamas had upped their game, hiring professional

matchmakers to train the girls what to look for in a man and how to catch them. So while those cats thought they were in control... truly they weren't. The machinations of many decades of practiced matchmaking held everyone in its sway.

The season is on, the game afoot—once more unto the breach, dear friends! She smiled to herself.

Ellie attempted to listen to the conversation of the other girls but became overly bored. Couldn't they, for one single minute, discuss something other than the men? She turned to Georgianna. "I believe I'll take a moment in the retiring room, Georgianna. Would you like to accompany me?" she asked, for they were never to go anywhere alone. Wolves and all. But Georgianna was obliviously batting her eyes at that blond who was perfectly terrified.

Ellie laughed behind her glove, then turned. She could manage one trip to the retiring room, heaven's sake. There were matrons everywhere tonight. She pushed her way through the crowds, occasionally pinching some immoveable person from her path.

"Maitland."

She turned at the voice and dipped a quick curtsey. "Mama."

"Viscount Mayjoy and his daughter are here tonight. Find her. She's well on the shelf but she's still invited because of her father so she'd be the perfect companion. Entry to all the biggest events without competition."

"Yes, Mother. If you could point her out I'll try, but for now I must go. I was with Georgianna and we mustn't separate."

"Of course," her mother said then shooed her on her way. Ellie wasn't of a mood for this.

She pushed her way into the retiring room and flumped herself into a chair, allowing her skirts to float around her as they wished. She watched the silk flutter to the floor. She'd no wish to return to the ball. It was the loneliest crowd she'd ever been in. Somehow in her mind it had all seemed so much more glamourous.

Water rushed in the attached water closet, and she straightened herself. She positioned herself coyly, knees together, feet to the left, tilting her knees demurely, her hands clasped on the reticule in her lap. She cocked her chin and gazed at the door to the main house as though she were awaiting someone.

She heard a gasp—not much more than an inhale—and turned to find the girl, *that* girl, the beautiful brunette from the potted palms. A shiver rushed her spine, sending her to her feet. "It's you," she whispered, then glanced behind the girl and waited to see if she were alone.

When her gaze returned, the girl was staring at the floor, straightening her skirts and her posture. Ellie knew this action well, as they were all constantly straightening, pulling, pushing, and arranging themselves to their best advantage. But the girl never looked up—and she wanted her to.

"I saw—" Ellie stopped; she shouldn't call her out. It was already obvious they both knew who the other was from that moment in the ballroom. "My name is Miss Rigsby, Maitland...Rigsby. Eliot. Maitland Eliot Rigsby." She shook her head, as though it would help un-jumble her thoughts. "My friends, should I have them someday, will call me Ellie." She shook her head again—she was making a mockery of herself, and the girl still wouldn't meet her eyes. Ellie walked closer and put her hand out in greeting then as a chill rushed her skin from the door opening, she snatched it back.

A gaggle of women entered the room, their chattering filling the small space as they pushed between her and the girl in blue. The women walked to the wall with the mirrors, speaking amongst themselves as if she and the girl weren't even in the room. The girl seemed to make no notice of it, and Ellie took the chance to inspect her. *If she would only look up.* Her dress was sapphire, not the deep blue of the crystal, but somewhere close to it, where the light refracted and tossed about its bright happiness, somewhere between midnight and the dusky summer sky.

The neck was higher than it ought be, if Ellie were being honest about their purpose here tonight, and certainly her purpose must be one and the same. She should be teasing, and yet the edge of this girl's dress wasn't one to tease, even as her unsteady breath pushed her chest against her stays and rose a flush to her neck. She wondered why she would wear it. She was young, clearly unmarried, and all the young, unmarried ladies had a singular purpose...

Her breath stopped suddenly, and Ellie tried again to catch her gaze. Her eyelashes, thick and black against her flushed cheeks, were the most beautiful things Ellie had ever seen. Like pieces of mink, perfectly placed and begging for her to run a finger against the tips. They would be so soft. Ellie closed her eyes and took a deep breath to slow her racing heart because surely, *surely*, this girl was beyond her somehow. Her beauty, her poise. Ellie should allow her to go about her business.

When she opened them, the girl was still holding her hands before her, and Ellie was certain she'd never once looked up. If she could only— A cackle from one of the women at the mirrors stopped Ellie from moving, and she saw the girl tense. *Please stay,* Ellie thought as she waited patiently, fervently praying the girl didn't take the opportunity to flee.

The gaggle turned, their chatter unceasing. *Please, please don't join that crowd. Please, please don't disappear from me now.* The crowd moved again, like a murder of crows, and Ellie held her breath as they moved between them and returned from whence they came, and the girl in blue waited still.

Ellie breathed. She watched as the girl closed her eyes, then opened them. She seemed to be composing herself, and Ellie was happy to allow it if it meant she would finally speak to her, because for some reason Ellie felt her entire future would hang on whatever this girl had to say.

When she caught her gaze, Ellie's breath was stolen from her— eyes she never would have expected shimmered like sapphires from beneath those lashes, and the dress suddenly made perfect sense. This girl's eyes were wide and wise and the deepest blue. Neither of them moved. "You'll call me Ellie," she said, and realized it was the most ridiculous moment of her life, but that it called forth a smile from this girl—oh, how she would give her life away right now to hear her speak, to know her name. Or to hear her own name on the girl's breath. Ellie stilled and waited once again.

It seemed too long a wait but she finally approached, feeling completely out of control of her own actions. She lifted one hand and took hers in greeting and leaned forward their cheeks were a breath apart, her skin warm. She lingered, closing her eyes and breathing of her. This was no girl, this was a woman, and didn't Ellie know it.

Louisa

You'll call me Ellie. Louisa had been so frightened at first that she'd smiled without looking. She hadn't been yet ready to meet those wondrous eyes, but the assumption Ellie'd made in that simple phrase was the most beautiful sentence in the history of speech.

She'd been terrified to meet her gaze, because this thing—it wasn't like anything she'd ever experienced in all her life. It's how she expected to feel when she met a husband. Explained time and again by happy wives everywhere before they bid their goodbyes and disappeared from her life because she was yet unwed...no longer of their set.

She was constantly losing friends. It was exhausting to begin again, year after year. She just wanted one friend who wouldn't abandon her because of her circumstance.

Louisa paused her maundering, closing her eyes and taking a deep, steadying breath. It wasn't the time for this.

She believed herself composed enough to be able to gaze into Ellie's eyes and not give away how incredibly flustered she was. And so she did. But she'd been wrong, so wrong, so very, very, wrong. It seemed forever before she could speak. She was trying so hard to find words, her name, *a vowel*...anything with which she could greet the angel before her. For she was an angel, haloed in the blondest hair, the only depth of color those eyes, those deep, mesmerizing lavender eyes. She blinked as though to clear whatever fog created the illusion.

She opened her mouth and willed herself to speak but "Lou—" was all that came out. She looked away again, a pinch of tension between her shoulder blades.

Ellie took her hand and said, "Lou is a beautiful name."

And Louisa melted, let the feel of it embrace her. Ellie pulled her to the settee as she attempted to speak again. "Louisa," she said, "Present. Louisa Present." And they sat together. She had so many questions but all she could manage was to gaze in those eyes and try to stutter some sort of explanation as to why she was behaving so terribly. "I... Your eyes," she said.

Ellie looked down as if to hide them, but Louisa ducked her head and fought for them because they were stunning...there were no other words and now that she'd braved meeting them, she refused to relent. "My grandmother, she said I was born a ghost. You know, all this pale skin...hair," Ellie said, "but a fairy kissed my eyelids, giving me these eyes as a gift to balance it out."

"Were I a fairy," Louisa whispered and Ellie smiled and it filled her tip to toe with a lemony sunshine she couldn't contain. "It's your first season?" Louisa asked more out of politesse than anything else.

"Yes... not yours though," Ellie said with a soft smile.

"No... no."

"Are you here with... anyone?"

"No, I—" Louisa realized she'd have to tell Ellie whose daughter she was—a viscount with a terrible reputation. "My father is here. Viscount Mayjoy." Then she held her breath, hoping she still had a friend.

"Mayjoy?" Ellie replied and though she stifled it, Louisa noticed the slightest sadness before Ellie caught herself. Louisa looked away, pulling her hands to her lap and threading her fingers together.

Ellie

"Mayjoy, I—I'm not familiar. You must not have an eligible heir in your midst," Ellie said with a smile, hoping Louisa understood her jest, and she did seem to relax a bit. She should tell say something but she wanted to know everything about this girl and she was afraid if she said something, anything, the wrong thing, that she'd be gone. She was like a butterfly shuddering on a leaf ready to take off at any moment, and Ellie didn't want to spook her.

Quite honestly, Ellie wasn't sure how to behave because Louisa was stunning in a way she'd never considered. Beyond knowing whose gown was made by which maker and such, she hadn't ever paid any mind to any other girls. But right now, with her...she'd never seen a woman with such blue eyes and such dark hair. It was intoxicating, and she could _not_ stop staring. She'd never thought much of her own violet eyes. They were unique for being a shade different from the rest, but to have blue eyes with such depth and variation—Ellie believed that to be truly unique. Like the sky and the sea had been painted there and only now fought for control. Or perhaps it was the way she felt weightless when searching the depths of them.

Her etiquette training demanded Ellie turn away, but she couldn't. Ellie knew it must be awkward; she knew she should be saying something.

Louisa spoke. "Are you enjoying your coming out?"

"I— Well, as I've only just... I suppose."

"I find it all rather tedious. Months of studying the news sheets and Debrett's coupled with years of lessons for proper etiquette and behavior. I honestly see no point in all this tradition. What's a woman to do with all these skills except to manage a man's household? Women are trained up with the sole purpose of finding and tending a man and his wishes." Louisa picked at a thread on her skirts.

"You've no interest in finding a husband?" Ellie asked then, holding her breath.

"I didn't say that, exactly...or at all, really. Though I suppose you could take it that way, and I... I don't believe this atmosphere is terribly conducive to finding someone with whom you'd be able to spend the balance of your life. That's all." Louisa smiled.

"Well, having a husband is quite different from having a companion is it not?"

"Is that what you're looking for? A companion?"

"Yes, I think, more than anything."

"A lady after my own heart," Louisa said. "I want the same."

Ellie let out the breath that had caught. Suddenly this felt like so much more than simple friendship. "Oh, I'm no lady, not like you."

"It's but a word, isn't it? I was lucky enough to be born of the right man, who was married to the woman, who birthed me. I'm not sure how much I hold to the God's hand interpretation of the peerage but—" She stopped and looked away.

"You have no interest in this?" Ellie waved her hand about as she gave up on finding the proper word for whatever this ridiculous event and all of its madding attendees should be called.

"The season?" Louisa asked. "Or society in general?"

"The season," she said with a smile.

"Not particularly."

"And not your first," Ellie said, more to herself as she noted the deeper color of Louisa's gown.

"No, not my first. My third, in fact. *Third*," she repeated, feigned terror on her face, and Ellie laughed. "Every year I find less and less reason to want to find a husband. Every year at season's end, I find less has changed and the urgency dwindles more—for myself, at any rate. I understand I need somewhere to live, eventually, but I'm not entirely sure marriage is for me. I understand my father wants to make connections, to further his control in government, but I don't feel that urgency in the way he does, even as he threatens to leave me destitute should I fail to secure a match."

Ellie knew her eyes widened.

"I apologize. That was terribly forward. That was… I shouldn't have said that. I've no idea what's come over me. It's as though we've been friends for ever," Louisa said as her spine straightened and she seemed to restore her socially required postures, creating a sort of invisible barrier between them where before they'd been drifting so cautiously the one toward the other. Something in Ellie sank the slightest bit.

"I feel that as well," Ellie replied. "Please don't stop now." She allowed herself to drift. "Just before I came in here…" Ellie took a deep breath and steeled herself. "Before I came in here, my mother told me to find you. Well, not *you* you, but Viscount Mayjoy's daughter. She thought you'd make a good companion."

"I see," Louisa said, the sadness in the words heavy.

"But that's not… I didn't come because of that. I came because of the potted palms. Not exactly that either. I came because of you, the woman I saw in the potted palms. Nothing to do with your father. I didn't know you were the same, but I don't want there to be anything between us so I wanted…"

"Wanted?" Louisa asked.

"I want to know you, to know Louisa. The rest of it is merely the fancy dressing of society."

"Shall we carry on as we've begun? As though we are good friends?" And Louisa leaned in, the slightest of degrees, but it was enough. "Perhaps the very best of friends?" she said without a breath to back it up.

Ellie couldn't believe her luck. Finally, she'd found someone she felt safe with. But she could see Louisa didn't feel quite safe yet. Ellie would strive to become a place she could. "Yes, please." Ellie squeezed her hand and never wanted to let go. She was desperate to tread lightly to keep this flighty butterfly on the same path.

They sat together, silent, for a time. Quiet when other women came in, assessed them, straightened themselves, and left. Ellie skimmed her fingers over Louisa's delicate gloves, following the embroidery and the pearl buttons without even considering how forward the action was. They were happy to sit and simply be, and for Ellie it was wondrous. She felt as though she'd been running for months now in preparation for tonight, but this...this peace was unexpected. She treasured it, wanted to settle into it.

The door swung wide again, and a smallish woman with blond hair and stunning dress entered. Louisa stood, tearing her hand from Ellie's as she did so. Ellie followed.

"Ma'am," Louisa said, her head bowed and knees bent in a respectful curtsey.

Not sure who she was, Ellie mirrored her movements. It would do no good to her season to upset a matron this early on, and she could tell this woman was of import, if not to Louisa then to society.

The woman stopped in front of them, and Louisa gestured to Ellie. "My Lady, might I introduce Miss Eliot Rigsby?" she said in a voice almost unrecognizable in its formality. The woman nodded, and Louisa turned to smile at her. "Miss Eliot Rigsby I present you The Viscountess Mayjoy." *Her mother.*

Ellie knew her eyes widened and she almost stumbled in her curtsey. Her family was money but theirs was power, and she could tell the difference by the way it oozed from this woman's presence. "My Lady, an honor to meet you," she said before rising. All this training for just such a moment, and she'd survived. Well, managed at any rate. She smiled warmly as the viscountess examined her tip to toe. She'd known the ladies of the ton were quite forward in their opinions. She waited.

"Well," the Viscountess said, her head turning to Louisa while her gaze continued to measure Ellie. "It seems you've a friend. How lovely." Ellie didn't believed her words. "You must invite her to tea," she finished, and her eyes left Ellie and she felt like she could breathe again.

"Yes, ma'am," Louisa said with a small dip of a curtsey. How many was that now? So formal. Was the family always so formal?

"Miss Eliot Rigsby, I will direct the invitation to your mother, Lady...?"

Ellie stopped breathing again. She was fit to pass out if she kept on like this. "Ma'am, my mother is Mrs. Eliot. She's often with her sister, the Countess Rigsby." Her mother had said to use the title only if she found herself in a situation in which it seemed quite necessary.

The woman's interest waned. "I know of Rigsby. He worked with Mayjoy on several occasions." The intonation inferred that Ellie's uncle, an Earl, was more of an assistant to the viscount than a higher member of the peerage in his own standing. "Well, Louisa, you've had enough rest. You should return. I'm certain Miss Eliot Rigsby has also been missed, as she's one of the lovelier of this year's set." The *t* of set was pronounced so hard Ellie flinched.

"Yes, My Lady," Louisa said, then nodded to Ellie and disappeared through the door to the ballroom.

Ellie waited a moment, out of respect, to be sure the viscountess was done with her, which she apparently was. She didn't give her a nod, a farewell, another glance, or by-her-leave. She walked to the mirror to asses her countenance then abandoned Ellie in the middle of the room.

Ellie gave the slightest curtsey to no one in particular and returned to the ballroom. She didn't catch sight of Louisa again, as much as she tried. As much as she wished to. Ellie was caught up by the crush and the introductions and the dances with men she now wished to be rid of. When she finally had a moment to speak with her mother, she told her of Louisa and the coming invitation. Her mother decided that had made the evening a success and they should leave early, as if to give the appearance of unaffectedness, or some such notion. Ellie wasn't sure, and to be honest she couldn't be bothered to care. All she could think of was that blue-eyed girl from the potted palms.

The invitation came two days later, and provided no warning. They were expected that very day. Within the hour, in fact. Ellie and her mother rushed to ready then took a hack and told the footmen to send the carriage along behind as soon as it was readied—to bring them home. Ellie had been told that peers were an odd bunch, expecting everyone to grovel at their feet, and her mother was none too happy to provide a knee to bend. Ellie was as well at the moment—anything for Louisa—for she knew, *she knew,* Louisa was someone she had to know.

Louisa's home was beautiful, and large, and rather… overwhelming. The house was on Gloucester street, facing Portman Square, minutes from Hyde Park. Ellie knew then that Viscount Mayjoy was powerful to hold such a property in London, perhaps even moreso than her uncle. The brick house was five stories straight up, and the public foyer held a beautiful neoclassical stairway that wrapped the circular entry from the main floor to the glass dome on the roof in spectacular fashion.

When she'd first seen Louisa at the ball, she'd been alone and quiet, and Ellie had assumed that meant Louisa was not part of the *haute ton*, but she quite obviously was regardless that Louisa was, quite plainly, an aspiring matron. Ellie tried to breathe as the army of liveried servants took wraps, hats, and gloves awaiting further orders for the arrivals from their masters. She was in well over her head, and her mother beamed.

"Oh, you've done well in this friendship, Maitland, quite well," she whispered. She was overjoyed and took Ellie's arm, giving her a squeeze. "You shall have entry to the best of the *Season* with this friendship. You must stick with this girl and make her happy to ensure she invites you to everything!" Ellie had never seen her mother quite so happy and while she understood, it soured her stomach nonetheless. "Well done, my daughter, well done."

Ellie heard footsteps like a metronome clicking on the hard floor of the balcony above them but wrapped around those perfect footsteps was a rather erratic rhythm, one that seemed to chase, relent, then surpass the other. She looked up to the balcony, attempting to see past the carved ornate balustrade that encircled the upper floors, to see a flurry of blue. Ellie shook her head at the sight of Louisa.

The blue calmed before Louisa came around the final bend and began to descend the staircase to the ground floor. Louisa beamed and it infused her blood, sped her heart, and rushed her skin in countless tiny pricks of electricity. Standing still in that moment was the most difficult thing Ellie'd ever endured, and she could tell Louisa was preventing herself from soaring down the balustrade with everything in her.

Ellie waited what seemed forever as she gave her mother a chance to inspect her friend. She attempted to hide her excitement, to no avail. Ellie knew her smile gave too much away. She stopped herself before she tapped an impatient foot. As excited as her mother was, her consternation should Ellie misstep now would be wicked.

But then Louisa was before her. She curtseyed to her mother as she greeted her, then she turned her full glory to Ellie. It was one thing to see this sort of beauty in a dimly lit retiring room. It was something else altogether to see this woman beneath the bright light of a colorful glass dome, where it filtered, bounced and wound its way down, lighting every small nook and cranny, creating a halo of light around her that matched the light she held within. Ellie exhaled with her curtsey, and Louisa took her hands and led her away while the butler spoke to her mother.

They went back up those stairs, but this time it seemed only a moment before they'd reached the top, turned to the left, went up the second case, rounded the walkway, and entered a parlor.

It seemed to Ellie that this visit was to be so many small breaths that put together would be a gust strong enough to lift her and cast her against the ground. As beautiful as that five-story entry was, this room was more. It brought the majestic beauty close where you could see it intimately and even touch it if you dared. From the velvet-patterned wall paper, to the delicately designed and painted woodwork, this room was created to give everyone something to contemplate, without ever seeming that they were avoiding conversation.

Ellie's caught up realizing she'd been presented to the Viscountess Mayjoy. She hadn't had time to consider her at the ball, she'd been so overwhelmed. She gave her best curtsey and as she inspected the woman, she realized Louisa must get all of her looks from her father. This woman was air, light, and simplicity where Louisa was all drama, depth, and color.

The Viscountess motioned to the settee across the tea butler, and her mother sat. Then the inquisition began. Where was their

home, where did they summer, what were her hobbies, who were her friends... She could only hope she fared properly as she delivered her rote responses, so well trained into her she hadn't even to consider them.

"Louisa," Lady Mayjoy said. "Leave us to our discussions."

"It was lovely to make your acquaintance ma'am...again," Elie said and she curtseyed to Lady Mayjoy, then nodded to the others in the room as she followed Louisa to the door. Once down the hallway, almost back to the grand staircase, she could breathe. It seemed to her that voices in the rotunda would carry so she didn't speak yet.

Louisa took her hand, leading her down the stairs and back up the opposite set instead of down the main case. Louisa rushed her to the end of the walkway and through a set of double doors. She released her, then turned, closing both heavy doors and throwing the latch across the top to bar entry.

"Finally," Louisa said. She walked toward her, lifting her hands. Ellie waited, unsure what her intention was. When her cool hands came to rest on her cheeks, Ellie took a breath. She closed her eyes and felt the cool fingertips coasting over the crests of her cheeks, then down her jaw, to her neck. The light shifted behind her eyelids, and Louisa kissed her cheeks beside her own lips, first on her left, then her right. Ellie felt those soft kisses all the way to her toes, like her body filled with bubbles and threatened to lift her from her shoes.

"Hello," Louisa said quietly.

"What was that?" Ellie asked as she opened her eyes to see this girl close enough to distinguish the threads in her eyes.

"Just a friendly greeting," she replied with a nervous smile.

Ellie needed a minute to compile her thoughts, so she turned to the room. Then she lost all thought. As if the great rotunda was not enough, as though the sitting room with all its delicate furnishing and intricate detail were nothing more than a simple room, as if even Louisa, in all her beauty, could not fully impress any of the visitors to this house. This room, in its vastness and grandeur, certainly could.

It relegated all other aspects of this home to mere introductions to beauty. Rooms meant to prepare you for what you were to be witness to.

Ellie stood, enraptured, no idea what she should do next. Louisa's warm hand wrapped around hers, and she squeezed back as though to steady herself. "I'm..." She didn't know what to say.

"This is my favorite place in all the world."

"I can imagine why," Ellie said. The ceiling extended the remaining three stories to yet another glass ceiling, but this one was tinged with pale colors, which created a pattern to the light that fell around the room. Like swimming in a subtle rainbow.

"My father prefers to view the sculptures with the torches lit, and my father's wife prefers the gas lamps. I prefer to see them like this, with the sun overhead through the ceiling," Louisa said.

"Yes, this...this is magical." At first glance, a pattern in the tile would look to be a certain color and pattern, but then a cloud would shift, the light would change, and everything she thought to be simply wasn't. As though this room, this world, was never the same. She walked to one of the massive sculptures and, reaching out, she looked to Louisa for permission.

Louisa nodded. "Never let anyone else see you touch them. It's not allowed."

Ellie stretched her fingers and warmed them in preparation then reached out across the base, where her toes met the marble. She slid her hand up one strong thigh, closing her eyes and feeling the shape of the muscle. She could imagine it shifting against her hand. When her fingertips met the abdomen of the man, she shifted away from the center of him, then skated her hand down the round of his hip, and back down his leg. "I've never— I can't believe... He's magnificent," Ellie whispered.

"Why do you go by Ellie?" Louisa asked as they moved to the next sculpture.

"I don't, exactly. I— I was lonely as a child. My mother kept me close. My older sister, the first Maitland, died when she was out with the governess and other children—"

"You were named for your dead sister?"

"Yes and I— I always wanted to be someone else instead of her."

"Middle name?"

Ellie smiled. "No. That was hers first as well."

Louisa stopped her, then hugged her. Ellie was...she wasn't sure what she was. Nobody'd ever reacted to her this way. She sank into the warmth of the arms around her and she wanted... For the first time in her life, she *wanted*.

She let out a shuddering breath as though to let go of everything she'd thought she wanted before. Then she breathed deep, taking this new want into her and holding it. Then Louisa let go, slow and a bit unsteady as though she wished to stay. Oh, but Ellie shouldn't read too much into this. They were friends and she wanted her friendship more than anything.

"I'm sorry that happened to you," Louisa said.

Her family had never understood why she didn't like her name, and it wasn't exactly that she didn't like it, it simply wasn't *hers* and somehow Louisa understood that so easily, with so little explanation.

"Ellie," she started again. "Ellie ellie Eliot... that's how the young kids teased. I suppose I started to pretend that... well I was young and—it seems strange, now. Anyway, I decided if I ever had truly close friends, they would call me Ellie. And now I'm rambling. I suppose it's not terribly imaginative," Ellie finished.

"It's beautiful," Louisa said. "Ellie."

"I don't want... Please don't..."

"It's our secret. I promise."

Ellie smiled and walked up to another sculpture, this one a woman. She was soft and round and inviting. She was laid out on a large pedestal, one knee out to the side as she lay on her hip, her body curled around that leg as though she held something precious in her lap, but there wasn't anything.

"I used to crawl up in that space with a quilt and sleep," Louisa said from behind her. "You can see the wear on her leg, unfortunately. But I always felt so safe in the lee of her strength."

"What about your mother?"

"Actually, Lady Mayjoy is not my mother. My mother died when I was born."

That explained why she'd called her her father's wife. "Lou—" She stopped, her words and her breath lost as Louisa placed two fingers to her lips to silence her.

"No, please. I never knew her. If I ever wanted for a mother, there were the nursemaids and nannies and governesses, and this lady here. She was my favorite because *she* never yelled at me."

Ellie's heart broke for the baby who'd never known a mother's love. She took Louisa's hand and pressed a kiss to her palm. "I'm sorry," she said, then let it drop when she realized how forward the action was. But she watched as Louisa curled her fingers into her palm as though to keep it. As she tucked it against her breast, Ellie turned toward yet another large piece of marble, determined not to react. "Do you look like your mother then?"

Louisa tweaked one of the marble man's toes, then reached for Ellie and rushed her through the gallery toward the far wall and a large portrait. A beam of natural light from the single uncovered window illuminated the painting edge to edge, and when Louisa stepped in front of it, she cast a shadow across the canvas.

Ellie stared. "This isn't you," she said, somehow knowing that this woman—the spitting image of Louisa but for some sort of knowledge shining through the eyes of the painted woman—was her mother.

Louisa reached up into the sunlight and let her shadow caress the cheek of her mother on the wall. "Mama. She was beautiful," she whispered.

"Like you," Ellie replied. "She looks like you. Or, I suppose, you look like her," Ellie said as she stood behind Louisa so as not to block any more light to the painting.

Louisa turned her face, illuminated by the sunlight just as her mother's was in the painting. She shifted her shoulders, straightened her spine, tilted her head, then relaxed her eyes and dropped her lips open the slightest bit.

"Oh my God," Ellie said. "Oh my God!" She'd never seen anything like this—as if the painting had come to life. As though Louisa had walked from the wall and into the sunlight.

Louisa smiled and broke the spell then swept a hand down Ellie's shoulder to her hand, and moved back into the gallery.

"I'm sorry. I... I suppose you do understand a loss that was never your own."

"I suppose I do," Louisa said. "I always wondered if that was why my father had no time for me, because I reminded him of her, because I know he loved her. At least I believe he did. In reality, it could have been that he hated her as well. I don't know. I should probably never know, in fact." Louisa sat on a long chaise, resting against the arm at the end, and waited for Ellie to join her. "You would wear blue today," she said, quietly fingering her own dress then Ellie's.

"It seems we had the same idea," Ellie replied as she sank to the chaise.

"I can only hope we do," Louisa said. Ellie watched Louisa, and a shiver coursed her spine and settled in her chest. She stared at Louisa's lips as they formed words, sounds, breath, but she couldn't make anything out above the pounding of her own heartbeat. Then her breath was close enough she felt it on her cheek, could smell the lemon and spice from her tea. She didn't know what Louisa had said, and maybe that was best because she didn't react when Louisa took her hand and ran a thumb along the edge of her palm and she possibly should have. Louisa ran her other hand from her shoulder to her elbow. Ellie stilled, couldn't move, and when Louisa's lips met her cheek, her hand resting on the opposite cheek, holding her there, Ellie nearly dissolved into a puddle at her feet.

She'd never had a friend, and she now understood why all the girls had them. She understood, finally, how very important friendship was. She'd never felt this close to another person in all her life. She didn't want to ever leave this moment.

Louisa

"Ellie, I—" Louisa said against Ellie's warm cheek, but Ellie turned away, a blush rising from her neck to her ears. She shouldn't have been so bold. "Ellie, please."

"No, I— I'm not... I don't. I apologize, I've never—"

"Ellie."

Ellie turned and took Louisa's gaze with her own, but it wasn't painful or judgmental or terrified as Louisa thought it might be. "Louisa, I've never in my life had a friendship where..." She paused, her brow wrinkled, and Louisa was afraid to say anything. "I guess I had no idea it could be like this."

"Friends kiss, don't they? They should. I don't see why not." Louisa thought she should say something else, instead of trying to play her actions as different. Was this merely friendship? She wasn't sure. This felt like...so much more than that, somehow, and perhaps Ellie did as well, but was just as afraid. "Ellie, I've never had friends, and certainly none like this. I'm so very blessed to have found you."

"And I you. I simply..." Ellie said, her hands in her lap.

"Please forgive my awkwardness. I don't know how to do any of this. All I know for certain is that I care for you. It may seem sudden, but..." Louisa said.

"Perhaps. But I care for you as well. I imagine we've plenty of time to figure it all out. That is something friends do, yes?"

"It's what I've always imagined, at least, that friends watch out for each other, they care for each other, they protect and support each other, they…they learn things together. I wouldn't ever ask more than that of you."

"You've truly never had friends? It seems so odd."

"I was kept home. They didn't want me getting any brazen ideas, I suppose. Nobody was good enough. My father wanted his family above reproach."

"That sounds very lonely," Ellie said, and the words settled in Louisa's chest as though she hadn't ever considered it. *Lonely, yes,* that was the word she'd never thought to use.

"Would you… Perhaps it sounds funny and—"

"Tell me, Louisa, please?"

"You have a name that nobody uses but me, would it be too much or too odd or…" Louisa chewed her lip.

"What shall I call you?"

"Only what you've already called me, even as it was by accident." She quieted for a moment, wondering if she should tell her how it felt. Holding back from this woman felt like lying somehow. She closed her eyes and inhaled deeply, the scent of violets making her smile. "Both times stilled my heart as I waited…and I long for that feeling again."

"Lou," Ellie said on a breath and then hushed.

Louisa beamed, knowing Ellie had understood. Accidental as it was. She nodded.

"Lou. I rather like that. I also rather like that not one soul will call you that but me. It seems only fair," Ellie said.

"Louuuiiiiiisaaaaa!" The name rang through the front entry, and they both stood, hands snapping to clutch at their own waists.

Louisa rushed to the entry of the gallery, unhooking the latch and swinging the doors wide to the sun from the foyer. "Here, My Lady!" she said. Then she walked forward, her heart racing inside her chest. She leaned over the balustrade to the group in the front entry. "I was showing Miss Eliot Rigsby the gallery."

Her stepmother looked up. "As you should. The gallery is extensive and quite impressive." She turned to Ellie's mother. "Your daughter is welcome here. The gallery is a good place to practice sketching. We also have an extensive library for practicing dictation and the like, and our music room, of course, is unparalleled. She would be welcome to join Louisa in her lessons."

Louisa watched, hopeful, nearly tipping herself over the balustrade as she tried to hear the response.

Ellie's mother brightened. "Of course, I've no doubt Maitland would benefit from such lessons and friendship. If there's anything I can do—" She stopped short, certainly realizing there was nothing the viscountess couldn't afford to provide for Louisa, and certainly Ellie's mother had seen that in her expression.

The ladies turned back to them.

"Mrs. Eliot is prepared to leave. Where is Miss Eliot Rigsby?" the viscountess said.

"Here, My Lady, thank you," Ellie said as she passed Louisa. She took Ellie's hand and squeezed, promising her entire world in that touch. Then Ellie moved away and Louisa watched her go, descending the steps in her lovely skirts.

When Ellie reached the group in the foyer they turned to the entry. Lady Mayjoy looked up to Louisa, then called to Mrs. Eliot. "We are going to the dressmakers this afternoon. Perhaps your daughter would care to join us?"

Louisa stopped breathing. She needed to stop stopping. She would end up in hospital should she not. Yet she waited for the answer without a breath yet.

"Of course," Mrs. Eliot replied with a too-grand smile.

Her stepmother watched, and Louisa could tell she was annoyed. "We shall be by around three in the Viscounts carriage to collect her. Please have her ready."

"Of course, ma'am."

Louisa stayed until they quit the house. She breathed then as well. Finally. Then she turned to enter the gallery, to retrace the steps she'd taken with Ellie earlier. To remember every turn of her graceful hand, every time the light through the glass had sparked in her eyes. She wanted to reach for it, to cast it to memory, to keep it forever and hold it dear. For while they were friends, and she knew they would be friends, this woman would marry and move to her husband's home to bear his children. She would not have access to her then as she did now.

But that was for later. She ran a hand up and down the leg of the sculpture, tracing Ellie's touch and holding the memories close.

"Louisa." She froze. She hadn't heard Lady Mayjoy enter the gallery. "I appreciate that you have a friend, even as beneath us as she is. Please have a care, however. You do still need to marry and get out of this house. Do not let your father see you wasting all your time looking to this girl for companionship, or

I shall be forced to be rid of her and her new-money family. Use her to help find a husband, perhaps someone of her set since you haven't managed with ours. You will both marry and can then remain friends."

Louisa's skin tightened, drawing her shoulders back, her hands tight. She turned to her and nodded. "Yes, ma'am."

She looked past Louisa, inspecting the portrait of her mother. "And when you move out, you may take that with you. It's no longer needed here."

"Yes ma'am," Louisa said. So that settled it. Her mother wasn't missed and her father must hate her because she only reminded him of her. The last thread of hope she had left in her heart snapped, and she pressed her hand to her belly as she curtseyed to hide her sadness from Lady Mayjoy. "Yes, ma'am. Thank you, ma'am."

Ellie

"Purchase whatever Lady Mayjoy recommends. Have the bills sent directly," her mother said in a harried voice. "Your father will complain, but this is quite obviously a test. Do whatever she says."

"Yes, mama," Ellie replied.

The knocker on the door sounded through the entry, and her mother nodded to the butler. He approached and whispered to her mother.

"They await you in the carriage. They don't think there's time to come inside," she said with a stiff smile.

Ellie took her mother's hand and squeezed it. "Don't worry, mama. I'm sure it's true."

"In which case you should hurry. Don't keep Lady Mayjoy waiting." Her mother took her shoulders and turned her for the door. "Go on now. Remember, don't refuse a thing."

Ellie walked down the steps then took the proffered hand of the footman as she stepped up into the carriage. She turned to sit on the rear-facing bench next to Louisa. She nodded. "Lady Mayjoy, thank you again for the invitation," she said respectfully. She felt Louisa's hand on hers with a quick gentle squeeze hello, then the door closed and the carriage lurched forward.

"We'll be visiting my personal tailor and haberdasher. If they have time, they may be able to fit you as well. It depends on previous appointments. They are very much in demand," Lady Mayjoy said.

"Of course, My Lady. I wouldn't want to put anyone out but would be happy to be fitted if time permits," Ellie said. She turned to the window.

"What is it your father does?" Lady Mayjoy asked then.

"Trade, My Lady. He has quite a prosperous business with India. My father helped to expand the representation of England."

Lady Mayjoy nodded, and Ellie hoped that was impressive enough for her. It was nothing but true.

"I understand India has been a profitable area for quite some time," Lady Mayjoy said.

"Yes, ma'am, but I don't pretend to know too much about it. My father would no doubt tell me more if I were a son, but as I'm not, I only know what he may discuss with others in my presence," Ellie said with a smile.

"I see. It is our place to disseminate information to the best of our ability in order to protect and help our families. Certainly you will become more adept at ferreting information as you grow into your own as a woman—at least, one would hope."

Ellie exchanged a glance with Louisa, not entirely sure why Lady Mayjoy would be so interested in her father's business. "I learn as much as I'm able, my Lady, and as you say I hope to only become more proficient at learning for the betterment of my family." Ellie looked out the window, watching as the busy London streets seemed to swarm about them as the carriage cut its way through the crowds. She leaned against Louisa whenever possible, around turns, when the carriage swayed, wanting the warmth of her, the tangible reality of her person so close. And when Louisa leaned back, Ellie couldn't help but to grin and to hide it as well to prevent any odd questioning, to protect this quietest of moments between them.

The bustle thinned, and the carriage pulled up to what seemed a private residence at the center of a block. The footman dropped the stairs and opened the door, reaching in and escorting Lady Mayjoy, first, from the carriage. Ellie followed behind Louisa, and they entered the beautiful residence that doubled as a dress shop. Tea was set in a small parlor on the left, and a butler was collecting gloves, bags, and wraps as a woman in a narrow black dress descended the staircase toward them.

"Lady Mayjoy, a pleasure as ever," she said as she took her hands and curtseyed.

"Marjorie. Thank you for seeing me on such short notice," Lady Mayjoy responded.

"For you, anything. What can we do?" Marjorie led them into the parlor and directed them to the settees around the tea butler.

"Louisa needs something new. She has yet to catch herself a husband. Obviously what she's been doing hasn't worked," Lady Mayjoy said. "This girl, Miss Eliot Rigsby, had a dress on the other night that garnered quite a bit of attention. Perhaps you could do something similar, though not in such a pale shade of course, as Louisa is far past the blushing youth stage. She isn't bound to fool anyone with a dress."

So she was here because of the dress. Louisa stared at the floor, and Ellie wanted very much to reach out and take comfort, but she dared not.

Marjorie smiled. "Tell me of the dress then?"

"Ma'am," Ellie said. "It was designed by Emile Pingat. My mother had several commissioned on our last trip to Paris." Ellie watched as the woman's eyes widened.

"Of course they're stunning, without doubt then," she said with the wave of a hand. Ellie smiled and saw Lady Mayjoy narrow her eyes. "Lady Mayjoy, we would be happy to create a few items for Louisa, in the style of Pingat, and of course we have many lovely imported silks and brocades to accomplish anything you wish." Marjorie stood and waved her hands at Louisa and Ellie, and they followed. "You may stay if you wish, but the fitting should be most of the afternoon."

"That won't be necessary," Lady Mayjoy said as she stood. "I'll send the carriage for her when I'm finished with my rounds."

The door shut behind her, and they all seem to breathe.

Then Marjorie turned to Ellie. "You must tell me everything about him! Did you actually meet Monsieur Pingat? Or was it merely his workers?"

"Oh, I met Monsieur Pingat, and he was lovely. The way his hands moved…it was incredible. We were in his fashion studio for nearly three days. He did all of the design and fitting of the dresses while we wore them so they would be exact," Ellie said.

Marjorie stood and put a hand to her mouth. "Of course… As intricate as everything is…as delicate the fabric…" Ellie could see her considering. "Tell me about the dress Lady Mayjoy is particular about?"

Louisa smiled then. "Marjorie, it's like an extension of Ellie herself. The color was…like a blush, and the style…long and elegant with curves that enhanced who she is. They didn't take away from her at all. It was stunning. The line in the back was high neck to floor with pleats the entire way, but the front was cut low, though at first glance because of the color you really had no idea until you were already looking too long. Perfect." She said, "Absolutely perfect."

Ellie caught her breath at the detailed description. At first she felt warm all over at the description, but then her skin tightened as she considered longer. Was she nothing but a dress?

Marjorie nodded. "Let's see what colors we have, then we can talk about design. I can only do so much. Certainly you ladies have no interest in standing while I create a dress around you."

"For a dress like that one?" Louisa said, then looked at Ellie and smiled. "I can see how it would be worth every minute."

"If you have a moment, I could send to my mother for the dress," Ellie said, and Louisa's eyes narrowed. "If that's all that matters is the dress." She felt cold and it had nothing to do with her state of dress because the temperature in here was near sweltering.

"If you wouldn't mind," Marjorie said then snapped her fingers and a footman approached. "Gordon, please see to Miss Eliot Rigsby's wishes." Marjorie walked to the back room, leaving them there, and Ellie gave Gordon the instructions, watching as he too disappeared from the room, leaving them alone. She needed space to think, but Louisa took her hand before she could walk away.

She pulled Ellie close. "What's happening?"

"I just...didn't realize that this—" She motioned between them, tried to calm her nerves before she broke. Attempted to steady her voice before it faltered. "Was all about that...dress." Her voice still broke on the last word.

"What do you mean?"

"This, our friendship. Is that the only reason I was invited to—"

"Oh Ellie, this, what's between us? Has nothing to do with the dress and everything to do with the woman who wore it. The dress was stunning, but you... Ellie, you're the warmest, most beautiful and lovely person and the dress pales in comparison to you. This—" she also motioned between them, "—is not at all about that dress," Louisa said, and Ellie took a breath, even managed a smile. "This about everything beneath that dress." And then Louisa blushed, quite ferociously.

"I'm fairly sure I'm more pale than that dress," she said weakly to break the tension, and Louisa laughed. As she looked into her eyes, Louisa leaned in and pressed a quick kiss to her lips. So quickly that Ellie hadn't a chance to prepare for it, or enjoy it, or even to remember the shape and pressure of her mouth. She touched her own nonetheless.

"I adore you, Ellie. Dress or no." Then Louisa took her hand and pulled her toward the backroom, while Ellie kept that hand over her lips and attempted to savor the remainder of the kiss that seemed to reach all the way to her toes. She wanted more...then thought better of it. She shouldn't want more of that, should she?

They moved to the back room, and Marjorie sent her girls to undressing both Louisa and Ellie, placing their clothes on a rack by the door so they wouldn't be scuffed. They were positioned on two separate pedestals in the center of the room, facing each other as they were measured, every inch, from their insteps to their earlobes.

Louisa giggled and shook several times, obviously ticklish, which made Ellie smile.

"I remember Monsieur talking about the pleats, Marjorie," Ellie said, wanting to help. "That the pleats must be perfect, that they must be an exact length to prevent dragging the floor, because it would damage them. He also said something about tacking them, to keep them pleated properly."

"Good, good!" Marjorie said as she swept a bolt of fabric before Louisa, letting the end trail in front of her. It was a deep iridescent blue, like that of a peacock, and it brought out all the tones in Louisa's eyes.

"Yes, that one," Ellie said, then looked away before anyone saw how much she cared.

Louisa laughed. "I like it too," Louisa said.

"It could work. The silk is watered so it could be structured enough to hold the pleats. Perhaps if we use another fabric under the bodice for stability…" Marjorie disappeared again, and Louisa reached out and took Ellie's hand.

"I'm glad you're here," she said.

"I'm glad I'm here too," Ellie replied, "even though I'm not entirely sure why I had to be undressed," she said with a grin. Louisa laughed again, and one of the girls doing the measurements stopped.

"Stop moving, please," she said.

"Of course. Apologies," Louisa said.

When the dress arrived, the shop girls helped Ellie into it. Marjorie stared at her as though she were a statue, taking in all the delicate pleating and beadwork. Running her hands down the seams and against the hem. "Stunning, just stunning. Lady Mayjoy was correct. This is a masterpiece. I cannot recreate it, but I can make something similar. If only I could let some of the seams to see how—"

"No!" Louisa said suddenly. "I mean, you can't possibly think to take it apart. Her mother would be incredibly upset I'm certain."

"Quite so. We'll do our best for you, of course," Marjorie replied, but Ellie could see the disappointment in her face. Marjorie wanted to take the entire dress apart in order to see how it ticked, like a clock. But they never quite went back the same, did they? Once pulled apart? Perhaps a clock did, but this dress was a work of art, and you couldn't undo a work of art and expect it to be the same once repaired.

She looked to find Louisa smiling at the shop girl, who'd apparently said something humorous. Ellie loved this dress. It was her favorite of all the dresses they'd had made in Paris. But when Lou looked up with joy in her eyes, Ellie would have torn it to shreds if she'd asked.

Louisa

ouisa walked the ballroom again, checking behind plants and decorations, hoping Ellie would be there. They hadn't a chance to talk about upcoming events after the dressmakers, so she'd been attending all the best of them for the opportunity of seeing her again. She moved to the halfway point, disappointed that in this ballroom there were no large plants to hide between. She took up a position next to one of the large marble columns and waited, watching the crowd, trying to catch sight of her.

"Hello, dear." The deep voice came from the other side of the column she leaned against. Baron Endsleigh.

She smiled but didn't turn. Ender was the only person who was able to sneak up on her—then again, nobody else was interested enough to want to sneak up on her. "Hugh," she said.

"Oh-so informal...we aren't trying to impress anyone tonight?"

She kept her smile to herself. "Ender then, and who on earth would I have need to impress?" She smiled and rolled her eyes at him.

He made a broad arch with his arm in front of him. "Isn't your future husband out there? Somewhere?" he asked coyly as he gestured to the whole of the ballroom.

Louisa laughed. She couldn't help herself. Then she turned and curtseyed to him. "You have me there, my friend. I do yet have need of a husband according to my family. And society. And apparently the whole of London and the world beyond." She

pursed her lips. "Tsk, tsk, tsk, for shame, an unmarried woman." She winked at him, and he laughed.

They'd an easy relationship since neither ever expected anything from the other beyond companionship. It was different from anything else she had in the *ton* and she loved it for the simple ease of it, for the companionship of it. He pined for someone promised to a duke, well beyond his meager barony, and she...well, she was undetermined. Though if she were forced to take a man, Hugh would not be a chore. At least he could make her laugh.

"May I fill your dance card? Or is the gentleman you seek here somewhere? You'll introduce us, won't you? I feel the need to extoll your virtues, secure your hand," Hugh said excitedly.

"No," she said. "Besides, I wasn't—" She caught herself but not before his gaze narrowed. "I wasn't necessarily searching for a gentleman. I was looking for my friend."

"A friend? Never say it. You've a friend? I find that impossible to believe, Louisa. Didn't your family teach you not to tell tales?"

"No, really! Hugh, she's absolutely lovely. In every way. Every way. Her eyes—" She felt her cheeks heat as Hugh watched her.

"Her…eyes."

Louisa raised her fan in front of her mouth as she tried to stop her panic. But why? She was allowed *friendship*. His gaze measured her before he spoke again.

"So you are yet in need of a dance partner. Good. I've no interest in dancing this evening either, at least not with these new chits," he said as he leaned a shoulder against the column.

"Don't be cruel, Hugh. It's beneath you."

"Become soft in our old age, have we, Louisa? My apologies, *the new set*. Better?" he asked and she wondered when she'd become so protective of the girls who've recently come out.

She turned back to him. "Thank you, yes. I am in fact in need of a dance partner. So you're it, as always."

"Perhaps even a turn around the balcony?" he mused, and her heartbeat seemed to speed up. "Since there's no fear of embarrassment now, will you introduce me to your friend? Perhaps she's in need of a dance partner as well," he asked, suddenly serious.

She measured him. She knew his attention was elsewhere, but part of her didn't want to introduce them. As stunning as Ellie was, if he became enamored of her it would break Lousia's heart. That was an interesting idea, though… Ellie wouldn't be refused her company if *they* were wed. Still, Hugh was set upon another. Whom he most absolutely couldn't have. "I suppose I should. Perhaps the two of you should be friends."

"Or possibly more, if she's that stunning," he replied. Her eyes snapped to his, shocked as he'd read her thoughts so effortlessly. He raised his hands toward her. "I jest! You know I'm not interested in anyone, particularly not a green girl. I'm much too occupied elsewhere," he finished.

"How is she?" Louisa asked then, searching to change the subject. "This girl of yours that you cannot sever from your thoughts."

"She's well, or as well as can be expected, I suppose. I miss her, Louisa."

"It's hard being so far from her?"

"Yes, quite," he replied, gazing across the ballroom.

She wondered what that felt like, that want to be close to someone at all times. She thought again of Ellie and began to cast her gaze once again around the room.

"What does she look like?" he asked. "I shall help you find her."

"I don't know if she's even attending tonight. I—" But then her breath caught as her eyes landed on the perfectly done blond hair she knew was Ellie's.

"Where?" Hugh said. "Show me her."

Louisa felt herself pointing her fan surreptitiously in the direction of the gardens as Ellie was lead from the ballroom on the arm of a tall gentleman with bright red hair. She shuddered– their children would never be in the sun for fear of the burn.

"I didn't see. Are you sure?" he asked.

Louisa felt herself nod. "Yes, nobody has hair like that, like an angel." She felt Hugh's stare on her again, and knew she was blushing. "I only meant— If you saw it you would understand what I meant."

"Careful, Louisa. I believe I do understand what you mean. For your sake and hers, please be cautious."

A chill ran her spine at his words. Did he know? He knew she wasn't much for marriage, but...could he know that she wasn't much for men altogether? She turned to him then for the first time, frightened of what she'd find, but all she saw was an anxiousness in his countenance.

His shoulders pitched, his jaw tight. He reached for her hand and took it. "I'm merely concerned for you. We're friends, Louisa. I'm concerned. Please be careful. Your father..."

She was sure what he meant by that last bit, even she'd never heard a woman speak of another woman in this manner... but there was no other way to speak of Ellie. And Hugh was the only person she felt safe in telling. And she had an idea as to why that was. And he was correct.

He kissed her knuckles as she considered that absentmindedly until he squeezed her fingers and cocked his head as he watched her. Then someone called to him. "Forgive me, my dear friend, but I must go as Trumbull has deigned to grace us with his presence and if left alone for long, he'll raise havoc. However, I am at your disposal should you need to present a strong front. If you need another champion tonight, I've no doubt Perry would happily oblige as well."

"I'm not going to be seen dancing with that rake. My father would lock me in a closet regardless how he wishes to be rid of me."

Hugh laughed again, and all tension left with the sound.

"Did someone say rake?" Peregrine Trumbull sidled up in all of his fitted finery, and Hugh closed his eyes briefly, then winked at Louisa before he turned to Perry, taking him by the shoulder and steering him away from her. She watched as they walked across the room so easily.

She wished to be a man if only to be at ease no matter where she went. She was required to be ever wary of her surroundings and behavior, and it was exhausting. The only time she could be herself...well. She felt some semblance of that with Ellie in the gallery. Hopefully that would happen again.

Ellie

Ellie stared up at the bobbing boy Lord and wondered how she could get away from him to find Lou. She'd seen her speaking with a tall blond man when she'd walked into the ballroom but had been waylaid by her mother and another introduction to some peer who had requested one. Her mother had been thrilled, of course. Ellie on the other hand, was exhausted. Over the past week she'd met, danced with, spoken to, ridden with and been taken to the park with no less than twenty eligible peers. She'd no idea they were in such supply. She also failed to understand why they were all so enamored of her.

Certainly she had money, but so did so many other of the new girls, and those girls also had titles and connections. Not so with her. Ellie was exhausted, and bored. Not a single one of these men caught her interest, and she'd expected to at least be entertained. At the very least. It wasn't so.

Most of these men took her out to discuss how much she was going to love taking care of their household, bearing their children, and minding their beds, *wink wink*. What was it with this courting process? Barely a week in, and she wanted out. So she'd insisted they go to the gardens, away from the noise of the ballroom. Because at least there she could enjoy the plants. Bushes. Grass. Perhaps watch it grow in the dark. Her shoulders drooped as she sighed.

Boredom.

"Miss?"

Damn. "Sorry...My Lord, I was considering my next cross stitching project. I thought perhaps a small pillow with a bible quote appropriate, My Lord," she repeated. Thank goodness they could

all be called My Lord, or Sir, because she'd already forgotten who he was. She smiled up at him. Way, way up at him. So far up his forehead was in shadow.

She wondered what Louisa was doing with that blond. He was beautiful—of that, she found herself jealous. Not that he was beautiful, but that he'd spoken with Louisa. She'd seen them across the room all smiles and banter, and her hands had itched to separate them. Though Louisa had been smiling, genuinely at that, so perhaps he was a friend, someone with a sense of humor? But she'd said she had no friends.

She looked back toward the house and wished to see more.

"Miss Eliot Rigsby?"

Damn. "Yes, so very sorry. Perhaps I should return to the ballroom because my mind is elsewhere." She shuddered falsely, pulling her wrap around her shoulders as he tried to see down her dress. He grunted and looked away, and she caught sight of the blond at the entry with another man. "Do you know him?" she asked, attempting to stay her curiosity a bit.

"Trumbull? Or do you mean Endsleigh? Either one should be avoided," he replied contemptuously, the boy Lord did, whomever he was. She really should practice paying attention if she was to survive these meetings.

"The blond?" she asked, ignoring his warning and his tone.

"That's Baron Endsleigh. He's young, not interested in marriage. More interested in shenanigans with Trumbull—*who is a rake.*" He enunciated each word with aplomb before continuing heedless. "You would do well to avoid the both of them. I have much more to recommend me. One day I'll be an Earl, after all."

"Yes, of course, my Lord," she replied, and he smiled at his success. Perfect, all forgiven. "Should we return?" she asked again, and his eyebrows came together with a sudden crash and she realized she'd offended him once more. She winced. She needed to do better, but this boy Lord needed a few years and perhaps a dead father before he would be impressive to anyone, even her. He didn't speak, only turned toward the ballroom and lifted his elbow to her. He wasn't all that bad. But he wasn't Louisa.

Once inside, Ellie searched for Lou, finding her where she'd seen her, leaning against the column. This time without her companion. She turned to Lord whoever and curtseyed. "Thank you, my Lord, for the walk in the gardens. It was lovely." She smiled, and he grumbled something in return then walked away.

As she turned back to Louisa, she saw them—the men and her mother—descending. It seemed she wasn't to have a moment's peace, and her mother was quite beyond thrilled judging by her smile. Ellie looked away then dodged through the crowd toward Louisa; she didn't slow as she passed her but reached out and took her hand, pulling her along through the crush, pinching and poking the people in her way as she ducked her face and went full steam ahead for the main part of the house. She didn't stop at the entry. She led her up the main stairs, only glancing back to see that Louisa was with her.

They reached the landing and Ellie paused, then Louisa led the way. "This way," she said breathlessly and like a slingshot they were off down a darkened hallway until Ellie, caught in a fit of laughter, pulled Louisa to a stop.

"Please," she begged through her smile. "Please, a moment to catch my breath?"

"Oh, I see. Now you need a moment. I hadn't a moment to pause when some wicked thing reached from the crowd and took me by the arm, pulling me through, and into, half the ton in the ballroom...but now *you* need a moment?" Louisa said with a grin.

Ellie smiled, her hand on her belly as she tried to still her breathing. "Yes, yes, I beg you. The rush is gone, please."

Louisa smiled at her and glanced down the hallway once more waving to an open room. "In here. Let's get out of the hall where someone might come upon us and force us to return."

Ellie lifted her skirts and followed her into the room, which, as it happened, was a library. "Oh, Louisa, did you know?" Once again her breath was stolen as she considered the magnificent collection, so many books she could live two lifetimes and never read them all.

"In a manner. I was here last season. I knew the library was down this way but I wasn't certain." She reached for the gas lamp switch and turned the lights up.

"We shouldn't. Someone will see," Ellie said, not wanting to be disturbed in here. Ever.

Louisa walked back to the door and closed it. "There, undisturbed. So you like to read?"

"Oh yes, I— Yes. Very much so."

"*Alice's Adventures in Wonderland*?" Louisa asked, and Ellie turned so fast her skirts caught on a shelf and wrapped around her legs.

"Yes, yes, I adore Alice. Could you imagine a world so colorful? So different and enchanting? They were all so wonderful."

"Except for the Queen of Hearts," Louisa reminded her.

"I think perhaps she needs a hug. Nobody can get close to her. She won't allow it. Sometimes I believe people need to be held."

"I don't suppose you would hold the jabberwocky, would you?"

Ellie laughed at that. "No, I shudder to think of something like that and I quite draw the line at jabberwockies. No, that animal I would not attempt to coddle."

"Good thing, that," Louisa said with a horrified look.

"Though he probably needs a hug as well. Perhaps the knight could attempt it? He has armor." Louisa laughed, and Ellie took her hand and pulled her to a settee in the middle of the library. "I couldn't wait to see you again, and I'd no idea when that would be. I thought to send a missive, but I didn't want to be too presumptuous, and certainly didn't want to annoy your father's wife. She seemed a bit put out by my mother. Which is understandable. I honestly don't see why I've been so popular this season, come to think on it. I mean, I have callers every day, all day. I—"

"You don't understand?"

"No I don't. Certainly I have money but nothing else to recommend me. There are plenty of titled girls with good dowries— What?" She stopped as Louisa's gaze turned enigmatic and she lost her train of thought. "Louisa?"

"Ellie, I can tell you exactly why they flock to you, and it isn't your money, though to be sure that is what's making it acceptable for the flocking. I believe even without it they would, Ellie. They would all want you. They all do want you." The last bit came on a breath and Ellie stilled, watching Louisa's lips as if it would help her to hear better. She startled when she felt a fingertip sweep a curl from her cheek and tuck it behind her ear.

"Louisa," she said.

"Ellie, you are... I don't know that there are words for what you are. To see you is to see the sun shining in a dark world. So out of place and yet welcome, warming, beautiful. And that's not even taking those devastating eyes into consideration. You could floor a man with your eyes closed and a gentle smile on your lips."

"A man?" she asked as her belly tightened.

"Any man," Louisa replied.

"I don't want any man," Ellie said then, and she lifted her gaze to Louisa's and held her. "I don't want..." Ellie breathed through the fear. "I don't want a man," she said without the slightest bit of breath to force it, for if she took a breath now, she may just cry.

Louisa

ouisa's heart jumped between her ribs, as though it fought, stretching between the bones to leave her body and latch on to the woman next to her. *Ellie doesn't want any man.* She shook her head, enough to shake the stray thoughts away and concentrate. *Ellie doesn't want* a *man.* Ellie seemed pale and a bit panicked. Louisa couldn't see her breasts rising against her corset and wondered if she breathed at all.

Then, and Louisa wasn't sure who had done it—perhaps it was the two of them drawn together as if on a wire—but Ellie's mouth was the softest, sweetest... Louisa pressed against her harder, and Ellie didn't pull away. She reached out and took one hand, and Ellie wrapped her fingers with hers, pulled the tiniest bit, and Louisa sank into the sensation, their hands intertwined, their lips together. She closed her eyes, no longer worried she'd frighten her.

Ellie's lips fell open. And when Ellie swept her tongue against her upper lip, Louisa thought for sure she would die. "You taste of sweetened lemon," Ellie said against her. "You taste of—" Her tongue reached into her then, touched her tongue the slightest bit, slid across the roof of her mouth toward the front, then retreated, skimming once again across her upper lip. "Spice and...sugar, so sweet."

And Louisa knew she would live and die a thousand deaths that night as she remembered this moment.

"Louisa?" She said her name against her lips, and Louisa felt the vibration all the way to her toes. Ellie's hand tightened on hers, and Louisa's chest compressed, her breath hitching. She realized, moments later when Ellie's hands took her face and she sipped the

tears away, that she was crying. They kissed. They kissed and kissed and…it sounded such a tawdry word of a sudden for something that seemed so much more, like a prayer, or a curse.

She let out a breath and it was shared as she twisted her hands in the back of Ellie's dress and pulled her tight and they tasted, licked and, yes, kissed. Like they hadn't ever before, and she hadn't truly. She'd been kissed but she'd never…she'd never given of herself like this. She'd never wanted to know the truth of a person by the flavor of their tongue. This was so, so much more than a mere kiss. She tasted salt and knew they were both lost. They would never be able to return to the ball if they didn't stop.

Louisa froze, broke the connection between their mouths, and dipped her head. Ellie's lips kissed her forehead, and she leaned into her, attempting to catch her breath.

"I'm frightened," Louisa said then. "I don't understand, I've never felt this before and I never expected it with—"

"A woman?"

Louisa looked into those magical eyes. "Yes. This, what we have here, I feel more for you than I ever have. Women are meant to be friends."

"They are," Ellie said. "And aren't we friends? Whatever we do, we can seem no more than friends to the world beyond."

"Is that what we are then? More than friends?" Louisa asked.

"I think…yes. Louisa, I don't feel very friendly toward you. What I feel for you is decidedly more than that."

Louisa wanted to scream, to cry, to curl into a ball and hide… to stretch long against Ellie with the beat of her heart against every inch of her skin, but then she thought about what Hugh had said and it worried her. "Perhaps we should remain no more than friends, Ellie. There's so much…there's so much danger." *My father…*

"Is that what you want?" Ellie's voice was so patient, at complete odds with Louisa's racing heart.

"No," Louisa said. "It's not what I want." She tensed at the thought and brought Ellie flush against her chest. "That's not at all what I want. I may not know what I do want, but I know that *that…*

is absolutely *not* it." She looked back into Ellie's eyes, attempted to trace the threads of deepest blue and violet she knew were there, but the room was too dark. She wanted to learned the pattern as if it a puzzle, she wanted to remember, to be able to recognize, possibly duplicate it in a painting or drawing, perhaps simply in her mind. She wanted enough time, staring into Ellie's eyes, to learn them.

"Louisa?"

"Yes?"

Ellie reached up and skimmed her hand down Louisa's cheek. "You're so lovely. I'm blessed to have found you."

Louisa had no response to that. She watched the other girl, her eyes searching in the way she knew her own were at that very moment. Because Louisa felt as though she'd been found. As if she'd lived the whole of her life at the back of a very dim cave, people standing in the light yelling at her to do, to be, to think, to behave, in so many certain ways. Then Ellie came along, wove easily amongst them, shifting the light at the entrance to the cave before ducking in, blocking the light and allowing her to adjust to the new reality.

She allowed the adjustment. Allowed the full weight of it to come down around her like a heavy shroud. It weighed not just on her body but her heart, and her soul. Louisa shrank against it, the prick of tears sharp in her eyes as she stared into those deep pools of Ellie's. Louisa watched as that weight seemed not to transfer, but to encompass Ellie as well and it pulled at her even more. Her hands tightened to white knuckles of pain.

"But... we both must marry. This is not good," she said.

Ellie

Ellie looked away, the immensity of their realizations taking on such a tangible power between them she could no longer bear it and Louisa's hold on her loosened. They wrapped their hands together. She traced a tear down Louisa's cheek with only her eyes, then watched it fall to their joined hands, the intense pressure of the knot of them painfully tight.

"We should have stayed friends." She heard the words and nearly believed she hadn't spoken them, so detached was she from her own self. She felt a twist as something wrenched in her belly and grew sour. Their hands released, exploded from each other as though they'd only realized they were still connected. Impossibly connected, and the separation had to be violent in order to be realized.

Ellie clasped her hands then, rubbed the blood back into them as she thought.

"We must… you and I both must marry," Louisa said, and Ellie realized the voice came from behind her, not knowing when she'd turned away.

"So we must," she replied.

"My father—"

"I understand. Believe me. Don't think I don't wish it weren't true, because I do more than anything. They expect me to marry a peer, to gain a small step into your world through that union. This is my responsibility to the family." Louisa's hand skimmed down her arm and she reached for it, pulling her back toward Louisa. Louisa took both of her hands, then watched her thumbs circling the back of her hands.

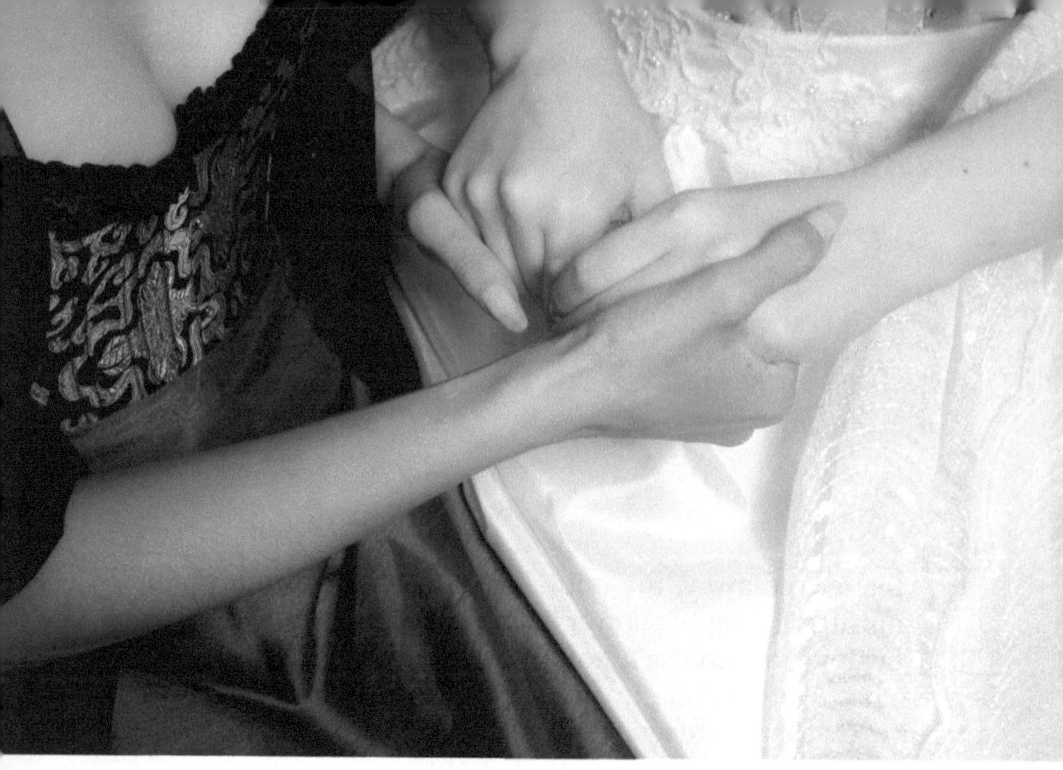

"I wish for a small life," she said. "I wish for a small house—a single room would be sufficient even. A cottage. I wish for a cottage, with a large garden, a patch of sunshine far from London where I can grow some vegetables, some herbs, some flowers."

"I would like a cat," Ellie replied, and Louisa glanced up then. "Because I do not like mice."

Louisa smiled. "It would be nice to have a small barn, perhaps a single cow and a few chickens. Occasionally raise a pig. I've heard people do that. I've read about it in books. I'm certain I could do that. They share them with other families, or with the local butcher, who takes a cut to sell in payment for his services. Because I could never kill an animal."

"I couldn't either. I could give it a good life while it was here, but I couldn't end that life," Ellie agreed.

"We could buy meat. Keep the cow for milk. Eggs would be fine. We can have chickens," Louisa decided.

"Perhaps a goat to tend the weeds," Ellie said as she leaned into Louisa's shoulder, searching for warmth. "We'll need a strong fence to keep him from the gardens."

"Whitewashed, of course," Louisa said.

"With a bell on the gate?" Ellie wanted a little bell that would go off throughout the day for the goat, or visitors.

"Absolutely."

"And a spring on the hinge to keep it shut."

"Is there another sort of gate?" Louisa grinned up at her and a shiver ran her shoulders and down her arms.

Ellie shook her head. "No, not for a cottage, in the country, away from London, only used for keeping a goat from the gardens."

"I wish..." Louisa said again.

"As do I," Ellie replied.

Louisa

Louisa hadn't slept at all that night, and it wasn't just that she'd brought herself off thinking about how lovely Ellie was. It was that kiss. That hard clash of teeth and tongue. Something she'd never experienced. Oh, how she wanted to be with her. Her mind turned, trying to find viable ways they could disappear as spinsters together, and the life they would live, quiet and happy far from London and society in their little cottage with the bell on the gate.

She couldn't concentrate on anything the following day either, and her cross stitch was suffering to the point that Lady Mayjoy was becoming annoyed with her. Louisa wasn't sure what she should do. She was mediocre at cross stitching to begin with but this was ridiculous; she'd be lucky if she didn't stitch herself to her work, as distracted as she was.

In all her life, Louisa had never sought another woman for the kind of love and companionship she was taught to want from a man. Yet here she was. She wanted Ellie, wanted to spend her life getting to know more about her...she hardly knew anything at all but what she did know was of such kinship to her she shuddered to consider how deep their bond could go— how deep it would go. Never had she felt this. She'd no basis for comparison. Part of her wondered if it was merely the need for companionship, a closeness she certainly lacked with any other woman, but another part of her knew that whatever this was, it was not simply friendship or companionship.

Never would she have assumed that Ellie felt this way as well. Louisa would have held herself back forever, if only to remain close enough—but they'd kissed, and if there was one thing she knew, it was that it had been no kiss borne of friendship. It was more, so very much more. She stabbed herself with the needle and sucked air between her teeth, bringing it to her lips as she bit the tip of her finger.

"Louisa."

"Yes, ma'am?"

"What has you so distracted?"

Damn. What was she to say? Louisa was not one who could think on her feet.

"What happened at the ball last night? You disappeared for quite awhile. Were you perhaps with a gentleman?"

"In the gardens, yes, for a time," Louisa said. It wasn't a lie.

"Perhaps there's a bit of hope for you yet. Go clean up that mess before you bleed on my silk chaise. The ladies will be here for tea soon."

"Yes, ma'am." She stood and carefully set aside her work, which was awful enough to not warrant using such caution. "Am I expected at tea?"

"Yes, that woman and her daughter are coming. You'll be needed to entertain the daughter so I will only have to deal with the one of them."

Louisa froze. More adequately, her heart skipped a beat, stopping her blood and freezing her muscles beneath her skin. She was quite unable to move. "Yes, ma'am." She forced the words, and the woman's eyes narrowed on her in consideration.

"Perhaps you begin to understand the difficulty of dealing with the new-money types in London. Go now. I can't have guests see you behaving in a such a manner."

Louisa curtseyed and moved to the door.

"And Louisa?"

She turned back. "Yes, ma'am?"

Lady Mayjoy didn't look at her. "I saw you leave the ballroom with her last night. I warned you, Louisa, have a care."

Louisa turned and rushed toward her room, all the while attempting to catch her breath. It was as if she'd fallen and had the wind knocked from her—it simply wouldn't come. She wasn't sure what would happen. Lady Mayjoy must know something— but Ellie was being allowed to tea today. Was it a trap?

They'd left each other the night before cautious and nowhere near optimistic. They'd dreamed aloud together of a lovely home, the two of them, their garden and their goat. Things Louisa couldn't find a way to. She had to marry, they both did. She would never be free of her father. Even now, three years into society, and he still held her beneath his thumb. She had no friends to take pity on her and give her a room, no family to run to beyond London. Save Ellie, she was alone.

"Maitland, you must sit still." Her mother yanked her skirt again to get her attention.

"Yes, mama." She held her knee and concentrated on keeping her heel from rattling against the floor. She hadn't expected the invitation to tea and wasn't sure why it had come about, but honestly she didn't care. She simply couldn't wait to have Louisa alone in that beautiful gallery again.

The carriage pulled up to the front walk and the liveried servants opened the carriage door, assisting her. She waited for her mother, breathing in counts of three to settle her nerves. What if Louisa thought she'd been too forward? What if Louisa realized how dangerous a mistake it was for them to pursue this? What if Louisa had been shocked and had only gone along with the kiss at the time? What if Louisa— *Oh, what if what if what if...* Funny how distance played such terrible tricks with the mind.

Ellie closed her eyes and remembered the last moments from the night before. That kiss, that amazing kiss, had been the both of them. She hadn't much experience in kissing, but that the kiss was amazing was a fact simple to decide. None of these concerns should be of concern. Everything was as she wanted, as she believed it to be.

What if Louisa wasn't planning on being here for the at-home today? Her eyes snapped open. Well then, she'd found a concern that was valid.

The front door swept open and Ellie followed her mother into that incredible foyer. She couldn't help it; her head fell back and

she gazed at the massive glass dome so far above as it sprinkled down rainbows on all who entered her keeping. She saw a dart of green on the upper-floor balcony and knew Louisa was in fact home. Ellie smiled. She couldn't stop even when the butler cut a glance from the corner of his eye. Apparently the servants disapproved of her demeanor as well. Fantastic.

She followed her mother up the stairs to the first-floor landing, where they would turn to the left to continue to the parlor, and she would need to control her want to go to the right instead, toward the gallery. The butler stopped there and spoke softly to her. "Miss Present will meet you in the gallery," he said, then turned and continued on with her mother.

Ellie paused, watching as they left her behind, and her heart raced. She looked to her right, the short set of steps that would bring her to the upper landing and the gallery. Lou had gone down a hallway here, not into the gallery. She heard the rise of voices as the door to the parlor opened and her mother was announced and greeted. It actually warmed her heart that her mother was welcome here. Well, somewhat welcome. Ellie understood how the *ton* felt about her family, that they weren't of the establishment and weren't particularly wanted in upper society. She further understood her distinct purpose in this, that Louisa's father, the Viscount, was searching for backing for a certain action he wished to see come to pass in the House. It all came down to money. It always came down to money.

Yet without it, where would she be? She shuddered to think. Certainly nowhere near Louisa. But money was also what would keep them apart, because they both had to marry in order to meet their true worth as daughters of powerful men. Tokens. Chess pieces. Chattle.

"Miss?"

Ellie shook off the thoughts. "I beg your pardon. I'll be going. I was...thinking."

He brushed past her and disappeared down the staircase into the foyer.

Ellie turned and shuffled up the steps, headed to find the only person she trusted for certain.

Louisa

Louisa stopped in one of the hallways near the gallery and sat on a small bench. She'd never understood why there were benches and small settees strewn about the house, but today she couldn't be more thankful to be able to sit and rest and think for one simple moment. She didn't want to go a single step further. She twisted her hands in her skirt and closed her eyes. She wanted to say a prayer, but she wasn't sure what she should say, or if God would even listen. If everything she'd been taught were true…

But she could hope.

How many people ask for a sign? How many people beg You to tell them that what they feel is real, and true, and what You've designed for them? I refuse to believe that You would create us only to watch some of us suffer, to catch our tears. Why would I feel this way if it wasn't borne into me? If You made me… If You truly did make me, all of me, why would You have made this part of me? Louisa swiped a tear from her cheek and pressed on.

I am not supposed to need, I'm not supposed to question, but at this moment I have nothing but questions. I'm so terribly lost. I could use a guide, something to follow. You gave Joseph a star… She paused, working up her bravery. She'd never asked for anything for herself. As a good and penitent girl, she'd only ever asked for blessings on her friends and family—for herself, only forgiveness. To ask for more than that, it wasn't something she was supposed to do. As well, she couldn't ask forgiveness for something that seemed a gift to her—she refused to do so.

Louisa took a deep breath.

Dear God, please give me a sign, some small piece of hope. I wish to be good and true, but right this moment I'm having a difficult time. I'm certain You're busy—I'm certain You're busy with so many pressing issues, but if You can see it in Your infinite wisdom that I should be on this path...please God, give me a star to follow.

The touch at her cheek was so infinitely delicate, Louisa wasn't sure she'd felt it until she heard the voice.

"Louisa?"

Ellie.

Louisa didn't move. She felt the bench sway next to her, the warmth of Ellie's body as it leaned into her side. She felt her press toward her, then her lips on her cheek as she kissed away a tear with such reverence that Louisa shuddered.

Dear God, please don't tempt me so in the moment you know me weak.

She couldn't open her eyes but felt Ellie's hand drift down her arms, her fingers tangling with her own.

"Won't you take me to the gallery?" she asked.

Please God. Louisa tensed for a moment, then opened her eyes on her lap, her hands clenched with Ellie's, their fingers a knot of tension. She shifted her gaze, following Ellie's arm, and stopped when she came to the fabric of her gown. The white linen was carefully embroidered with hundreds of diminutive bursts of color in a pale blue silk thread that shimmered against the plain background. Once again Louisa couldn't move as her breath stole from her.

"You're covered in stars," she choked out the whisper, breathed it really, so quiet she hadn't even heard the words though she knew she'd formed them. "You're...you're covered in stars." The tears came readily then, coursing her cheeks and skimming her neck and collarbone. Ellie's eyes widened, and Louisa hid her face in her hands, so fretfully overwhelmed she had to stop everything. The sounds, the sights, the scents, and dear God but Ellie smelled delicious.

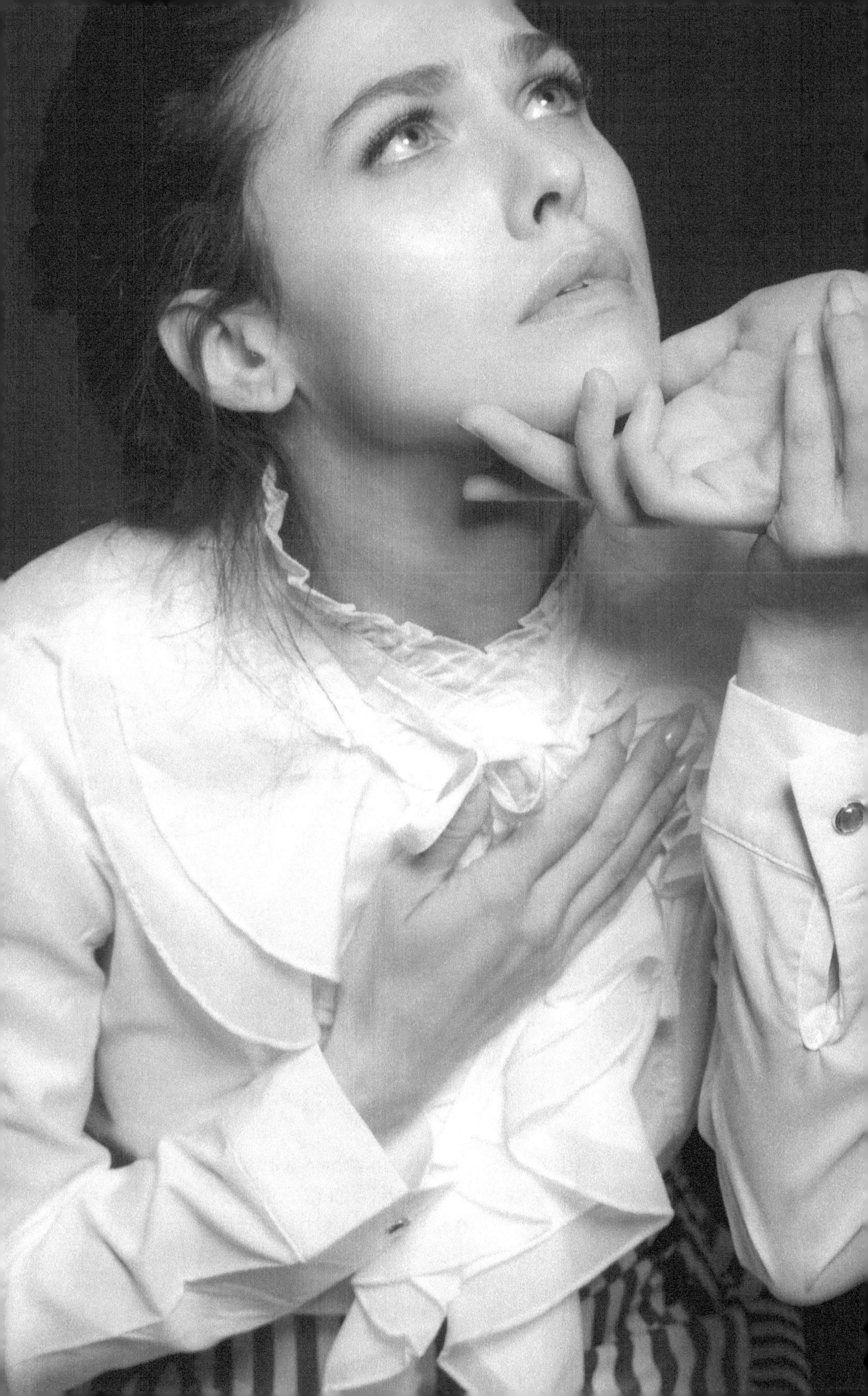

Ellie took her hands away and tangled them with her own again, and Louisa turned her face away, tucking her chin to her shoulder. *Not yet.* She simply couldn't...not yet.

"This gown made me think of you," Ellie said. "The color of the little bursts, the blue of your eyes." Ellie pulled one hand away, and Louisa heard the rustle of fabric. Louisa turned to find Ellie fingering one of what must be thousands of tiny shimmering bursts.

"I'll follow you anywhere," Louisa said and searched Ellie's eyes. Ellie stood and pulled her toward the gallery, the hold on her hand growing tighter as they moved through the open foyer.

Louisa shut the door behind them, then paused with her back to the room, both hands on the seam of the door as though to seal out the whole of the world. She felt warmth against her back, the raised silk of Ellie's stars tickling the skin at the backs of her arms. "Ellie, I—"

Ellie took her shoulders and turned her.

"I think we should simply do. Enough talking, enough debating, I just... I feel, I feel so very much and I need to know what it means because I—I don't. Do you?"

"No, I don't, I've never... This is... I can't—" Ellie closed her eyes, a line of tension coming between her eyebrows that Louisa tried to soften with her thumb. Ellie relaxed, pushed her face into Louisa's hand. Held it with her own.

She closed her eyes and breathed of Ellie, sank into the sensation of skin on skin and wished for more...so much more. Then she tasted the warm sweetness of Ellie's mouth as it met with hers, their breath mingling between them. She felt as though the stars were here, her skin reflecting the tiny bursts of light. She wanted to float away on them.

"Kiss me. Just—" Ellie paused, her breathing hard against her. "Kiss me."

And so she did. Louisa skimmed her tongue across Ellie's lips, smiled at the now-familiar taste of chocolate, *it's chocolate!* She pulled her lower lip into her mouth with a gentle suction then wound her hands around Ellie's face and held her there so she could taste more of her. Ellie's hands wrapped around her waist, twisting the fabric of her dress as she held on to her as well.

This, this was everything. This moment was her entire world, and Louisa wished to live in it for the balance of her life and never leave. "Oh God, Ellie, what is this?" Her chest filled with a million tiny sparkling stars.

"Love, Louisa. I think this is love."

"We only—"

"But I've been waiting for you the whole of my life."

"I had no idea," Louisa said. "I had no idea you would ever find me. Come settle with me," she said, breaking the kiss and pulling Ellie toward the settee. They sank together, and Ellie's heart beat against Louisa's chest, then she pressed her face to her neck. "Ellie."

Ellie cupped her head and held her there, and Louisa reached up, kissing along her jaw.

"I'm home." She kissed and sucked and licked every bit of her uncovered until Ellie was leaning against the end of the settee, splayed beneath Louisa. And Louisa wanted more of her. She trailed her hand from Ellie's hip, up her ribs, across her breast. Ellie arched beneath her, her gaze unfocused, so beautiful Louisa had no idea how she was supposed to react.

"Please," she said, and Louisa leaned into her again, kissing her with such abandon neither of them would be presentable if they didn't stop soon. She loosened the neck then wrapped her fingers around the edge of her corset and pulled gently until her chemise-covered nipple peeked above the edge of it.

Ellie stilled to her core as Louisa stared at her breast, trapped behind the thin fabric. Her skin so pale, tipped by a bud the color of rose. She skimmed a thumb across her nipple and Louisa thought she'd unspool like so much thread tight on a bobbin from watching the tiny bud furl, the blush spread from that small connection to all of Ellie's skin.

When Louisa's mouth on Ellie's breast replaced her thumb, Ellie took in a lungful of air and Louisa covered her mouth—a quiet reminder not to be loud. Ellie's hands wrapped around Louisa and pulled her tight as she leaned back into the bench, and Louisa followed.

Her hands...everywhere. Everywhere. She had to touch her everywhere. Louisa couldn't think straight. She couldn't think at all; streaks of fire rushed from her skin to her core igniting something deep inside she'd never known would be touched by another. And Ellie held on, allowed her. This woman who was so brave. So much braver than Louisa had ever dreamed to be.

"Ellie—" she started but was cut off when Ellie removed the hand on her lips and brought them together, the wet warmth of her mouth arrested any thought. They kissed and kissed, and Louisa didn't think she could ever get enough. "Ellie, God, Ellie, you kiss me like, like I've always imagined I would be kissed someday."

"Louisa, I feel like I'm falling."

"I've already fallen. I fell the moment I saw those eyes of yours. I fell. Come with me. Come, come with me," Louisa breathed. "Oh, please, come with me."

Ellie tensed and Louisa pulled back, her face pinked, hot and alive. Her eyes lit from inside, the vivid color black with excitement. Then Louisa started gathering the fabric at her knee until she met the soft silk of her stockings. Ellie studied her face, the soft tips of her fingers on Louisa's neck. She slid her hands up. Slid beneath the scalloped hem of her drawers and along her leg until they skimmed the very edge of her stocking, the softest skin there at her fingertips.

"Ellie." She was frightened, excited, concerned, frightened, frightened... Louisa stopped. "I'm not sure what—" She wasn't sure what they should be doing or where they should be going. Stopping or starting. She leaned forward and kissed Ellie again, spreading her legs as she did, and her hand slid further until Louisa thought for sure her heart would stop beating.

They both stopped moving and gazed at each other. Louisa watched as Ellie's eyes lightened, and she felt her heartbeat slow, her breathing settle. Louisa pulled her hand from beneath her skirt, pulling the fabric down as she did so, then shifted the top of her dress, covering Ellie's breasts. Louisa then reached for Ellie and pulled her in tight, her arms wrapped around her.

"I'm sorry. I don't know what's come over me. I—I shouldn't have..."

"Please don't. Please don't take it back," Ellie whispered.

Louisa held her gaze. "Never."

They sat for a bit, helping each other return to decency, smoothing fabric and straightening seams until it was as if they'd never been.

Louisa stood, needing to move through the pervasive nervousness. She took Ellie's hand and knotted it with hers as they walked the gallery again. They spoke of nothing of consequence, but her shoulder brushed Ellie's often, and Ellie's elbow tucked tight into her side, and their skirts tangled and required extra steps to kick them free.

When they reached the far end beneath her mother's portrait, Louisa looked up. "Mama, I would like for you to meet Ellie." She pulled her close, wrapped her arm around Ellie's waist, and tucked her chin against her shoulder. "I love her," she said.

She felt Ellie drop a kiss on her forehead, and she returned the kiss to Ellie's collarbone, and her neck as she turned into her hold.

Louisa took her face in her hands once again, exploring those eyes. Those eyes that could hide nothing from her. Louisa skimmed her thumbs over her eyebrows, then across the crest of her cheeks. She dropped her gaze to Ellie's mouth. "I love you," she whispered and kissed her again, and she put every single piece of her soul into that kiss. "I want...I want to spend my life getting to know you." She studied Ellie's eyes. "I don't know how this works. I've never... I don't know either way. But I want to know you." Louisa placed her hand on Ellie's chest. "Your heart, your soul, your mind." Her other hand skimmed down the side of her face. "Everything. I want to know you."

Ellie smiled. "I want the same, but—"

"But?" Louisa asked.

"How...can we? We'll be ostracized."

"Or forgotten."

"We should be so lucky."

"A bright possibility after all," Louisa said as she soaked in the warmth of the sun, "We can find a way, can't we? I'm nearly a spinster, even as my father is determined. You're so much more brave than I, Ellie."

"I have to marry," Ellie whispered. With those words, they released each other and stepped away. "I must, I can't... My father will not allow me to walk away from a match. I have no choice, and I am his for another three years. I cannot..."

Louisa walked toward the large windows. "Then the time we have is all the time we have. Until that changes. But until that changes, Ellie—" she turned back toward her, "—until that changes, you are mine, and I'll not let you go. And I'm already yours and I will always be yours."

Ellie rushed her, wrapping her up in a tight embrace. "If only..."

"No...only now."

"Only now," Ellie whispered. "Right now." The doors to the gallery opened, and they moved apart. "Or perhaps later," Ellie said with a grin.

"Later," Louisa whispered.

"I've an idea."

"Maitland, it's time we should go. Lady Mayjoy is exhausted by her visitors. Let's not wear on her," her mother said, the butler holding the door.

Ellie turned to her. "Mama, might Louisa come to our house? Perhaps go with us to the ball tomorrow evening, then stay the night?"

"That sounds like a fine idea, Ellie, so long as it's acceptable to Lady Mayjoy," her mother replied with a smile.

Ellie slid her hand behind her, and Louisa squeezed it, then she turned and walked toward the entry, following her mother and the butler from the room.

Louisa breathed. Then she melted in the puddle of sunlight like iced cream. She sat on the floor, inspecting her hands, smelling and kissing them and thinking of all the places those hands had roamed just now. All the things they'd felt and done. *Ellie.* Louisa had one reason for living at this moment, and that reason was Ellie. She stood and headed to the parlor to ask permission to go to Ellie's house the following night.

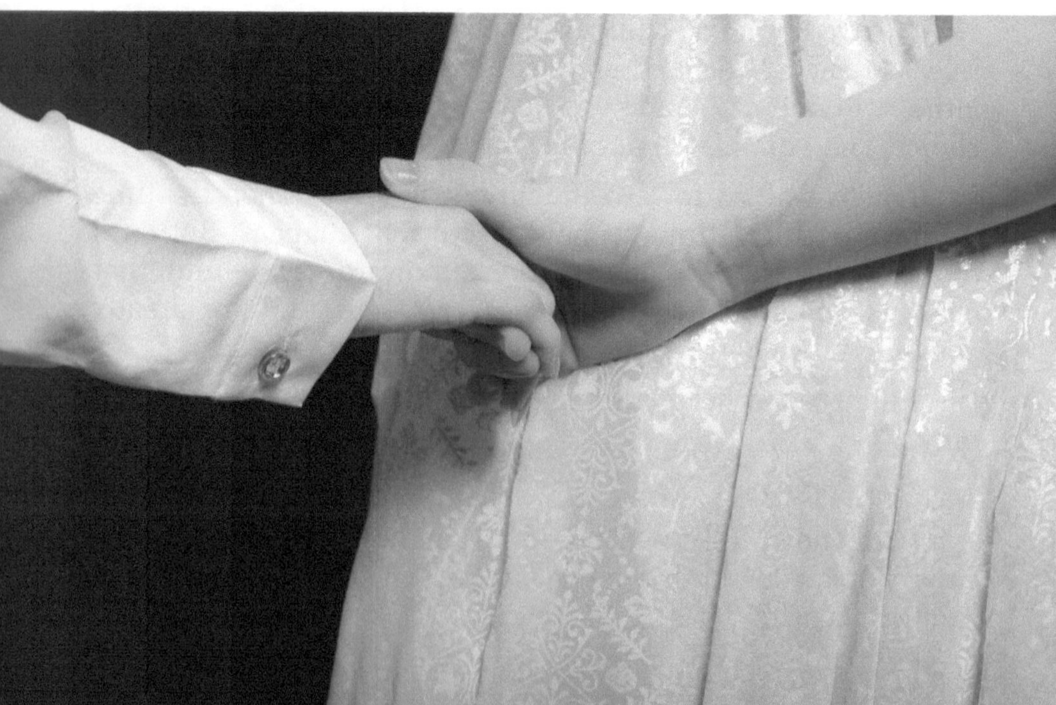

Ellie hadn't been nervous for her first ball. She hadn't been nervous when she'd been introduced to countless peers, from dukes to barons and viscounts. She hadn't even been nervous when Edward, the future king, had attended the opera and had spoken with her from his private box next to theirs. Right now though, her hands were clammy and shaking, her knees felt unstable, and her jaw was tense.

Louisa would be at her house any moment now, and someone would show her to the parlor where Ellie was standing, regarding the scene outside the window expectantly. Nervously.

As though she were a virgin on her wedding night...or so she'd been told she would be. The whole thing seemed all too perverse to her and she'd never paid it any mind, until now.

Until Louisa.

Her knees knocked and she sat hard on the window seat as thoughts of a naked Louisa in her bed coursed her mind and sank into her belly. Way down low in warm, wet, places she wasn't sure she'd known were there. Ellie hoped Louisa would allow her touch. Not just her hands, or her shoulders. Her mouth or her hip. Ellie wanted very desperately to touch Louisa in such an intimate way that the actual idea of it sent her insides to flipping around beneath her skin like a fish in the shallows. She couldn't even consider being touched by Louisa again; she'd flame out of existence and never have the chance.

"Maitland?"

She turned to her mother.

"What's with you, child?" she asked, forcing Ellie to pay attention. She rushed over to her, placing a hand to her forehead. "You're flushed. Are you ill?"

"No, Mother, it's from sitting in the window. I'm fine, really."

"What has you so wrapped up in thought that you didn't hear me?"

"I'm looking forward to this evening is all. It's supposed to be one of the best events of the season. The dinner is the biggest and most extravagant, the dancing going well into the night. I suppose I'm happy to be included," she said.

"Your cousin Bertrand will accompany the two of you to and from Lady Greensborough's. Please listen to him, and to his wife."

"Yes, Mother."

"He'll introduce you to several men of the gentry," she said happily. "Perhaps if I'm not there to call attention to your status—"

"Mama, please don't." Ellie turned to see her mother shaking her head.

"Maitland, just go with Bertrand, make the acquaintances, try to find a man you can tolerate, and marry the damn thing before he figures out you're nothing but a pretty face with money."

Ellie stared as her mother turned and left the room. Then the butler entered with Louisa behind him. Ellie couldn't force herself to her feet. Her mother had never talked to her in such a way, and something inside her slipped. Like a cube of ice had cracked and shifted along the fault. Louisa took the space next to her in the narrow seat.

"What happened?" she asked.

Ellie shook her head. "A simple reminder that I am not my own, and I must marry before I lose my looks or my father's money," she said plainly.

They stayed there for a long while, watching the carriages pass in the street as the sun began its descent from the crest of its journey. Until a maid came in and reminded Ellie they needed to prepare for the ball.

By then Ellie was strong enough to stand without hesitation. "Were your things taken to my room?" she asked Louisa.

"No, your mother said I would stay in the guest suite. I assume you'll be allowed to stay with me?"

"The guest suite? I've...never been allowed in there."

"I'd prefer to be in your rooms, but I don't want to cause a fuss."

"Not at all. I'll—"

"Unless you'd like to stay in the guest suite?"

Ellie thought about it. She knew she didn't have to impress Louisa, but she also knew her mother was doing her best to do so, and this was her only chance to stay in the most lavish rooms in this house. Rooms she'd only ever peeked in through an ajar entry while the maids were cleaning.

Ellie nodded, reached out, and squeezed Louisa's elbow, then led her from the room. Her parents' house wasn't nearly as regal as Louisa's but it was one of the nicest properties overlooking Green Park on Arlington. Ellie led Louisa up to the second floor and down the left passageway. She opened the first door on the left to the suite of rooms, and Louisa followed diligently. Once inside, Ellie turned to her ladies maid and with a simple nod, she began to lay all of the clothes out for both of them.

Ellie had chosen a pale green gown of silk with lavender pinstripes. It was a bear to keep straight as much as the fabric attempted to wrinkle, but it was one of her favorites. It was also her most impressive. The bustles were enormous, intricately set with large purple satin-edged georgette bows that matched the purple striping of the fabric. It was truly a showpiece of a gown, as it was meant to be. Her mother had been promised it would be one of the most exquisite and singular gowns of the season, as well as one of the most expensive. And everyone would know it.

The maid then pulled Louisa's gown from the wardrobe where they'd placed it and flounced the fabric to release the wrinkles from the trip over. Ellie nearly lost her breath. It was nearly the same color as Louisa's own skin, and as she wore it, she would seem completely naked in places. The fitted corset top was trimmed in the deepest of sapphire blue, highlighting Louisa's natural curves, while the edge of the dress, the place where it met the skirt, and the bustle at the back were decorated with sapphire blue rosettes. This dress had no spare decor. It was spare and simple at first glance, all the detail going into the construction of the bodice, and the way, Ellie knew, it would highlight Louisa's figure. She turned away.

"It seems we will both be at purpose tonight," she said.

Her maid piped in. "Oh yes, these dresses will catch many a man's eye tonight. I've never seen two their equal. You'll both be the belles of the ball, without doubt."

Ellie turned and smiled at her. "Thank you, Abigail. Would you leave us for a moment?"

She nodded. "Yes miss. Ring when you're ready to dress. Bertrand should be along with the carriage in about two hours, so we should hurry getting you both ready." Then she left the room, closing the door behind her.

"You heard her," Ellie said. "We need to dress quickly." She stood in the center of the room and stared at Louisa, as if waiting until one of them worked up the courage to move. Heavy breaths floated against the backdrop of the busy household outside the doors.

"Might she return?" Louisa asked.

"Not until I call for her."

The silence floated down over them like a soft sheet pulled fresh from the line. Then Ellie moved. "You called me brave," she said.

"I did," Louisa responded.

"Why do you think me brave?" she asked as she put her hands on Louisa's ribs, holding her gaze.

"Because you are. If it weren't for you... If it weren't for you, there would be no us," she finished on a whisper.

"Is there an us?" Ellie asked.

"Yes."

"I find the opposite to be true. I believe there to be an us strictly because of you."

A light spread from her center filling her veins with a warm glow that she wanted— no, needed to share. Louisa spun Ellie around until her back was to her, then she started to undo all the

buttons, pins, ties, clips and knots that held her into her clothes. Ellie helped as much as she could until she stood before Louisa in her corset, chemise, drawers and stockings. Ellie lifted a hand and fidgeted with the pendent on the chain at her neck.

"Louisa," she said. "I may not be as brave as you think."

"I'll help you," Louisa replied. "You're so beautiful." She swept a hand across her collar bone and down the center of her chest, her arm grazing her nipple. Ellie hissed a breath as it peaked tight and Louisa stared down at it. The long case clock in the hallway struck six times, and each toll resonated through her belly and across her skin. Louisa stared at her as if she'd no idea what to do next.

"We should ready," Ellie said.

Louisa nodded, and Ellie moved to the pull, notifying Abigail that she needed to return. Then she sat at the small dressing table, sorting through the jewelry case placed there searching for pieces to match her gown. The door swept open, and Ellie turned. Louisa still stood where she'd left her, in the middle of the room. And Abigail walked straight to Louisa and started undoing her dress, then her skirts, and finally her petticoats, letting everything fall to the floor as Ellie held her gaze and her breath.

"The bath has been run," Abigail said, and Ellie's breath caught.

"We'll share it," Louisa said, "to save time, if you wouldn't mind readying the rest of our things?"

"Of course, miss. Let me pin Ellie's hair up." She went to the open wardrobe and pulled out a threadbare chemise. "Here's a bathing chemise for you."

Ellie stood but turned away as Louisa changed in order to hide the blush she knew was rising. Hands came to her back, first untying the laces, then loosening the corset with a slow, methodical pull. Ellie thought she'd die. It seemed all her bravery had suddenly left the room. Why did this make her nervous?

Louisa's arms wrapped around her middle, squeezed her hard, and released the clips at the front of the corset, and Ellie swooned on the thick rush of air to her lungs. Her hand flew out, and Louisa took it, spinning her around to face her as the corset fell to the floor. Ellie closed her eyes and waited. Louisa's hands

were on the chemise, skimming up her thighs, meeting the skin at the top of her stockings. Her knuckles grazed the skin over her ribs as she lifted the chemise up, and the warm heat of Louisa's mouth was on her nipple before she stood, sweeping the chemise off and dropping it to the floor.

Ellie stared. Then her world went dark as a different chemise was pulled down over her from behind. *Oh.* And her drawers were untied, pooling at her feet the her stocking were pushed to the floor, Abigail lifting her feet one at a time to remove them.

Louisa took Ellie's hand and led her through the bedroom, to the bathroom, and the bathing room. She'd never been in here. It was beautiful, a large tub at the center with brass fittings. The windows were all stained glass for privacy and created a patterned light much like the dome of Louisa's house. A magical room like this was here all along, and she'd never been allowed to enjoy it.

Louisa led her to the tub, helping her over the high edge and into the milky water, then she followed. They sat facing each other, knees up, the fabric of the thin chemises clinging to their bodies, loose threads of hair pasted to their necks.

Louisa inspected the vials of oils and bottles of dried herbs on the tray, reading the labels and smelling them as Ellie took a sea sponge and washed her arms, her shins, and her toes. Then Louisa tilted a bottle and let a rill of oil float along the water. She replaced the stopper and mixed the oil and the water, and the heady smell of roses bloomed around them in the steam. She leaned back against the rolled edge of the tub and breathed.

Enraptured, Ellie watched Louisa, eyes closed, face serene, body relaxed. She couldn't relax in her end of the tub in the same way, but she was perfectly content to wrap her arms around her knees and watch. Louisa shifted her knees together, moving her legs next to Ellie's, then stretching them out as much as she was able in the small space. Ellie's mouth went dry. The thin fabric of the chemise plastered itself to her body when she moved, her own breasts barely visible through the milky water that was nearly the same color as her own skin, making her appear to disappear entirely.

But Louisa's skin was warm enough as to shadow the milk bath and make Ellie wish for a clear running stream. When Louisa opened her eyes and found Ellie bound in a ball of tension she laughed. The sound of it bounced around the tiled bathing room, echoing joy. "I could spend the rest of my life here with you and need for nothing," she said.

Ellie smiled as southing unwound in her belly loosening the knots in her shoulders. "It's a lovely room. But any room you're in is lovely."

One of Louisa's hands broke the surface of the milky water and she leaned forward, taking Ellie's hands and pulling her closer until their lips met somewhere between them, reaching while they shifted awkwardly, hands searching and knees bumping.

Ellie grabbed the edge of the tub for traction and Louisa pulled her closer, her body curling and slipping until they were breast to breast, closer than they'd ever been, nothing between them but fabric so thin only the wrinkles mattered. Their legs tangled, and Ellie had a momentary concern for being discovered. But only momentary, because this moment was worth whatever she'd have to get through to savor.

Her nipples tightened against Louisa's skin and she shifted, the drift of skin across the coiled buds sent a shock through her body straight to her pelvis, where it warmed and bloomed like the

roses she breathed in. She couldn't explore with her hands and it frustrated her; if she released the edge of the tub, they'd slip and sink, and then they'd be in trouble for ruining their hair on such an important night. Ellie had enough awareness to know they couldn't do that. But she held herself to Louisa as she explored her mouth and inhaled, and it was...everything. In that moment, she was determined to find a way to know Louisa the rest of her life.

Louisa shifted in the water, their legs tangling further, and when her thigh brushed Ellie's vulva, she threw her head back and moaned in a way she'd never heard from herself or anyone else. "Oh God, Lou, what..." Louisa shifted again, and her breath caught, and Ellie's head snapped up as she focused on Louisa's face. "Lou?"

"Miss, do you have a different corset for this dress?" Abigail asked from beyond the bathroom, and the two of them were on their knees facing each other faster than Ellie had any idea how they'd managed. Louisa nodded, her chest heaving, her breasts pressing against the folds in the fabric, her nipples tight, her face flushed, her eyes wide and bright, the blue aflame.

"Yes," Louisa said finally, breathlessly. "Yes, I do. We'll be right there." Then she caught Ellie's gaze, held it. The water began to cool, and shivers coursed Ellie's skin, sending ripples of water out to lick at Louisa's belly. Louisa reached for her, wrapped one arm around her waist, the other tipping Ellie's chin until their mouths were lined up. She licked her lower lip, then her upper lip.

"Lou," was all Ellie could say, the sensation of the cooler water, the heat of her body through the chilled fabric, then Louisa's hand sliding between them and cupping her mons as she gasped, and Louisa swallowed her breath like it gave her life.

Ellie held on, one hand on the edge of the tub, the other wrapped around Louisa, the fabric of her chemise a knot in her fist.

"Come off for me, Ellie," she said, and Ellie tasted the sweetened lemon and spice on her tongue. "Close your eyes, Ellie. Let go."

Ellie nodded and allowed her body to sink against the sensations. Louisa's fingers played with her folds through the fabric, and it seemed her body generated enough heat to boil the water around them. Louisa shifted, moving one leg between them, bringing Ellie closer to ride that ridge of muscle, and her hand slid back up between them and plucked at her nipple like a raspberry. Ellie pushed against her, chasing something she couldn't see. Using Louisa's thigh in way's she'd never considered. Louisa wrapped an arm around her waist, held her tight, helped Ellie move.

"Come, Ellie, let go. Let go."

And as she gazed into Louisa's eyes, she understood, at long last, what that meant. "Louisa?" She threw her head back and Louisa kissed her way down her neck, taking a nipple in her mouth and sucking hard and she held steady, and Ellie bore down on her leg unashamed and wild, the pure abandon blooming from somewhere inside, reaching for Louisa and tangling them together in a way Ellie had never known possible. Louisa lifted, catching her cry between them and holding her close as her body rocked, convulsing madly, the bloom of ecstasy filling her veins until she was weak, slipping.

Louisa adjusted them, drawing Ellie back down into the bath on top of her, cautiously shifting to keep their hair above water as they sank together and let the water wash it all away.

Ellie knew then, living without Louisa was an impossibility.

"Can I help?" Ellie asked once they were both dressed in their fresh drawers, chemises and stockings.

"You might as well." Abigail's voice was sweet and joyful. Ellie had always liked her voice. She never did seem unhappy or upset. It was nice.

"Only tell me what to do," Ellie said as she walked up to Louisa and put her hands on her waist and surreptitiously slid her hands up Louisa's belly to her breasts, skimming the underside with the backs of her hands through the chemise. Louisa bit her lip and closed her eyes as Ellie's fingers wandered and she smiled. After what they'd done in the bath, Ellie wanted nothing more than to have Louisa completely naked and beneath her on the bed. She wanted to play Lousia's body in the way Louisa had clearly played hers. She wanted to see the effect she had on her. She wanted to feel it.

Abigail turned back, and Ellie dropped her hands, then took the new corset as Abigail wrapped it around Louisa from behind, and Louisa opened her eyes. Ellie clipped the front of the corset together, smoothing the chemise below it, her hands pushing into Louisa's belly, her chest, her knuckles rubbing her nipples as she worked to get the top clasp done so Abigail could lace her up, and Louisa seemed ready to swoon. Their eyes locked and Ellie carried on.

Louisa stopped breathing as Ellie helped one nipple to furl tight, then the other. Then she reached into the corset and chemise, scooping Louisa's firm breasts against the corset, adjusting the round tops at the crest and making sure her tight nipples were tucked behind the edge, until the corset was snug and she had to move her fingers or be trapped. Then she held Louisa's waist as Abigail tightened the laces, and Louisa swayed against the tension.

Ellie grabbed the caged bustle and pulled it around her waist, their chests pressed tight together as she peered over Louisa's shoulder to make sure she had it centered, then kissed her neck where it met her shoulder and watched the blush spread across her skin as she smoothed the ties around her waist to the front to attach it. Louisa reached up and held her

arm, steadying herself. Her breath came faster as Ellie teased. But so then, did Ellie's.

"Stand back, miss," Abigail said, and Ellie took a step back as Louisa finally broke that connection when she glanced over her shoulder. Abigail tossed the first of many skirts over her head. When that was done, Abigail brought the last of the skirts over, and Ellie held that stunning dress.

"Whose idea was it to make this gown the color of your skin?" Ellie asked.

"My father's wife," Louisa replied. "She said it would attract all the gentlemen."

"It will. You'd better not leave my sight," Ellie said. She helped Abigail bring the dress down over Louisa's head, then turned her. The buttons started at one hip and traveled across her back to the opposite shoulder. The lines were exquisite and reminded Ellie of a barber pole, or a lollipop, or a carousel. Something mesmerizing to watch, taste, or ride.

Abigail handed Ellie a button hook, and she did the buttons one by one. "Well," she said when she finished, "it appears you have forty-six buttons' worth of back." She smiled at Louisa as

Abigail worked to bustle the skirts and fix them to the underskirts so they wouldn't slip when she lifted them to sit down.

Then Abigail stood back. "We made a good team," she said with a smile.

"I should say so," Louisa replied as she examined herself in the tall cheval mirror. Then she caught Ellie's gaze in the glass. "But now it's my turn."

Louisa smiled wickedly, and Ellie rethought everything she'd done. Abigail handed Louisa the corset then started pulling underskirts from the wardrobe with the caged bustle. Ellie stopped. She hadn't thought about this. "If we must," she whispered as Louisa stalked toward her.

Ellie turned away from them, once again hiding the blush she knew was rising. Then Louisa's hands were at her back, placing the corset on her spine and dancing her fingers through the laces. When Louisa came around to the front, they simply watched each other as Abigail tied Ellie into her corset and finished dressing her. Their eyes never wavered again, not once.

Louisa

ouisa tried to concentrate on the dinner. In all of her years of being allowed to this particular feast, it was absolutely her favorite because of the incredible selection of foods. They served everything. Pheasant, duck, partridge, peacock, steak, several types of fish, lamb, and that was just the meat. The salads were even more abundant in all their assemblages and presentations. It was remarkable and one of the biggest suppers of the season because everyone wanted to see the incredible food.

Unfortunately, Louisa had been seated directly in front of a peacock paté, which had to be the most disturbing dish of the night. A fully feathered bird in all its wondrous glory had been relieved of its insides, only to be stuffed with those of other birds. She wished she'd been seated anywhere but here. But she hadn't been paying attention to the bird when she'd come in; she'd been watching Ellie.

They were close, about the width of one stuffed peacock between them. Truth be told, Louisa had enjoyed most of the dinner. Ender was there with his friend Trumbull, and they had most of the dinner party laughing with jokes about their rather inappropriate exploits. She wondered if Ender really would agree to marry her when the girl he loved married someone else. Louisa just needed a husband, and he wouldn't want to marry someone who wasn't Amelia, not if it was to be a true marriage. She and Ender could retire to his far estate. Live a ridiculous hermit-like existence and simply fade away. Without Ellie as an option, it sounded nice enough.

She watched as Ellie picked up a candied pear slice and sucked the end of the sweet treat. Then stared. Then gaped. She only realized she was doing so when the gentleman—if you could call him that—next to her cleared his throat.

"She's quite charming," he drawled from between two floppy jowls of cheeks. "You'll have to introduce us." He sneered as he took yet another large helping of the stuffed peacock.

Louisa shuddered. She wouldn't introduce them. She would avoid it. She cut her gaze to the man, then away again.

"Your father, he's a friend. He mentioned you're nearly on the shelf and may need some help in finding your way."

She cringed. What the hell did that mean? "Sir, I am quite able to find my way, thank you. Regardless, we have yet to be introduced ourselves. This entire conversation is..." Her thoughts drifted away as she watched Ellie spoon a giant puff of whipped cream into her mouth, then give her a wink. She was doing this on purpose. It wasn't a show for the men—though they heartily believed it may be. She sat over there acting all sweet and innocent, but in reality she was baiting Louisa the whole time. Lou closed her eyes and smiled, then jumped when she felt a hand at her knee. She stood suddenly, her chair falling back to the floor with a resounding clatter that stilled the whole of the dining room. Louisa blanched. "I beg your pardon, I..." *Don't insult the hostess...* "I believe I might swoon from so many wonderful dishes. Won't you excuse me?" She turned, then heard Ellie.

"I shall go help her."

When she entered the retiring room, Louisa checked to be sure nobody was in the attached water closet, then she turned to the door. As soon as she saw Ellie enter the room she took her shoulders, pushed her back against the door as it closed, and kissed her. Damn, it felt good. To push her up against the wall and have her mouth. She could taste the sugar and ginger from the pears, the cream from the dessert, the sweet wine she'd had with dinner.

She swept her tongue across the roof of her mouth and sucked that lower lip into her mouth, savoring every last taste she could. Then Ellie changed everything and next thing Louisa knew, she was pushed to a settee and Ellie was on top of her, her hands crushing the satin of her own skirts as she tried to push them out of the way.

"Ellie... Ellie!" Louisa said. "Ellie, you have to stop. We can't, not here." Louisa took Ellie's cheeks between her palms and caught her gaze. "Sweet, beautiful Ellie, not here. Even if we can dress each other, we'll never escape without some rumor."

Ellie sat up as she straddled Louisa, pouting. Then she stood from the settee and pulled Louisa up to try to straighten her dress. "Stop making it so difficult then," Ellie said stiffly.

"Me? I wasn't the one who was sucking on every piece of candied fruit I could get my hands on," Louisa replied.

"I wasn't sitting across the table making eyes at some gruesome gentleman."

"You can't be serious. That man..." Louisa shuddered. "No."

Ellie turned Louisa and started to straighten the silk of her bustle so it wasn't so terribly rumpled. "Do you think dinner is over yet? I don't want to go back in there."

Louisa popped her head out the door. "I hear the orchestra tuning, so I imagine it's nearly done. We could go to the ballroom and wait, or out to the gardens." She didn't want to return to that table either. The man next to her had been abhorrent, and watching Ellie flirt had been beyond frustrating.

"Did you really want me because of the fruit?" Ellie said.

"More than you can know, Ellie. More than you can know."

Louisa watched Ellie across the ballroom, wishing she could do more than just gaze at her from afar, but calling attention to her...attentions was out of the question. Her father was here tonight, as were his friends. She wished they could manage to get out to the gardens so they could walk, alone, perhaps chat a bit, get away from the crowd.

"Louisa!" The exasperated voice came over her shoulder.

She peered at him...up at him. All that blondish hair flopping too long against his crown, his smile without want or insistence. "Oh, you are well in your cups, aren't you?"

"Absolutely...yes. I suppose so."

"What do you need, Hugh?"

"Nothing. Would you like to dance? You haven't been seen with a suitor yet this evening."

"Are you offering?" She cocked an eyebrow at him.

"I... To dance, yes. The rest? Not particularly. I just figured, you know, once around the floor for friendship sake?" He shrugged. He seemed terribly unsure of himself at the moment and while she knew she wasn't the cause of it, something in her called to be the resolution. "I'm serious. Think about it," he said then and his demeanor shifted from sadly jovial to truly heartbroken. "And when there are no other options..."

"No other— Ah, yes." She wasn't about to list with specificity his impending broken heart.

"Yes. Well. When there are no other options, I think we would make fine spinsters together."

"Is it really that dire for you and Amelia?"

"I'm afraid so. I've always known she and Charles would marry. The contract, after all, is nearly as old as we are. It's that... it's soon, and I only just realized...I only just realized it was no longer some awful thing that would happen one day. That *one day* will be here— sooner than I'm prepared for."

"Well, when that day comes you may call on me."

He looked at her confused for a moment, then smiled, "Ah... my very own spinster wife."

Louisa giggled. "I think my father would allow it. You must be better than nothing, wouldn't you think?" she said stoically. Hugh laughed, and it filled his face with a joy she hadn't seen on him in a while.

He took her hand and pulled her to the dance floor without another word. "So, do we have a pact then?" he asked as he recovered quite well and swung her vigorously through a turn. "If neither of us can find a suitable match, we'll have each other."

"Yes, precisely," Louisa replied. "You know, eventually, if certain things don't work in your favor," she said.

"You already assume nothing will work in your favor?" He sobered. Louisa's heart skipped a momentary beat, then she nodded. It seemed all she could persuade herself to do for an answer. "In that case I could be persuaded to offer for you," he whispered.

The music ended, and Hugh bowed to her as she scanned the ballroom for Ellie. She must have been taken to the gardens by some man. Louisa waved Ender off as Trumbull approached, then returned to her chosen potted palm.

"Louisa." The deep voice sent a steel rod up her spine, stiffening all of her muscles as she turned to her father and curtseyed. "Daughter, I would present Lord Hepplewort. His lands at Shropshire are extensive and in need of a mistress. You would do well to consider him."

So it was like that, was it? Not even a how-do-you-do? All business. Just a gruff get-yourself-married-and-out-of-my-house-this-man-will-do-fine. Her father didn't even smile. She curtseyed to the man who'd been seated next to her at dinner out of requirement more than respect. The man known as Hepplewort was more porcine than human in manner and his dress was frankly quite garish.

She raised her hand for him, "My Lord."

"The pleasure is mine. Perhaps a walk in the garden?" Hepplewort said.

"My Lord, I—" she started but her father cut her off.

"I think that a lovely idea," he said stiffly, then he nodded to Hepplewort, gave her a look that chilled her to the bone and turned and left her with him. A sense of dread washed over Louisa like thick black ink spilling across her diary, blotting out all the words and permanently destroying any thoughts she'd written down.

Hepplewort took her hand and placed it on his elbow, holding it there when she tried to jerk away as he waddled them toward the exterior doors. She glanced over her shoulder for Ellie but didn't see her anywhere. She saw Hugh but he was turned from her, chatting with Trumbull across the room. The last thing she saw before looking forward was his head thrown back in laughter at something Trumbull said.

"Your father tells me you're interested in getting married post haste," Hepplewort said.

Louisa shook her head. "My father believes I should be," she replied. "But I'm not particularly ready for that shelf quite yet."

"Oh, that, my dear, is obvious. I am betrothed regardless."

"Why would my father attempt to marry me to you if you already have a wife in waiting?"

"I didn't make your father aware of it. Seemed unnecessary." He motioned for her to precede him through the door, and she was relieved to release his arm and move swiftly away from him.

"But when he introduced us—" Louisa said.

"Necessary for propriety's sake, of course. After all, a young, marriageable woman shouldn't be taken to the greens by a man who has no interest in her future, now, should she?" he said from right next to her.

She should have felt better knowing he wasn't interested in marriage to her, but she didn't. "Where is your lovely betrothed this evening then?" she asked, hoping to divine some reason for this farce.

"My wife is in France. She's being trained in proper comportment for a lady. When she comes to England, she'll be the most respectable bride imaginable."

"Will she, My Lord?" She walked to the end of the terrace to put more distance between them, hoping to find another couple with which they could converse, but there was nobody.

"Most definitely. She's in seclusion in a convent. She won't be of an acceptable age for another year or so. But she'll be well worth the wait," he said, once again much too close.

Louisa felt a stone form in her chest that slowly sank to the pit of her belly, sitting there like bread without yeast, too heavy to digest. It sounded as though he was betrothed to a child, and she wondered how much say the girl had in this decision. Most likely none at all. Louisa felt his dry finger run from her shoulder to the top of her glove, and fear slivered through her. She moved down the steps to put some space between them, once again searching for someone else with which to buffer the conversation, he followed.

"My Lord," she said, attempting to keep some sound, simple words, *anything,* between them. Something another person could hear and attest to, inane conversation of any sort at least, but her throat closed and her hands began to shake. The rock in her belly expanded and her lungs compressed, no room against the corset to make up for the loss. She felt a trickle of sweat run the length of her neck, soaking into the edge of her corset and starting a chill.

Her gaze darted about the gardens for anyone they could move toward. She heard laughter around the corner and turned in that direction, only to realize she'd come to a small courtyard garden and the laughter she'd heard came from an upper window that was cranked open. She turned back—but he was there, his fetid body much too close. "I see no reason to remain here, since we've no interest. As you're betrothed and my father has made his interest in my finding a husband clear, I should be returning—"

"My purpose for being here isn't to marry you."

"But my father— My Lord?" Louisa's heart raced. He moved much swifter than a man of his stature should be able.

"Your father knows exactly what he requested of me. Don't play coy—this is your third season. There aren't many reasons for that. You've no longer your maidenhead to barter with, or you need to learn your place. So let's have a sample and find out which it is, shall we?"

Louisa was trapped as he grabbed for her skirts and pulled her closer. If she screamed, she'd be ruined and truly trapped with this man—for life. She had to get away from him quietly and without incident. She side-stepped but felt the cold stone of the house and she closed her eyes for a moment and tried to think. "Please, My Lord," she begged.

"Yes, do a bit of that, won't you? I do like it when they beg." He ran his tongue across his lip as he watched her, pressed into her, and lifted her skirts with one hand.

She pushed against him but his feet were anchored and his weight too much. "Please." She watched as the light from the windows above cut across his face and his eyes flared in the light. "Oh, God no, please."

His hand ran up her inner thigh, and she took a breath, all hope gone, nothing left but to scream for help now, but his other hand slammed up into her chin before she could muster her breath—closing her mouth with a violent snap while his fingers pressed against her lips to stifle any sound she made. He pushed into her face, the force of it turning her into the cold stone as he crowded her against the wall. "Be silent now, would you? We wouldn't want to be interrupted. Think of the consequences then," he said as he forced one leg between hers and pried them loose.

She fought, her hands hitting his shoulders, his chest, grabbing at his coat while he somehow kept his face out of her reach. She wanted to dig his eyes out, but she couldn't move her head from the wall, couldn't shift her gaze enough to see where he was. It seemed he was everywhere.

"That's the way," he grumbled. "Fight me."

The words made her freeze. Her hands clenched on his jacket as she tried to catch her breath behind his hand. She closed her eyes and wished, hoped, for someone to find her. She cried hot, stinging tears and closed her eyes. She whimpered.

His hand found its way between her legs again, and she lost all semblance of propriety. His hard, calloused fingers forced through, and she pushed, fought and kicked with every part of her. She was no longer in control of herself; she didn't know who she was. She felt so completely separate from everything she knew herself to be, from her past, from her present, from her future.

One moment she was up against the wall and the next she was on the ground, her skirts around her thighs, the cage of her bustle cutting into the backs of her thighs, and this man, this man in a place he had no right to be.

She closed her eyes and tried to expel him from her body, tried to force him off her, tried everything she could, but there was nothing, and then his hand slid away and she screamed. A shadow fell across him, and she realized someone was leaning from the window above.

She heard angry voices but had no idea what they said—then she was cold. She was still on the ground but he was gone. She rolled to her side, curled into herself and lay there. In the back of her mind, she knew she needed to get up, she needed to set herself to rights, to make herself presentable, to run, to get away before someone discovered her here—before she was ruined. But she couldn't move.

The light shifted again, and she covered her face with one arm as she flung the other forward in defense and sobbed. "Please, no." Her voice was hoarse. Hands were on her and she pushed them away preparing for another battle. Her eyes flung wide in terror as she cursed herself for not running when she had the reprieve.

"Louisa."

She held her hands out at arms' length as she tried to concentrate on the voice.

"Louisa."

Her name was so quiet, so calm, so... "Hugh?" Her voice caught in her throat and she looked up into the light from the window to see the outline of a man bending down to her, lifting her from the ground, then holding her close. Relief like a flood in the marsh washed over her body and took all rational thought away, and all she could think was, *Thank God for this man.*

"Perry, get my carriage to the mews. The gates are beyond the gardens," he whispered.

"What about her father?" Perry asked.

"Don't," she said, physically and mentally exhausted. Louisa closed her eyes and let Hugh take charge of her. "Don't go to him. I didn't come here with him. I came with Maitland and her cousin," she managed. She grabbed on to Hugh with all her remaining strength.

"Perry, we have to get her away from here as quick as possible. She can't be seen with either of us. You cannot tell her cousin unless you're of a mind to marry—"

"No."

"I thought not. So bring my carriage. We'll get her home and send a note. Louisa?"

She didn't answer. She had nothing to say.

"Louisa, I have to ask you a question, please." He held her tight in his arms and spoke softly, his mouth at her ear, the words questioning, his tone brooking compliance. She nodded once, and he waited. "Do you have need of a physician?" Hugh whispered when Perry's footsteps receded.

"I don't... I don't know," she said, wondering what sort of question it was, and that was when her body started to wake up and report pains she was unaware of only moments ago. Her face stung, probably from being pressed into the wall. Her fingers hurt from grabbing him and scratching, and fighting—

"Louisa, I need you to tell me if he forced himself inside you. Did he take your maidenhead?" he asked.

Oh... oh, God. "I just... really have no idea," she replied. Because she didn't. It had hurt, his hands. They'd hurt when he'd forced his hands between her legs. Whatever had happened there on the ground...it had hurt, it had all hurt, but she'd no idea what he'd done to her. Louisa heard the rattle of a team of horses behind them and felt Hugh turn with her and move toward the sound. "Wait— Ellie. I was to stay with—with Maitland tonight. Maitland Eliot Rigsby."

Hugh spoke with his driver, then spoke to Perry and placed her carefully in the carriage. She didn't let go of him, and when he sat next to her, she melted against him again. She couldn't let go. "Perry, find a way to get word to her cousin that Louisa has taken ill. Do not go yourself—find Miss Eliot Rigsby, have *her* tell the cousin, then get her to this carriage. We'll wait here. Do *not* let anyone see you with her."

"What do you take me for, a novice?" Perry asked plainly.

"Perry," was all Hugh said, and Perry raised his hands in acquiescence then ran across the lawn toward the house again.

Louisa didn't want to feel anything more. She didn't want to know what had happened to her. She wanted Ellie, she wanted to go home, and she wanted to leave London and never return. She felt Hugh tip her face up to him with a gentle hand.

"Louisa." His other hand rubbed circles into her back then smoothed the hair from her face, his thumbs skimming her cheeks. She opened her eyes. "What happened?" he said. "If he ruined you, I'll marry you. I will protect you. I only need to know if it's necessary."

Louisa felt tears scorch her cheeks and she shivered. "He touched me."

"How did he touch you? Louisa, I ask because I wish to protect you. I'll do whatever need be done to protect you. If he took your maidenhead—"

"How do I know? It hurt. That's all I know." She clenched her eyes tight, tucking her head against his chest, suddenly ashamed.

"Louisa, this is not your fault. Don't be afraid to tell me—let me be your friend."

She nodded stiffly and began to speak again, closing her eyes and telling him everything she remembered.

"Was it just rough? Or did it feel like flesh was torn?" he asked. As if he'd asked about cream or sugar. As if he'd asked her preference for dinner. As if he'd asked whether she preferred blue over lavender.

She kept her eyes closed tight and nearly cried anew. "I'm torn," she whispered. "I don't... It hurt. What he did, it hurt. That's all I know."

Hugh nodded and skimmed the tears away with his thumb. "I will call on you tomorrow, Louisa. You will tell me if there's blood. That's how you'll know. If there's blood...I'll marry you. I wish for you to be sure, Louisa, because I know this marriage isn't what you want, but I'll not abandon you. I'm so sorry this has happened. Do you know who he was?"

Her eyes snapped to his then as she thought back to her father, and the introduction.

"Something Greek," she said.

"Hephas—"

"No."

"Hippocrates—"

"No."

"Hippolyta—"

"No. Hepple—something. He's from Shropshire," she whispered. "But my father made the introduction. My father knew... I must be confused. I don't understand," she finished.

Hugh's arms tightened around her, pulling her into his chest.

She stiffened at first and he looked down to her, but she shook her head and relaxed into him. "Just take me home."

He nodded against her crown.

You will tell me if there's blood, Louisa. If there's blood, I'll marry you. Louisa closed her eyes against the thought and hid her face against his chest, nodding once. His hands tightened on her to let her know he got the message without another word. She could take no more.

The carriage door opened then closed. She heard the crack of a whip and they jolted forward. For a moment, they were silent.

Louisa opened her eyes to find Ellie, pale as a ghost in the passing street lamps, a look of horror on her face. Louisa turned back into Hugh's chest. What had Perry told her? Louisa wanted to hide then, to pop right out of existence. She'd been manhandled before, but never to this extent. She wasn't sure how she'd allowed it to get so out of hand this time. She stared out the carriage window as the light from gas lamps slipped across them, one after the other, and thought about the last hour.

"I am going to see the two of you to the door. I'll call on you tomorrow. Will you be well on your own tonight?"

"I'll not be alone," she replied as she glanced to Ellie. "Will I?"

"No," Ellie whispered, frightened but sure. "You're not alone," she said, and Louisa filled with a warmth that emanated from her chest, wrapped her up in a way Hugh's arms could never do, and made the pain fade. His hands tensed against her back and she knew he wished to do more, but there was nothing more he *could* do at least not tonight. Really, there was nothing at all that he could do for her now.

Louisa yanked at her dress, flung her slippers from her feet and across the room, tugged at her stockings, and started to cry. Ellie felt helpless in a bone-deep way she never had. The man, Trumbull, had only said they had to go, that Louisa was in the carriage at the mews with Hugh and that something had happened and they needed to leave. Ellie hadn't had to guess once she'd reached the carriage and had heard what Hugh had been saying to her.

Now she only wanted to comfort her, to make her know she was safe...wasn't she? Ellie had no idea. Louisa had said it was an acquaintance of her father's. Certainly her father hadn't known he would do...what he'd done. Ellie stopped and shook all thoughts from her head. Louisa, Louisa needed her now, and she was standing here like a dumbstruck fool. She walked to her, wrapped her arms around her and held on. "Hush, Louisa, we're home and you're safe. I'm here with you. I'm here," Ellie said softly. She kissed her cheek, stroked her back, listened to her sob into her neck, Louisa's tears streaming down her back and chest from her shoulder. "I'm here, and you're safe," Ellie whispered.

At least for now, she thought, because what about tomorrow? Or the next day? What then? Louisa would have to go out in society again, and certainly this man would be there. That was how it worked—the men were free to do as they wished; the women were not. The women were victims who had to remain silent or be shuttled off to prevent a scandal, an embarrassment to their family. She felt Louisa's breathing calm, the hitching of her chest from her sobbing slowing as she settled.

"Get these things off of me, please," Louisa whispered.

Ellie leaned back, brushed the remaining tears from Louisa's cheeks then turned her gently and started on the buttons at the back of the dress. She worked slowly, diligently, carefully. She kept her touch light and loving, not wanting to remind Louisa of the man who'd violated her person. A tear dropped to her moving hands, and Ellie realized for the first time that she too cried. She swiped it away and breathed deeply, continuing on her task. When the dress fell to the floor with the underskirts and bustle, it was behind a blur of tears.

Louisa stepped out of the circle of fabric, then gathered it in her arms and tossed it out the window to the streets below. "I never want to see these things again," she said, then turned her back once more so Ellie could unlace her corset.

"That may cause a ruckus in the street tomorrow," Ellie said, trying to smile.

"Doubtful. The workers are out all night. It will be gone before anyone of importance sees anything," Louisa replied and she was correct. The common people who worked the night would never pass up the chance at such finery, and that gown and the trappings with it would bring quite a fair price wherever they attempted to sell them.

The corset slipped and Louisa caught it, flinging it out to join the dress on the street as the door to her room opened and Abigail entered. Louisa jumped at the sound, and Ellie turned to her.

"A bath, please," she said, then Louisa sat on the bench at the dressing table and removed her torn stockings. She really did have good aim; not a single thing hit the edge of the window. It all went straight through.

Ellie knelt beside her as she sank in the tub and she wished she could go back in time. That they could go back to when they were here last, together, peaceful and whole. Untouched, unruffled, undressed, unabashed, just her and Ellie and nothing between them but love. She curled toward the side of the tub, her hand against Ellie's. Everything had changed.

"What can I do?" she asked, and Louisa didn't have an answer for her. She wished she did. She wished this was something that could be easily fixed, something that could be forgotten.

"I don't know. Ellie, can I have a moment?"

"I'll be right back," Ellie said and she walked out of the room.

Louisa watched her go, then stretched out in the bath, let her hands search. Her cheek hurt, her neck—he'd shoved her face into the wall. She ran her hands down her arms. Her shoulder hurt—she remembered it hitting the ground when she fell. Her legs hurt like she'd been riding all day; she was sore like that, like she'd done too much. But it was more. She ran her hands up the insides of her thighs and remembered his rough, hard hands there. She would have bruises tomorrow.

She rested a hand on her mons, simply held herself and closed her eyes and tried to remember how violated she'd been. Would she be forced to marry Hugh? Would he be forced to marry her? She looked down and saw the pink tinge of blood in the bathwater, and knew Hugh would do as he promised. But she didn't want that. She didn't want to ruin both of their lives. If there was any hope for he and Amelia, he should have the freedom to pursue her.

She washed herself, determined. She would deal with the consequences if they came. But that man would never offer for her. If she was sent to a convent or a school, then so be it. At least it wouldn't be here in London with all eyes on her.

Ellie came back to the bathing room, a towel in one hand and a flowing cotton nightgown in the other. She'd managed to get out of her own clothes and dressed for bed.

Louisa stood and allowed her to wrap the towel around her. "I think... I think I should return home. If anything comes of tonight, I don't want any blame to fall on your family."

"Louisa—"

"Ellie, I should go," she said again and because it was Ellie, she nodded and without another word helped her to dress enough that she could leave quickly.

Ellie

Ellie watched the carriage pull away from her house, her footman nodding to remind her that they'd report back soon. All she wanted was to make sure Louisa returned home safely. She wished Louisa had stayed, but she couldn't make her do it. She didn't know what to do. She felt so helpless faced with this situation, the one that all the matrons harped on but none of them—not a single one of the young ladies—really believed would happen to them. *And it didn't, did it?* It had happened to Louisa, and Ellie could do nothing to repair that.

Louisa

ouisa heard the knock at the door and gazed down to the front drive from the window seat in the gallery. All she could see was a top hat and capes over a tall, narrow frame. But the familiarity of the way he moved had her shifting forward, her hand pressed against the chilled morning glass.

She went to the entry, preempting the need for the butler to find her, but when she walked to the balustrade and saw Hugh removing his capes and hat, she heard her father's name and backed away until her back was pressed to the wall.

He'd promised. He'd said he would come to her. He'd said nothing about speaking with her father unless she... Didn't he need to know how she felt before he spoke with her father?

Heavy shoes clicked across the entry as he was led to her father's study, but she didn't hear the door close. She waited until the butler shuffled off to whatever closet he stood in while awaiting his service then rushed the stairs and approached the room.

"Baron Endsleigh. I'm not certain your suit is welcome."

No. She stifled any words by holding her breath, pushing a knuckle between her teeth.

"Interesting, as I haven't offered yet. I came to call on Louisa and thought it appropriate to speak with you first to make you aware I was doing so."

When she released the gush of a breath, she nearly toppled. Of course Ender respected her more than to go behind her back.

"I find you calling on her unnecessary." He was too calm.

"She has a suitor then?"

"I don't see how that's any of your business." Her father was his ever-staid presence. He filled the room with a quiet menace, and she knew how dismissively he treated Ender. Probably sitting at his desk, continuing to write in his ledger while Hugh stood at the edge of his massive desk, not even asked to sit.

"I'm confused as to how it isn't. You've soundly rejected a suit I haven't offered and refuse to let me speak with her altogether?" God, but Hugh was lovely as he stood his ground.

"I haven't refused to let you speak with her, yet. I'm stating that your suit isn't necessarily welcome here, so you should tread lightly."

"I'd heard that any suit would be welcome at this point."

"Falsity. I'm Mayjoy. My daughter will wed per her station. She's in no rush to see it done. We await the most appropriate offer, and it is not a lowly baron."

"Ah, I see. I appreciate your candor. So I'm welcome to your daughter, but not to marry her. Is that what I'm hearing?"

"Sir, you try my patience."

"I'm attempting to discern to what purpose you believe my business if there is no purpose in seeing if Louisa and I would suit."

Heavy wooden chair legs scraped along the ruts long worn into the solid wood beneath the desk. Hugh had overstepped, and a shiver ran her spine. "You, sir, hang with the likes of Trumbull, who would be useful if he had anything to recommend him beyond his rakish behavior. He has little but money and connection to power. If you were friends with his brother Roxleigh, I might perhaps consider it because that family—"

"Is one of the most powerful in England, as we all know."

"Yes. Well. Trumbull is the least of them, however."

"By your count, perhaps. But his worth isn't determined by you."

"It is where my accounting purpose is for an advantageous marriage for my child. You have connections to Castleberry as well, childhood friends if I'm told correctly, and I usually am."

She knew Hugh tensed at the name of the man who would marry the woman he loved. An old contract to be sure, but apparently a contract the Duke of Castleberry intended to exercise soon. "Sir, yes. Our far estates bordered. We did grow up in the company of each other."

"I would be more willing to exploit that relationship than the Roxleigh clan—"

"Because Roxleigh has shown to be inexploitable?"

"If you are here solely to poke at me with your wiry fingers, you may see yourself out."

Louisa shuddered, Hugh shouldn't annoy her father so; if he decided she wasn't to speak with him ever again, she wasn't sure what she would do. She'd be lost to the ballroom without comrades to protect her. Except Ellie...but there was only so much Ellie could do. They needed men to be truly safe, men they could trust, and Hugh was one of a very short list of...one. She thought Trumbull was honorable but his reputation precluded any sort of ability for her to even converse with him in public. That left Hugh alone.

She turned back when she heard footsteps heading for the door. She hadn't been paying mind to what was being said and should have. She ducked around a corner as a servant panel opened and the butler walked through like a clockwork soldier ready to mark the time.

"See him to the front parlor and find Louisa, but they aren't to be left alone," her father said from the hall. So he couldn't even be trusted to ruin her and force marriage? That was the contempt her father had for a decent man. Well. She'd see about that.

She waited for them to pass and again until she heard the butler's shoes clicking up the staircase and went to the front parlor, checking to be sure her father wasn't still in the hallway.

She slid through the door to the parlor and turned to find Hugh with a creased brow and tense fingers, awaiting her, and she remembered. She remembered the night before in perfect clarity. "Oh," she said, then she took his hand as he helped her to the settee. She couldn't meet his face. He knew. He'd seen—horrible things, God knew what all. She flushed and turned her body away. Perhaps he should go. Perhaps she couldn't be around him anymore. Her chest tightened, and she felt a hand on her knee.

"Louisa, I'm so very sorry for last night. I'll never have the words to express how I wish it hadn't happened. I won't force you to look upon me if all you see is that. I'll see myself out as long as you believe an expedient marriage isn't necessary."

"No," she said, and she shrank into her clothes. He was only here for propriety, not for comfort. She'd read much too much into their ballroom interactions, she supposed. "It isn't necessary." Whatever came, she would find her way on her own.

"Louisa." She felt the warmth of him when he shifted closer. "I wish there was more I could do. I wish I knew what I should do."

She turned then and gazed into his eyes and saw those gentle, smiling eyes she always felt safe with. "I'm...frightened," she said, and then she swayed and he caught her, holding her in his warm, gentle hold. This was what she needed. A friend. She needed Ellie. She'd left her last night and...oh, Ellie was probably overwrought today not knowing what to do.

"I spoke with your father."

"I heard you. You test him too much, Hugh. I can't lose what small bit of friendship I have. You don't understand. If you anger him, he will see to it to ruin you."

"He would try. He seems to think himself more powerful than he is and he puts on a good, blustery show, Louisa, but let me tell you, darling girl, he is not the great and powerful man you think him to be. He's merely good at performance. And now with the link between he and Hepple—"

"Hepplewort." She straightened and shifted, and Hugh's hands fell away from her shoulders but rested close by. "That was his name. Hepplewort."

"Yes. He's not a good man, Louisa. You should not be seen near him. I need you to be even more diligent than ever that you aren't alone where he could find you and harm you again."

"And how am I to do that? My father handed me off to him as though I were a gift— I..." A chill ran her spine and she wrapped her arms around herself and squeezed tight. *My father handed me to him.* "Did he know?" she whispered, but Hugh didn't answer and Louisa feared looking at his face to find the truth for herself. A sob broke her resolve, and Hugh caught her up, holding her close once again.

"Louisa, my friends and I, we'll watch out for you, but we can only do so much. And Perry, well, he's doubly challenged because he can't be seen to be watching you or an entirely new set of rumors may start. He's sent word to his brother, but who knows if he'll make it to London for the season, as he's such a dedicated recluse."

"Perry doesn't seem like much of a rake if he's willing to help protect my chastity."

"Perry...is definitely a paradox," he said, and she knew he was smiling at his old friend.

"Please do tell him I appreciate his help and his discretion last night. I'm not sure what I would have done—"

"Don't worry, Louisa. I'm certain he's aware."

She sat back but stayed close, the warmth of him a comfort. It struck her as so odd that she felt so comfortable in his companionship, but it was that he wanted nothing more from her than words and smiles. She turned her face into the small bit of sun cutting through the window, and he inhaled sharply, his hand coming up to her chin and tilting her face.

She covered the bruise, but he wouldn't allow her to turn away this time.

"Louisa, do I need to arrange for a doctor? We can find someone discreet. Do you have more injuries?"

"No," she said, and he ran a thumb along her chin until she winced, not from pain but from the inspection of it. "No, this is the ugliest of it. I don't need to be pawed by another man." He pulled his hands away, horror on his face, and she smiled and took them. "Not you, Hugh. That's not at all what I meant."

"And yet I shouldn't have handled you without permission, and for that I apologize."

He brought tears to her eyes, and she shook her head against the sweetness of it. "You'll make someone a fine husband someday, and if it isn't Amelia, it will be her greatest loss." She took his hands and kissed the backs then held them. "I don't know what I would do without you in my life, my dearest friend."

"Laugh a bit less, I imagine," he said with a halfhearted grin, and she managed a smile. "I, um...I must get going. I'm meeting Trumbull at the Iron Duke for lunch. Will you be all right?"

"I'm well enough. I need to catch up on my correspondence."

"Perhaps Maitland can come by and help with that?"

"You may need someone to dictate your letters too, because your handwriting is abhorrent, but sir, I promise you mine is remarkable."

"Oh, of that I have no doubt. It's nice to have someone to talk to when going through the tediums of the everyday, isn't it?"

"Yes, I suppose it is." She snuck a glance at him and knew he was concerned for her being alone, but him staying here was inadvisable. They'd already spent too much time alone. She stood and walked to the window, the clicking of shoes growing louder before the door opened and he stood.

"Louisa, you shouldn't be in the company of a man alone," her father's wife said.

"No, I shouldn't. Perhaps speak with the butler who brought him to me then abandoned him here. Though I imagine it's possible he didn't know I was already in the parlor, as I was expecting a visitor today."

"Yes, well."

Hugh bowed before her. "Lady Mayjoy, my apologies. It's my error, as I should have immediately left when I realized. But Louisa was quite cordial, while keeping the furniture between us."

"And you are...?"

"Hubert Percival Garrison, Baron Endsleigh."

"Endsleigh. Have you spoken with Mayjoy?"

"Yes, ma'am, when I arrived."

Her eyes slid between she and Hugh, and Louisa knew she had no idea what was happening.

"Well," Louisa said. "I have correspondence to catch up on. It was lovely to see you, Endsleigh. I hope to see you at the Trentham event next week."

"If you would be so good as to save me a dance, it would be much appreciated," he replied. Then he walked to her, took her hand and bowed over it, but before he released her he gave it a warm squeeze and winked up at her. "At your service, Miss Present."

Then he turned, nodded to the viscountess and left.

"Would he suit?" she asked when he was beyond the range of the parlor.

"He would do, though I don't believe father approves. Baron, you know."

"Perhaps his standards are slipping. I was actually coming to find you because...well, I see you are attempting to find a match. So it's irrelevent. Will you need a new dress for Trentham's?"

"No, ma'am. I haven't yet worn the blue that Marjorie made. It will suffice." She was making awkward small talk, and Louisa wasn't sure why. "So, my correspondence then," she said and she curtseyed and went to her room.

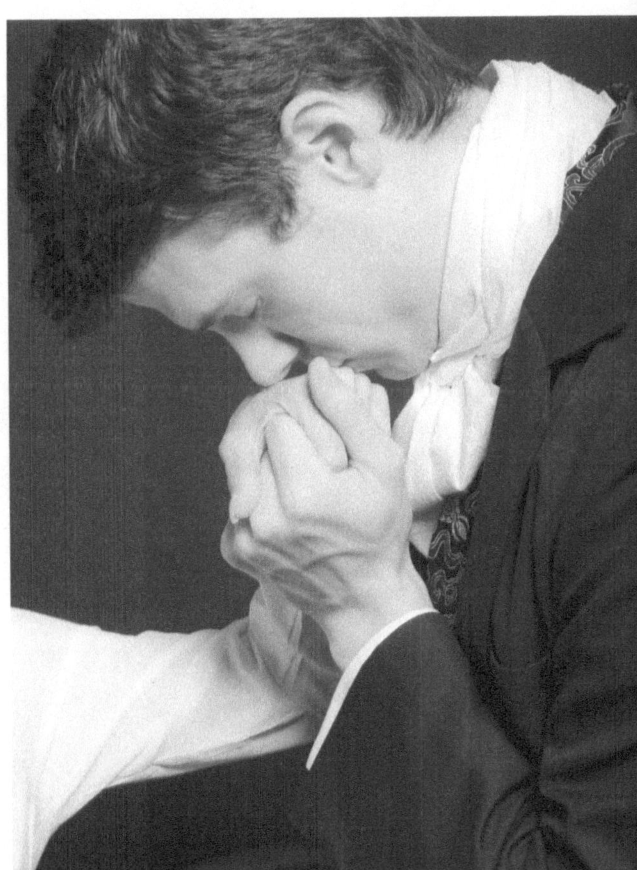

Ellie wanted nothing more than to hold Louisa. She wanted to hold her and never let go. She wished she'd refused to let her leave the night before but she hadn't known what to do, and so she'd let Louisa do whatever she wanted. She wished, so very much did she wish, that they could go back before the ball and simply choose not to go.

She'd had such plans for that night, and the bath when Louisa had brought her off had been...something she'd never even thought to want for, but oh how she wanted now. She wanted so much more. She wanted to bring Louisa off in the same way, to see her lose control by her hand. But now...all that had been taken from them, wiped away like chalk words on a chalkboard.

She wanted to write to her, but what could she possibly say in a note that might be read by someone else? It was impossible. So she waited for word. For two days, she worked on her cross-stitch and played with her needlepoint and twiddled her thumbs as she waited any sort of news.

"Maitland, you've been requested to tea," her mother said when she entered her room.

"Have I?" She dared not hope, but who else could it be? *Please, God, let it be her.* "And will you be accompanying—"

"No, they've quite seen to my name being left off. Probably something to do with their daughter sneaking off from our house in the dead of night to return home."

She closed her eyes and thanked God in that moment. "I'm certain they didn't mind. We took every care to be sure she was safe."

"Never mind now. At least you've been invited."

"I am sorry, mama, but really it must be an error."

"Maitland, there's no point. Let's get you ready. I refuse to keep the Mayjoy girl waiting regardless of their thoughts on me."

Louisa

Louisa took Ellie's hand and led her away from the parlor and all the chattering women. She drew her down the familiar half set of stairs and back up the other side to the walkway across from the parlor. It took all her will to walk. As they entered the massive gallery, she let out a breath, closed the doors, and locked them then turned.

She needed her. She'd come home two nights ago and had immediately wished she'd stayed, but then she'd no idea how to fix it. To bring her back. To go back.

Ellie took her face in her hands and pressed her against the door before she could even get a word out, and how lovely, how lovely it was. Her cool fingers skimmed up her cheeks and into the hair at her nape as she fell into the kiss, allowed the access, parted her lips and held on. She curled her fingers into the thick fabrics against Ellie's hips, pulling her ever closer.

She allowed herself to feel for a moment what this was like. "I'm sorry I left," she whispered against her cheek. "I should have stayed."

"I'm sorry you left too. I didn't know what to do, I didn't know—"

"You couldn't. How could you?"

"It was awful, Louisa, seeing you like that, seeing how he'd ruined your dress and wondering, just wondering—"

"Oh, Ellie, don't," she whispered, and a chill ran her spine. "Don't think on it please, don't."

"Whatever you need of me, Louisa, I'm here for you."

"Just please don't— Can we go back? Can we go back to before, back to when that horrid man hadn't ruined me, before he touched

me, back to when you—" She sobbed and her knees buckled, but Ellie caught her up and led her to the small settee.

"Louisa, we can go anywhere you want." She wrapped Louisa in her arms, rocking her gently. "The bath was so warm, and you were so beautiful. I've never seen anything so beautiful in my life as you. I've never experienced anything so beautiful in my life as that moment. The scent of roses surrounding us—can you smell them?—the full headiness of rose on steam. The warmth of the bath, the beautiful milky water that hid your body from mine. Allowed you to play, allowed you to tease, allowed you to show me things I never knew possible. Remember that?"

"Yes," Louisa replied with a warm sigh. She cuddled into Ellie, allowing the space to feel the words.

"After, we dressed in soft linen nightrails and built a bed of pillows in front of the fire where it was warm and the light made your skin glow like honey." Louisa smiled at the change, happy to rewrite their history. "And you allowed me the same exploration that I'd allowed you, and we stayed in that room. Together. The whole night through, just you and I like we are now. Safe, secure—"

They heard a beat, then another, and Louisa pushed back from her lover, her hands trembling at the steady sound of heavy footsteps coming toward them across the gallery.

"What...what is the meaning of this?" the deep voice boomed from deep inside the gallery beyond the sculptures—the loudest she'd ever heard. The angriest. She tangled her hands in Ellie's skirts, torn between pulling her close and pushing her away. She listened as his heavy boots continued to stride the length of the gallery toward them. "Louisa, what have you done?"

Ellie was frozen still and pale white, her hands clenched tight, the fear on her palpable. They should have been more cautious. They had always been so cautious... Why hadn't they—

"Louisa!"

Her lungs froze in her chest and spread the chill through her blood to the tips of her fingers. "I'm so sorry," she whispered to Ellie, releasing her skirt and patting her knee. "I am so sorry. Go, run, don't look back."

But Ellie didn't move. She stared forward as Louisa's father approached them from behind.

Louisa hadn't turned to him yet. She didn't need to look to see what she already knew. She could hear those boots like a countdown to her destiny. "Ellie," she choked. "Ellie." She shook her hands, pulling at the skirts to get her attention. "Ellie you need to go," she whispered as salty tears stained the words she spoke.

She saw Ellie's head shake and then she was naught but a whoosh of fabric— her skirts violently snapped from her hands as her father took Louisa by the arm, pulling her up from the settee. She didn't look at him, she couldn't turn away from Ellie. She wanted to see her go, see her run to safety. "Ellie! Go! Please!" she begged.

Her father shook her until she lost her breath and was silenced. He turned to Ellie, who was getting to her feet.

"Leave her be!" Ellie screamed, but he pushed her away, a gnat to his fury.

"You'll leave this moment. You will return to your mother. You will never speak of this or my daughter again, or I will ruin you. Do you understand me, chit? I'll not merely destroy you, but your entire family. Think not that I am unable to do so."

Ellie's beautiful lavender eyes met hers then like a storm, wild, dangerous and terrifying.

"Ellie," Louisa managed then. "Ellie, go and don't look back. Save yourself."

Ellie started to shake her head, but Louisa's father took one step toward her and Louisa could see Ellie's fear in the way she shook, in the storm in her eyes, in the white tension of her hands. "Louisa, I can't leave you with—"

"You can, and you will," her father said. "She is not now, nor has she ever been, of your concern. "Save yourself, as Louisa said, or I will happily ruin you in her place."

"Ellie, I'll never forgive you if you do so. Go. If you love me—leave."

"Love? Love?" her father screamed as he turned to her. "You dare not speak of love in the midst of the unholiness you have cast upon my house!" He turned back to Ellie once more. "Get out now, or you shall both be ruined by my hand."

And Ellie turned and ran.

And Louisa forgave her.

And her father turned back to her.

And it was the last conscious thought Louisa had for quite some time.

Louisa

When Louisa awoke, she was being bundled unceremoniously into an unmarked coach. Her father spoke with the coachman then gave instructions to one of his outriders, who would be accompanying her. She leaned against the side of the coach but groaned at the pain in her arm and sat upright again. She'd no idea her father could become so angry. So very angry.

She moved her limbs to take stock of her soreness and noted that the worst of it was her right knee and shoulder, her elbow, her cheek, as though she'd been thrown against a wall or pushed down to the floor.

She remembered him jerking her around by her left arm and reached up to it was very sore where he'd held on to her.

She dropped her hands to her lap, and as the carriage lurched forward on its old, worn springs, she noted that the clothes she wore were not her own. They were older, bland, heavy, ill-fitting and somewhat itchy. Her head dropped to her hands, and her chest heaved in a sob that was arrested by a sharp pain in her side. She wouldn't even be allowed the pity of a cry then. So be it. This was her fault. She hoped her father would do as he'd said he would and leave Ellie alone. She would suffer whatever it was he had deigned for her to keep Ellie safe.

Louisa watched out the window as the houses went by at a much slower pace than she was accustomed to in any of her father's well-sprung coaches. They crossed the Thames at Vauxhall but kept going south, farther than she'd ever been in her life. She'd never traveled south in London, always north. The streets were more rutted, the houses drabber, the paint more worn, and the brick heavier until the city seemed to dissipate and expand to country.

Perhaps she was being sent to the country house? They'd only ever gone there by train and she was certain it lay north of London, but how was she to know the direction? It wasn't her responsibility to know these things. She'd never paid attention to these things. She was always taken; she never went.

She watched out the window and vowed she would forever pay attention to direction from here on out. She hated being ignorant and had previously thought herself intelligent, only now realizing that her intelligence had been limited by the immediate world in which she lived.

She leaned back in the hardened squabs of the carriage and allowed her body to move with the rocking of the rusty springs. After a while, the carriage made a slow turn and she glanced out the window to see it pulling into a courtyard surrounded by large buildings. The front of the central building had a name, carved above the curved entryway. It read *Magdalen Hospital* and Louisa knew then she'd been written out of her family entirely. She wondered what story her father would tell society about her. Was she now dead? Or had she been married off to some distant peer? What was the story of her life as it would continue without her? She couldn't disappear from London without a word, could she? She thought of all the young women who'd come out and were then sent off to take the waters at Bath, or to mind to their great aunt in Florence...what had truly happened to them?

And what about Ellie? Her heart wrenched at the thought. How would she manage? What had she been told, if anything, and what had she heard? She hoped Ellie did as she was asked and kept quiet for her own sake, even as part of her wished Ellie would come and get her. Take her away so they could find their little cottage with the goat and the bell and the...the stupid cottage, from the stupid dream of an ignorant girl. Why hadn't she checked the gallery as she always had?

Outside the carriage window the outrider was speaking with a woman, accepting a folder with papers and a bundle of bank notes. The woman looked at her. She couldn't move. Not to run, not to breathe, not for anything. Her father had sent her away to be housed with prostitutes and pregnant women nobody wanted.

The door to the carriage opened, and she sat staring out in disbelief. Sure, he'd beaten her, but this? She watched as the woman at the steps waved toward her, and her father's outrider reached into the carriage and pulled her out. She thought she heard him apologize, but she wasn't sure of anything at the moment, her eyes glued as they were to the letter and the money in the woman's hand.

"What did he tell you?" she asked.

"It's none of your concern," the woman replied.

"Do you know who I am?"

"You're nobody now, like the rest of us."

"I'm not. I'm…" she replied; she couldn't take her eyes from the letter, her father's signature clear and perfect at the bottom. The woman spoke to the outrider, who still held her arm—luckily, she supposed, her right arm, and not the left arm that was still sore because of her father. Her father. She looked at the outrider. She didn't even know his name. She recognized him only by the color of his livery, and was suddenly ashamed of that. She'd no idea if he'd known her for a day, or for her entire life, wound up in herself as she'd been. "I'm so sorry," she said, then realized how ridiculous she must sound. This was all much too overwhelming.

He released her arm and spoke to her. "This way my la— Miss." But her legs weren't working. Exasperated, he picked her up like she was nothing but a sack of potatoes and took her into a parlor and dropped her to a settee that was very old, and quite worn, then he turned and left.

Louisa inspected her own hands, the only thing within her sight with which she was familiar. These were not her clothes, this was not her home, there was nothing around her that was comforting.

The woman came in and spoke with her, the words flowing over and around her, the basic idea of them settling with her, but the actual words spoken lost to her forever. Her family had abandoned her to the Magdalen Hospital for the Reception of Penitent Prostitutes with the explicit directive she was never to contact them again, and if she did, they would notify the authorities of what she was.

And what was that exactly? A woman who had done her best to find a decent man to marry? A woman who had fallen in love with the wrong person? She was nothing but a woman; she'd done nothing wrong, nothing. She'd loved and cared and tried to be a good daughter. That was all that she had done.

"I'll have a cot in the attics readied. You can stay here for the moment. The doctor will be along shortly to check you for lice and disease. Can't have you bringing anything unhealthy into this home. Can we?" the woman asked, but it wasn't one that required an answer.

Louisa looked up at the realization that yet another man was to have power of her person, and it was something she wasn't prepared to allow for. She felt it begin as a tick in her finger against her elbow. Then it slid along her bones, gathering with it the chill of the room until she shook uncontrollably. Every inch of her being screamed for her to leave. But to where? And to what end? She had

nobody. There was no way she would put Ellie in danger by trying to get help from her. Her father had promised to leave Ellie be as long as Louisa did as she was bade. That was all that mattered. She had to trust at least that much. After all, she was the one who'd betrayed his trust. She was the one who was…

Louisa twisted her hands with the handkerchief she held. It was the one thing she had that belonged to a woman of means.

The rest had been taken and replaced with these clothes from God knew where, by God knew who. Who had touched her when she'd been unconscious? Louisa clutched it to her chest as if to hold back the sob that attempted escape.

Once again she heard heavy footsteps and they crawled up her spine, knob by knob until they wrapped around her neck and forced her to standing. Once again she knew exactly what they signaled. The end of everything she knew. She turned toward the door to the parlor. She could see the front entry from here. She could run through the door, down the steps, and be gone forever. She saw the shadow that came before the woman who heralded those steps, and she did, she ran.

Louisa ran for the steps she'd only recently been carried up. A man's voice yelled from behind her and she turned back, tripping over the skirt and tumbling forward—but the ground never came. She'd been caught up, warm arms keeping her from hitting the ground. Louisa took in a deep breath to scream when his arms closed around her, but the scent of cinnamon and rich cigar underscored by a bit of brandy... He lifted her, and the scream stilled.

He set her on her own feet and took a step back. "Miss Present, we really must stop meeting like this," he said.

"Hugh?" He kept one hand on her arm to steady her, and she peeked at the entry to see the woman and the man she assumed to be the doctor, and shied, leaning into Hugh.

He held her securely. "Louisa."

"How did you—" She inspected him, examining him, wondering if she'd lost her mind. She turned back toward the house she'd just run from. The woman pointed at her, her eyes narrowed. "I've got to go." She grabbed his lapels. "Please."

Hugh lifted her, placing her in his carriage. "Isn't that convenient, as I came here for you, Louisa?"

She sank into the thick cushions, not daring to inspect the world outside the carriage. She felt the carriage sway as he mounted the step, then rock back into the tracks as it pulled away from the curb.

"Louisa, you're safe." He took her hand in his and held her tight.

She'd been terrified and alert for much too long, and his hands around hers completely overtook her. She felt more safe in that moment than she had in all her life. There was nothing more she could do, so Louisa closed her eyes and allowed sleep to take her.

When the carriage stopped, he lifted her out and carried her into his home. He loosened her skirt, carefully letting it fall and leaving her in one of her own long cotton chemises. Apparently the farce was only surface deep. He helped her into a large soft bed. "You're safe, Louisa. I'll watch over you. Nobody will disturb you here. Sleep for as long as you need."

She kept her eyes shut and tried, tried so hard to sink back into that happy blackness, but there was no respite to be had yet. Sleep wasn't possible while you cried, even as exhausted as she was—the tears, so hot, so heavy...they demanded her attention. She sat up from the bed, took Hugh's hand and pulled him down next to her, then she curled up in his lap, wrapped herself around him and cried. He held her without a word. He knew more of her story than most people. He'd saved her, after all. Twice now, in fact. Once from that man, and once from her father. It seemed Hugh was forever saving her and she didn't know how to thank him.

The thought shocked her silent, and she sat up, moved away from him. She backed up against the headboard and tucked her knees under her chin. "What are you expecting from me in return?"

"I don't... No, Louisa, it's not like that, please believe me. I expect no favor from you. I'm here to help you. Nothing more."

Louisa watched him. What she knew of him in the past had been genuine, and she craved so desperately some sort of human contact that was genuine. Craved it like a piece of her had gone missing with Ellie and there would never be a way to replace it, so she wished to fill it with any temporary thing she could and he was here...rescuing her. Filling her up. And he had rescued her. And he had offered for her. And what choice did she have at the moment? "Thank you," she whispered and reached out to him.

He held her hand and seemed to be happy to sit and wait for her to decide what was next.

"How did you find me? How did you know?"

"I had someone watching your house. The conversation with your father put me off, and the fact that the man who attacked you is known to him, he introduced you, yes?" She nodded and dipped her face to hide behind her knees. "It didn't sit correct with me. So I had someone watching. They saw Maitland run—"

"Ellie, oh God!"

"Maitland is home safe. She's with her family, and to my knowledge nothing else has happened. But I'm watching over her too now."

"Why?"

"Because, Louisa, you were always a friend to me. As odd as it seems—our ridiculous ballroom friendship—you're the only one who listened to my maundering and pining for Amelia. You're the only one who ever understood that."

"I've lost everything."

"You have me, and I'll do everything I can to help you."

"Hugh, you're too good to me...I don't understand how you came to be such a gentleman."

"Please don't call me that. It hardly signifies what it should these days. I don't wish to be tossed in with the lot of them at the moment."

"You're not the same as them. I cannot fathom why I've been so blessed as to have met you, if you truly wish nothing in return."

He smiled then, and part of her knew he was aware she would never bring herself to fully trust in him, though it would be rude of her to so bluntly state it.

"I'm not sure I know how to trust anymore. What will come of me? I cannot stay here in your home."

"You cannot, that much is true. Though I may have an idea."

Louisa froze, her fingers turning to ice, and she started to pull away. "So you do want something from me?"

"No, Louisa, not like that. I know you need somewhere to go, and if you have somewhere, I will help you get there. I'm not without means, even as meager as they are. But if you have nowhere, if you have no one, I would help to place you with my friend. It's at least two years until she'll be coming to London, so quite safe. Far from here. Somewhere nobody would ever think to find you. Somewhere I could see you, and check on you. Somewhere I know you would be safe and cared for."

"No one is searching for me regardless, I fear."

"Someone will always be searching for you."

"She shouldn't."

He stopped at those two definitive words and watched her for a moment.

She was too tired to hold herself up anymore and allowed her body to slide against the polished headboard until she was lying against it, and she stretched her feet out beneath the cover. "I am so terribly lost."

"I found you, and I won't allow you to be lost again. No matter what you decide for your future. We can discuss it later. You should rest. Please know I expect nothing, and you are safe. You are not lost, you are here, and I will care for you."

"I don't understand why."

"Because I'm able." He squeezed her hand one last time, then pushed up from the bed. He pointed out a glass of water, the doorway that would lead to his water closet, his dresser should she be bored and want to rummage...which made her smile, and he returned the smile then turned and left, shutting the door so carefully she almost didn't hear the click of the latch.

Her eyes fell shut and it was then she slept.

Ellie stared at Endsleigh across the parlor and wondered what he'd come for. She couldn't possibly hope for word about Louisa, could she? She nodded to the butler and shut the door. She was no lady and her father's money was what was going to buy her husband, not some preconceived notion of chastity society deemed important for ladies.

"Endsleigh?" she said, and he turned from his position staring out the front window.

"Miss Eliot Rigsby." He bowed then motioned to the settee and sat next to her. "I'll cut to it, shall I? I have a letter for you to read. You may read it here in this room with me present. The moment I leave, it will come with me so I can be certain it will be destroyed. If these terms are acceptable?"

"Do I have a choice?" she asked, knowing the answer but needing to hear it nonetheless.

"No, sadly. This is the single option."

"So be it."

He took her hand in his big, warm one and squeezed, then he reached into an inside pocket of his coat and pulled out a tightly folded letter, handing it to her. She took it and stood, walking to the window and unfolding it. It was warm from the pocket against his chest and the words were smudged, like...tears on wet ink, and Ellie knew this was going to hurt.

Ellie, my love. I have to leave. I am so sorry to have involved you with my family. If I had any conscience at all, I should have walked away from the first time we met and never looked back. I knew what I was doing, bringing you into my life. But I am selfish, and I wanted. So very much did I want.

You are the most beautiful woman I've ever met. You are brilliant and brave and wonderful. I'm blessed to have known you in the ways I have, and I want you to know that I will treasure every moment we shared for the rest of my life.

I am safe. I will be safe. Please do not ask Hugh to say anything more, for he won't, and it's for your own safety as well as mine. Don't ever give up on your dream of finding someone to spend your life with. You can find someone to share that cottage with still, but it won't be me. My heart breaks as I write this but I cannot leave you with any hope for the future, because we don't have one. We cannot be together, not ever.

This hurts, it will hurt, but it will ease for both of us with time. We've only just met. You'll find another. You'll be happy. And I will safe, far from London and the family I trusted to protect me.

Ellie, Ellie, my beautiful, brave, brilliant love. I will always love you. I will forever miss you. If I had known those last kisses were to be our last, my love, I would never have stopped kissing you. If I'd known the last I saw you would be the last forever I would never have blinked.

But I must go and I will live along the memories of you for the rest of my life.

Yours always,

Lou

She read it again, then again, until her own tears streaked the ink as well. She ran her fingers over the ink, feeling the words placed there by Louisa and knowing she would never see her again. She read it once more until it was so smudged as to be illegible, but still she tried. staining her fingers with blue like blood from a pain that came without a cut.

"Maitland." He reached for her shoulder, his hand reminding her he was there.

She sobbed, crushing the letter to her chest. "My Louisa," she said as she looked up to him. "I'll never see her again, not ever?" Saying the words aloud sent a spear of pain through her chest, splitting her open, the pain spreading like wildfire though her veins.

"No, Maitland, it's impossible."

"But she's safe?"

"I will ensure it, always."

"She gone?"

"She is."

"She's gone. It feels like a dream. Like...a dream." She shook her head, unable to explain how the whole thing was fading already, as though it were nothing but momentary magic, brought by the fae. "She's gone," she whispered, clenching tight on the letter, the last vestige of her life. "I should have kept something. I have nothing. I had no idea she would be gone so soon. I had no idea. I'll have nothing to remember her...from when she was mine."

She heard him sniff and glanced up in time to see him turn away, a hand wiping at his cheek. "I should go," he said, and she knew this was it. The one thing she had, this simple note, these words that she'd made with her own hand. The one thing that was left. She lifted it once more, the ink dried in a watery pattern of sadness. Their tears mixing on the page as their legs had once tangled.

"Tell her I will always love her."

He nodded and put his hand out. She stood before him, clutching the paper in her hands, memorizing the words, the way she'd written her name, the name she would never hear again. She tore the letter, removing her name written by her Louisa, and tucked it away in her corset. She said goodbye to Louisa, and she said goodbye to Ellie, and she placed the ruined paper in his hands, then turned and walked from the room.

After

Three years later

London, England

1881

LOVE
—BITTERSWEET, IRREPRESSIBLE—
LOOSENS MY LIMBS AND I TREMBLE.

~Sappho

Ellie

Ellie thought if she could get to Endsleigh that this time, maybe, he would relent. It had been three years. Three very long years, and he'd managed to avoid her at every turn. She attended balls she knew either Endsleigh or Trumbull would attend, even dancing with Trumbull once by pure accident when he was attempting to distract society from the fact that his brother had proposed in the middle of a ballroom. Then once again at that brother's wedding all the way up country at the Eildon Hill Estate in Roxleighshire. That had been a very long trip to be ignored and avoided incessantly, though the wedding had been spectacularly glorious.

But tonight was the night—she could feel it in her bones. Something was different in London lately, and it wasn't simply because Endsleigh was back. There was something electric in the air, and it felt to her like possibility.

Society was abuzz with speculation because of the particular attendees of tonight's ball, which included Endsleigh but also a Lady Amelia and Duke of Castleberry. You couldn't go outside without hearing someone gossiping about the elusive Lady Amelia, daughter of the Duke of Pembroke-by-the-Sea.

Tonight Ellie planned to attend that ball, to corner Endsleigh somehow and speak with him. To make him listen. She needed Louisa like she needed breathe. It did not lessen, and it certainly hadn't passed. It never would. She wrapped a hand around the locket that carried the torn parchment with Louisa's name on it. She would never walk away, and if Louisa had, she would find her and she would run.

She'd pestered her aunt, begging her to take her tonight until she'd relented. The carriage bobbed around a corner, and Ellie couldn't stop grinning.

"You should be married by now. I shouldn't have to see to you at this point. You had a miraculous coming out and immediately botched it for whatever reason, refusing every invitation, and here we are three years in and you're still my problem."

"Yes, ma'am. I appreciate you accompanying me though."

"I'll be seen as a failure for my part in your refusal to marry."

"I would never lay blame—"

"How could you? I'm blameless."

"Yes, of course, aunt."

The carriage came to a halt and they disembarked, Ellie following close behind her aunt. The ballroom was full and brimming, and the first thing she saw was Endsleigh dancing with a beautiful woman in white, her deep-red hair in a tight swirl around her crown, with a massive diamond brooch pinned through the curls at her nape. She was stunning and they moved together in perfect unison. But it almost seemed as though the woman didn't wish to be dancing with him.

"Maitland."

"Yes, aunt," she said and followed her through the crowd to where she preferred to stand—close enough to the punch to make her trips less obvious. She watched them dance, then watched them walk outside to the bordering gardens and when Endsleigh returned alone, she saw her opportunity. "Aunt," she said, "I'd like to dance with Baron Endsleigh."

"Well, girl, then let's see to it."

Ellie pointed him out, and her aunt dropped her punch to a tray and made a beeline, taking her hand and following him. Then as he paused and glanced over his shoulder, she pushed Ellie in his path and stood aside.

When he turned, he stumbled over her. "Pardon me—"

"No, my lord, I'm entirely at fault," Ellie said, and his eyes narrowed on her.

"Lord Endsleigh, at your service."

She curtseyed, taking his proffered hand. "Thank you, my lord. I am—" She stopped, glanced at her aunt. "Miss Rigsby." She smiled. She was afraid to say her full name if he hadn't quite recognized her yet. She needed to get him alone to have a conversation.

He released her hand and took a step back, his gaze unrelenting, and she thought perhaps all was lost. "Miss Maitland Rigsby?" he asked, and she nodded. His eyes closed, then opened on her once again, and everything she knew, and he knew, about her and about Louisa was there in their depths. "It has been delightful to make your acquaintance." He motioned to the entry. "However, I was on my way—"

"Why, Lord Endsleigh, I wasn't aware you'd been made known to my niece," her aunt said from behind him. He stiffened. Caught. Thank goodness for meddling matrons.

"We had not previously been introduced, no. We managed well enough after I tripped over her," he said. "She's a delightful young lady. You should be proud." His tenor was slipping; it was obvious how hard he was attempting to maintain his politesse. Ellie stared at her aunt, pursing her lips and widening her eyes in request.

"Perhaps a dance? Miss Rigsby is quite popular this evening, but I'm sure she has one dance available...for you."

Ellie celebrated inside, deep deep inside. Her aunt was a master.

He nodded stiffly and when the music shifted, without a word, he took her hand and led her to the dance floor. Her aunt gave her a wink as she passed and headed back to her abandoned punch.

Endsleigh swept her around the ballroom, his attention clearly on something other than her.

"Where is Louisa?" she asked without preamble. She could only keep him here for so long and didn't want to lose this opportunity.

"Maitland, I cannot... You promised."

"I know I did. I know I promised. But I cannot do this, I cannot. I will not. I cannot marry some doldrum and pretend I didn't hold everything I ever wanted in my hands and allow it to slip away."

His gaze slid over her head once again to the doors to the gardens, and she wondered who he was pining for. "Endsleigh."

"Call me Ender," he said. "If we're to be involved, you may as well call me Ender."

"What do you mean?"

He let out an exasperated sigh. "Louisa is here, in London. She's been a ladies maid for a...friend of mine for the past three years."

"She's here?" Ellie choked on the words, and his arm at her back tightened when she stumbled. It was more than she could hope for. She darted her gaze around the room, searching for the deepest black of her hair, only realizing she'd stopped dancing, in the middle of the dance floor, when another couple brushed a bit too close and Ender pulled her back against himself, moving almost without her cooperation.

"Yes, Maitland. Please mind the steps before you make a scene." His tone was gentle and it shocked her. She found her footing, the dance continuing to little notice. "She is here, in London. Not here tonight. She's now a ladies maid, no longer a lady. The woman she works for has come out tonight, in fact."

"That's why you're here. You're here for her."

"I'm not. She's betrothed to another. She's just a friend." He sounded rather put out for that all to be true, but Ellie allowed him his maunder. "Louisa is not here tonight." His attention came back to her, and she felt the weight of it like a heavy blanket.

"I see. How can I find her?"

"You shouldn't, Maitland. The both of you are still in some very real danger from her father, do you not understand that? Both of you have been safe for three years now. Do you truly—"

"Yes. And you're pining for a woman betrothed to another— unless I've misunderstood, and I don't believe I have. Now. What I understand is that I've secreted away my pin money for the last three years, and it's enough to buy a small cottage far from London. I understand that I cannot live without Louisa. I understand that this is my one chance for happiness and I understand that it may be hers as well. And I further understand that you know exactly where she is."

Hugh inspected her. "What kind of pin money does your father give you?"

"Enough for dresses and carriages and books and needlepoint and horses and...whatnot. Enough that I simply had my dresses freshened up instead of getting new dresses. Enough that I undid my old needlepoint and redid it. Enough that I can steal Louisa away from London, from being a maid. Enough."

"Please don't do anything rash," he said. "Please be cautious as you go about this. You can't understand the danger if you think it this simple. You cannot steal Louisa away from Amelia. It won't work. I cannot allow you to crash into her life and turn it inside out—"

"And who are you to keep us apart? It sounds as though you care more about that girl than the both of us."

"I won't argue that point, but you must know that my concern is for everyone. If Louisa was to up and disappear..." He didn't finish the sentence, but she understood the implications. There was too much at stake and for them to be gone for good without causing a ruckus. It would have to be done with care.

"I see. But Ender, I must see her. Please. You go to her. You obviously have access. Go see her and then...then tell her to meet me."

"Where?"

"I don't know. I don't exactly have—"

"I'll figure it out. I'll send word. Do not let your mother read my invitations. No matter how she reads them, she'll not understand, and it will cause a whole other mess that none of us need right now."

"Oh...all right." A warmth spread through Ellie's limbs at the very idea of seeing Louisa again. She would not let her go this time.

"Can you manage that?"

"Can I? Oh, yes. I can manage," she replied, her breath stilled in her chest at the possibility of Louisa.

"Fine, then. I'll send word. Or I won't and we'll be done with this, and this time you'll not track me down again."

"Yes, My Lord."

"Ender."

"Ender, thank you, Ender."

The music stopped, and he bowed over her hand then disappeared into the crowd without a second glance. As she watched him walk away, she saw the woman again, with the red hair, but this time she was on the hand of another gentleman, a man who was taller than any she'd ever met and had a countenance of power that sent a shudder across her shoulders. The woman was searching where Hugh had gone, and the man was staring at her.

"Stop staring at Castleberry. You don't want to draw his attention. Regardless, he's contracted to marry that girl already," her aunt said, startling her from her gazing.

"Oh I was... I thought maybe she knew Baron Endsleigh."

"She does. The three of them have bordering estates on the coast. They grew up together, but I believe there's been a falling out since Castleberry is to marry Lady Amelia. The ton is abuzz... Haven't you paid the least bit of attention?"

"Ah, yes, of course," she replied. Then she wrapped her arm around her aunt's. "I think I'm ready for bed. Are you tired?"

"We only just arrived!" she argued.

"Yes, but I've done exactly what I came to. It's better to leave early and leave them wondering, yes?"

"I suppose," her aunt said with enough of a sideways glance to put Ellie in her place.

Ellie couldn't keep her eyes from Amelia as she and Lady Rigsby walked from the ballroom—stunning as she was—but her excitement at finding Louisa far outweighed any interest she had in society and its rumors.

She stopped as she watched Amelia and Castleberry walk the room. *Louisa is with her...she's Amelia's ladies maid.* That was where she'd been all this time and why she was back now, but she wasn't sure where the London residence was. The Pembroke title didn't have a male heir and was therefore not one of those studied by those of interest.

Ender hadn't outright said it but it made perfect sense, and she wasn't sure why she hadn't put it together until now. She knew where Louisa was. Her skin tightened and she tried to calm, not run from the ballroom and cause a scene. She couldn't possibly change her mind now and stalk Lady Amelia. Her aunt would have her head.

"Where does Lady Amelia live? If she's the belle this year, shouldn't I invite her to tea?"

Her aunt glared at her suspiciously, and Ellie did her best to maintain her poise. She wasn't sure she was doing a good enough job, by her aunt's stare.

"You haven't had interest in this game for three years. What's got you?"

"I'm ready, aunt. I'm simply ready to begin my life."

Louisa

The thought of returning to London had scared Louisa. The very mention of it over the last three years had sent strings of fear through her blood. She always knew she'd have to return; it would be a requirement of her position. But the sheer terror—the unadulterated force of that fear that quaked her very insides—had not lessened with time as she'd hoped it would. Hope, it seemed, was all it was, all it would ever be, for here she was and every step she took felt like falling through the very ground beneath her feet, only to be caught up and thrown again. At any moment she expected her father to burst through the door and toss her like a rag doll once more.

Louisa watched from the upper windows as Amelia's carriage pulled up in front of Pembroke House. She knew this night would be difficult, that this night would either make or break her mistress. Amelia stepped from the carriage and shook her skirts straight. She was distraught as she walked briskly into the house, and Louisa knew tonight had not gone well.

How had it come to this? A mere six years past, Louisa had been the belle of the ball. A mere three years past, she'd stood in the ballroom and watched her world change with the tilt of one woman's chin. She was a lady no longer, now a lady's maid, and Amelia was her lady.

Louisa sat on the edge of her bed. She'd give Amelia a few minutes to gather herself before she'd see to her. That way, Amelia wouldn't fall apart— at least that was what Louisa hoped. Louisa had spent years attempting to help Amelia be stronger, braver.

Hugh was right; Amelia was different. She obsessed about things and she fixated on other things. She had a difficult experience most of the time, and Louisa really only saw Amelia calm when she was with Hugh. It was lovely to see, the two of them together. There was an intimacy borne of years of understanding and friendship that left much to be jealous of. It was almost like Amelia was locked in there somewhere and Hugh helped her come out. Louisa had learned a lot from watching them together, and she was able to help Ameila when she had an episode to a certain extent now too, but not like Hugh. Never like Hugh.

Louisa couldn't imagine being like Amelia and managing a true society ball at the height of the season. Louisa's heart wrenched for her as she closed her eyes and thought about the night her own life had been set on an entirely different path. The night she would stray from the path of society darling to something altogether different.

And yet— And yet...

She wouldn't have changed it for the world. Those moments with Ellie would always be the most treasured moments of her life, and she wouldn't give them up for anything. She'd told Hugh long ago she didn't want to know anything about her; she wanted to assume she was happy, and unless something horrid happened, it was better she not hear a word. It all hurt much too much and not knowing had worked for a time, but returning to London—

"Amelia!" The shriek lifted through the manor to Louisa's room and chilled her to the bone before she made it to her feet. She'd been sitting here daydreaming for too long, and Amelia's mother had returned.

Louisa ran. She had to intercept her. She couldn't let her near Amelia, not right now while Amelia was upset, because if Hugh was the key, her mother was the lock.

Damn, damn, damn.

Louisa vaulted down the upper stair with her skirts held high. That anyone would be able to see her drawers wasn't even a consideration in her hurry to get to Amelia first. It was a good thing her rooms were closer than the entry, but that woman was spry. She'd snuck up on Louisa countless times like a wraith. Louisa jumped the rail when she was within ten stairs of the upper landing then dropped her skirts as she bolted down the hallway, skidding around the corner to Amelia's room, all the while listening for that woman's horrid shrieking voice.

"Amelia!"

There. Louisa slipped to a halt, her hand shooting out to the wall to steady herself. Lady Pembroke had just made the upper landing. Louisa took a deep breath, attempting to still her racing heart. She patted her hair and tucked it back into her mobcap, straightening her apron across her chest and skirt and turning back toward the landing. "Your Grace," she said as she met her in the hall. "How lovely to see you. I wasn't expecting you so soon. Amelia said the ball was wonderful and she was a success." Louisa knew she could pull this off when Lady Pembroke stopped and assessed her, her hand going to the pearl buttons on the high neck of her dress.

"Did she." It wasn't exactly posed as a question, so Louisa knew she would need to press harder.

"Oh, she said the Duke was there, and they had a grand time. She sai—"

"The Duke?"

"Yes. The Castleberry, I assume?" *Please, oh please* let him have been there.

"She mentioned that?"

"Yes, ma'am. She was looking forward to seeing him again. She's resting, exhausted I'm afraid."

"I expect to see her at breakfast, Louisa. No excuses. I want a full report. She should have known to wait for my return. *You* should have known to wait."

"I beg pardon, ma'am, I assumed that since the evening had been successful, it wasn't necessary. I am terribly sorry." Louisa curtseyed and bowed her head and hoped.

"It's always necessary. Keep that in mind."

"Yes, ma'am." Louisa spoke to floor; she didn't think she could look at the woman with a bland eye. She waited. When Louisa saw the woman's skirts swirl around her feet and disappear down the corridor, Louisa straightened, took a genuine breath, and turned for Amelia's room. She followed the long hallways and turns and finally arrived. "Your mother is the very devil's undergarments!" she grumbled as she burst into the room. Louisa was immediately repentant when Amelia's entire body jerked as though she hadn't known where she was, and of course she didn't. She was considering the night, all of it, in detail. *Damn.* She shouldn't let her mother get to her like that.

"Louisa, dearest, my mother is as she is, as you should be aware by now."

"Promise me you'll not leave me to her when you're well and married. Please, take me with you," she said.

Amelia giggled and stood, and Louisa started to pull at her trappings, efficiently removing in a mere moment what had taken nearly an hour to place earlier that evening. "I would never do such a thing as leave you, you know that," Amelia said, her voice halting as Louisa pulled the corset strings loose. She'd been with Amelia all this time. Louisa had spent almost every day and every waking moment in Amelia's presence...she thought she might now know

Amelia almost as well as Hugh. Not quite as well, but close. So Louisa could help Amelia manage her feelings, and that was often enough. Unless her mother got to her.

Louisa shook her head again. "Viper, she is. You'd think the world was at an end simply because you left the ball."

"Ah... Is my mother home, or did she send a footman to check on me?"

Amelia was calm at the moment, so Louisa knew she'd be able to play with her a bit. She twisted her face into a ridiculous expression. "Send a footman?" Louisa squealed. "Send a footman! Why, the very— And leave the ball with only three liveried men to accompany the coach? You cannot be serious, Amelia. The very idea. I mean, really." She gave her a grand smile and put her hands on her hips.

Amelia collapsed back in her chair with a grin. "Goodness me, the coachman and outriders must be dizzy from circling London. Mother must have been waiting for their return."

"Hush now," Louisa said, leaning in. "She'll hear you, and then where will we be? In the stocks in the grand courtyard, that's where." Louisa lifted the skirt she'd just removed from Amelia to the light, poking her finger through a hole Amelia must have made while fidgeting, as she was wont to do.

"Louisa, the stocks were removed to the attics decades ago," Amelia said.

Louisa tossed the dress aside, knowing that calling attention to the damage was unhelpful. "Oh, my lady, don't think for a minute that she'll not pull them out simply for this transgression. Truly, you sound like a schoolgirl in this fit of giggles. She'll think you've become much too far gone and have you off to Bedlam by morning."

Amelia calmed then, rather suddenly, and Louisa knew she'd overstepped.

"Oh there, milady, I've gone too far. I always do. Come, come, never fear. If she had off with you, I'd be at your side to take the brunt of it." She saw Amelia try to smile, and Louisa let out the breath she'd held. "All right now, up with you. Here's a great soft bed calling to you."

"Louisa, don't leave me," Amelia said when she leaned in to hug her.

"Don't start now, milady. You know no good will come of this. Just simply take me with you. I'll never leave." God, what would she do if she lost this girl?

Amelia smiled and nodded, then crawled into the bed. Louisa fussed with the sheets and the counterpane, tucking her in nice and tight, and Amelia relaxed. Louisa felt it in her muscles as they melted under her fingers like warming butter. "I will," Amelia said.

Louisa prodded the fire and dimmed the gas lamp left in the far corner of her room to chase the shadows. "I know," she replied. She put out the remaining gaslights as she left, the heavy door clicking shut behind her. If only she could chase her own shadows as easily as she chased the shadows from Amelia's room.

Louisa turned down the hall and headed for the gallery where all the family portraits were. She went there to sit amongst all the ancestors of her employers; it wasn't her father's gallery by any stretch of the imagination, but it had the same feeling. She sat on a chair beneath a large portrait of some old woman painted to seem younger. The moonlight cast a pattern across the tiles at her feet, and Louisa thought about Ellie again. Her mind had been so clouded—thoughts of Ellie tangled with thoughts of her family.

Louisa wasn't sure she'd survive this return to London. Her heart was always racing, her nerves were on constant edge, and her brain was running away with her at every moment. She followed her gaze down the crossbar shadows of the window, the pieces of light forming shapes and patterns on the tile floor, cutting across the ordered tiles in a diagonal pattern. The floor in her father's gallery had been black-and-white marble, large, veined tiles. It had been her favorite place in all the world for such a long time. She used to sit on the statue's lap or at the foot of her mother's portrait and talk to her, and cry, and work through things on her own.

Perhaps it was still because regardless of the pain remembered in that room, it had also been witness to such beauty and such joy. She tucked her feet under her and leaned against the arm of the chair. She'd shared her first kiss with Ellie in that room. She'd shared her mother's portrait with Ellie. That was the first time Ellie had ever come to her house.

Ellie had said, *"She looks like you."*

Louisa bolted upright. She'd forgotten her mother's portrait until now. Surely it had been destroyed after she'd been abandoned. There would have been no reason to keep it. Her step-mother had made it clear that it wasn't wanted, and now the only thing she had—or that she would have had—of her mother was gone.

The heat of a tear fell on her cheek and Louisa brushed it away before it could fall, before the feel of it could spread across her skin and along her nerves and seep into her bones, where it would become permanent. She couldn't have that. The portrait was gone, just as she was gone. There was no use crying over it.

She stood and stared at the portrait of Amelia's grandmother that looked nothing like her. These were the faces she would see for the rest of her days. Strangers. She would do well to get used to it.

A shudder ran through her. She needed to forget Ellie, but she couldn't force her from her mind. She could feel her. Everywhere she went. Everything was a remembrance of her, and it hurt. It hurt so very much. She was hot and tight, stuffed into the clothes and the corset. She turned to the window and opened it, trying to get a fresh breeze only to be reminded that she was in London and there were no fresh breezes here. She closed her eyes and breathed the cool night air anyway. At this rate, she wasn't going to last until they left London.

Ellie stood in the park outside Pembroke House wishing they were less careful about their privacy. One of the largest private residences in London, the house was massive, taking up most of the west side of the park. And all of the curtains were drawn. She'd wandered around to the mews as well, to find that the house had wings that extended far into the gardens, but she couldn't see much more than the upper floors and the rooftops.

She shouldn't be back here. If someone saw her, it would end very badly. Ladies didn't belong wandering the mews of London. She kept the hood of her cape low on her brow, hiding as much as she could, and searched for something she could stand on to get a better view when a carriage rumbled through the mews and the stable door swung wide.

Ellie hid behind the door, out of the way as the men unhitched the horses from the large carriage. She leaned back against the brick mews, closing her eyes and allowing the sounds of the tack and stomping hooves to settle her nerves.

What was she doing? This was insanity. If someone discovered her they'd…well…they'd either ruin her in society or something much worse, where society's opinions would no longer matter to her.

She heard the driver and stable hands yelling as the horses were managed. The carriage was left there, half in and half out of the stable doors, the wheels grinding rock and dirt as they shifted it. She opened her eyes and waited to be discovered when a hand wrapped around the door to close it, but then someone called and the hand disappeared. She peeked out.

She'd gone from a terrible situation to a horrible one in the span of a breath but she couldn't help herself. She walked through the stables, head down, her black cloak as deep as the shadows around her swishing over her toes. When she got to the garden wall, she pushed the latch on the gate and pulled it open, slipping into the back gardens and pulling it closed.

What was she doing? She was supposed to be sleeping. She was supposed to be home. She wasn't supposed to be breaking into the gardens of a powerful duke. But if there were any chance that Louisa was here... She stopped and inspected the manicured paths, the shaped hedges and trimmed rosebushes looming in the dark like tangled claws. It was a nice garden, but it wasn't particularly a welcoming one. She ran down the path to a small trellis covered with vines and hid herself there.

She should leave. She should go back to the stables and slink her way back through the mews and back home before she was discovered. She peered around the corner column and up the brick of the house where here, the windows were shrouded by georgette as opposed to heavy brocades one could not see through. Somewhere in that house was her Lou. Maybe. Hopefully. Oh, how she wished.

She found a music room, the harp in the window. She found a library, the walls of books. She found a study, perhaps, with paintings on the walls. She searched the lower floors but there were no signs of habitation of any kind. Nothing. She examined a higher row of windows over the gardens. She could see faces in the moonlight—paintings. She took a step forward, the hood of her cloak slipping back as she lifted her chin and stared at the shadow she was certain had moved.

Her heart stuttered against her ribs, her fingers tingling with awareness and she reached, heart first, with all the hope in the world, that it was Louisa. The shadow shifted, stretched out taller in the moonlight, and Ellie followed heedless. The gallery. Of course, the gallery. She would find Louisa in the gallery amongst the art; of course she would. She reached out to the edge of the trellis to steady herself as the shadow above moved, then the window opened.

As the moonlight washed over Louisa's face, Ellie crumpled to the grass, no longer able to support her legs as her heart raced and her lungs fought against her constraints for air. "Louisa." But it wasn't even a whisper, her throat was so dry. She swallowed tears, trying to whet her throat as Louisa gazed down to her.

"Oi!" a man's voice yelled, and Ellie fell to the grass, curling beneath her cape as she froze. "Dun ya know how much coal's needed on that house, miss?"

"Jerrod! My apologies," Louisa said, and it was everything Ellie could do to not cry out now. "I needed a bit of air."

"We're in London, miss. No air here," Jerrod replied, and Ellie could hear the smile in his voice. She managed to remain silent as she shuddered beneath her cloak on the cold ground. Her heart felt like it would beat right out of her chest and if she weren't curled in a ball, she thought it might.

"Right, of course," Louisa said, and Ellie heard the window wind closed, then the click of the metal sash as it seated in place. She peeked out and the last thing she saw was Louisa's hand pressed to the glass, lifting away until it was naught but the four tiny pricks of her fingertips lit by the moon.

Jerrod chuckled, and she covered her face once more. She had to get out of the gardens and back home before anyone discovered her. She listened to his footsteps fade toward the stables and stood, shaking off her cloak and dress as best she could. It didn't do much; she looked perfectly ruined.

She glanced back up to the window once more but it had gone dark and still. For a moment, she considered trying to get into the house, but a noise from behind her sent her running straight to the mews as fast as her feet could carry her.

Louisa tossed Amelia's skirts over her head then arranged them at her waist. She was doing her absolute best to forget the dream from the night before. She needed to stop going to the gallery—she was conjuring Ellie in her dreams and she was set to go mad, and then where would she be? But seeing Ellie kneeling in the garden... She was haunted. Right now she needed to concentrate and listen, because Amelia was having a conversation with nobody and that was unfair.

"—I fear he won't wish to marry me unless I'm truly done with Hugh."

Louisa stilled, frozen behind her as she fastened myriad buttons at her waist. It didn't seem fair, how much women were forced to give up. Always. In every way.

"Louisa?"

"Yes, I...I heard you. Amelia, I know how much Ender means to you but—" She shook her hands out and went back to fastening buttons. It wasn't fair, and it never would be, but more than that, Louisa wasn't sure Amelia would survive without Hugh. Perhaps survive wasn't the right word. Of course she would survive. She just...wouldn't be the same.

"Louisa?"

"Yes?" She needed to stop maundering and pay attention. She stood when she finished the buttons, and Amelia turned toward her.

"I feel so terribly lost. I... He's my—"

"I know." Louisa took her in a strong embrace, unable to not comfort her, and knowing that if she held her tight, Amelia might find enough solace in that to carry on today. She wrapped her arms around her and squeezed, and Amelia let go and relaxed into her before Louisa released her. "Let's leave that for now, shall we? Today is merely a trip to the park with Charles. That's all. Today is not the wedding, and it certainly isn't the day you lose Ender." She leaned back and took her shoulders. "And you are absolutely lovely. Come, turn back around let me finish your bustle."

Louisa fussed a bit more then handed Amelia her reticule, which she glanced at disdainfully—it was a bit over-decorated, and Louisa would be surprised if it still had all the beads on it when Amelia returned.

Louisa turned her toward the door. "Enjoy the park, you love the park," she said, then the door clicked shut. Louisa turned to straighten Amelia's things and put her nightclothes in the laundry. Then she sat before the fire.

She knew what it was like with someone new, that spark of... *something* that fluttered inside, made your fingers tingle and your heart race. Though Amelia's feelings for Charles were a bit more complicated than all that, Louisa knew what she'd felt like, because the first time she'd felt it—that night in the ballroom— she'd latched on to that feeling and refused to let go. At the time, she'd no idea it would be wrenched from her so soon.

Louisa stood. She'd felt that again last night when she thought she'd seen Ellie in the gardens. It had been a dream—of course it had. How could Ellie possibly end up in the Pembroke House gardens? But the moment she'd seen Ellie glowing like seraphim in the moonlight, her heart had skipped and her toes had gone numb. But then, she'd been so concerned with Amelia, she hadn't even considered what being back in London might mean for them. She'd shoved it away, too dangerous to consider.

She couldn't go to Ellie because if anyone saw her—if her family saw her... But nobody else in London would remember her. Though...she was now a ladies maid. In her work dress, she could move through London without anyone paying her any mind.

She sat back down. Ellie was safe—not trolling ladies gardens in the dark of night. Beyond that, Louisa knew nothing. Hugh

hadn't said anything. What if Ellie had quit London? What if she'd married? What if Hugh couldn't bear to tell her the news? All these questions. She shook them off and stood.

She should stop thinking about Ellie and forget what happened between them. Certainly Ellie had already done so. It wasn't as if they could ever be together again—after all, she'd been the one to tell Ellie to move on.

Louisa sank once again. She pulled the letter from the pocket she'd sewn at the edge of her corset and held it. It was so fragile at this point, the soft vellum no competition for all the tears and handling. The unfolding and refolding. She read it once again to remind herself of what she'd said, and she cried anew. There was no going back.

And yet...she couldn't fathom Ellie regarding someone else the way she'd regarded her. Those eyes like ametrine in the sun. Threaded so perfectly. She wondered if anyone else knew her eyes were woven with gold in the purple.

She wanted her mother. A mother would tell her what to do, she was certain. A mother would know. Even though she'd never had a mother, Louisa knew that a true one would help her, guide her, and if all else failed, would hold her and let her cry until the world felt somewhat more bearable.

Louisa stood again, this time determined. If she stood far enough away from her father's house she'd be able to see through the gallery windows. She could wear a shawl over her hair and keep her head down—nobody ever paid any mind to the help.

Louisa went to her room and removed her apron, but she kept her simple black work dress on. She took her ragged shawl and headed out. She knew she was being ridiculous. This was dangerous. Going to her father's house was not a good idea and she knew it. It had been three years since she'd been banished from that house, from London, society, her family, everything she'd ever known—

But then...nobody would remember her now, not like this. She'd been cast from memory the night her father had discovered the truth and sent her away.

Louisa found herself standing in Portman Square across from her father's house and dropped her head, hiding her face. It was as though her feet had known where to go without her consciously making the turns. Her heart knocked wildly against her ribs and she did her best to steady her breath.

She cast her eyes about, but there weren't many people. At this time of day, they'd be out calling on others, or riding the row, or shopping in some fashionable district... Portman was a smaller, more private square; it wasn't one of the destination parks where the ton went to see and to be seen. For that she was thankful.

She walked to a park bench and sat down before her knees forced her to the ground, then she lifted her chin until she could see the front entry to the house. It was as she'd remembered: the white marble portico over the entry, the flat-red brick façade, the wrought iron gates before the full-length windows, the exterior balconies on the upper floors that nobody ever used, and the whitewashed window trim that was touched up. So many windows were a statement, money to burn while the chimneys pushed out a bleakness that covered the roof, tarnished everything.

It was so cold. Louisa shuddered, pulling the wrap tighter around her shoulders.

Nothing had changed. Except that it was no longer her home, if it ever had been. If she had to choose a place to be her home, it was wherever Amelia was. Because that was when she felt safe.

She looked higher, only to have her line of sight blocked by the branch of a tree, and it took a few moments of berating and watching the sidewalks for people before she could convince her chin to lift further again, but when it did, her eyes went to the window on the second floor. It was dark inside, the clouds today heavy with coal dust and smoke from the trains and London. The sun wasn't making its way through the glass ceiling of her father's townhouse, that was certain.

She could see some of the shapes inside, the human forms that were larger than life, denoting her favorite sculptures as opposed to the members of her family—former family.

She shouldn't be here. Even the rare chance that she be recognized was too much to risk and she suddenly knew it. The last time she'd left this square should have been the last time forever.

Louisa turned away from the house and started back across the park. She shouldn't even be out in London. If anyone saw her and recognized her...

This would lead to certain disaster. She twisted her hands together and attempted to steady her breath. She needed to remember the past; she needed to remember. If she forgot—even for a moment—she could end up dead or worse. She and Ellie had forgotten to check the gallery the one time, and that was all it had taken to ruin her entire life. She glanced up as a carriage cut across her path. She needed to return to the house, to see to Amelia. She pushed all thoughts of the past to the back of her mind. She needed to concentrate on Amelia now. Amelia was her life.

Ellie couldn't bring herself to rise from bed. She begged off all her mother's plans for her and lazed about in her room reading, drinking tea, and staring into the fire thinking about Louisa's hand on the window and what it would feel like to have those fingertips on her body once again.

A shiver slipped through her system and she melted into the settee, one hand between her thighs, the other on her heart trying to convince it to calm so she could breathe.

The biggest reason she didn't dress today was she didn't think she could manage a day of breathlessness inside a corset, because every time Louisa crossed her mind—which was too often at the moment—she couldn't take a breath. She didn't need a steel-boned corset hindering her further. What she wouldn't give to wander corset-free and happy in the cottage they'd built in her dreams.

Did Louisa still dream of it? Or had shut out even that small piece of her when she'd gone? She needed to talk to Hugh and she hadn't heard from him yet. Nobody had rung the bell. No messages had been brought to her. No hope delivered.

She closed her eyes and remembered last night, the earlier part before the latter part. She'd never felt so much in her life and hadn't felt as much since. She hadn't even been able to bring herself off the way Louisa had, and it shocked and saddened her. She wanted that abandon, that pure joy, the release and absolute surrender, but she couldn't find it.

She closed her eyes, her breath steadying as she remembered the water wash over her. The smell of roses heavy on the air. And Louisa's kisses of sweetened lemon and spice. She wanted, how very much did she want.

She could go to the house, could wander by. She couldn't wait here for Ender to make up his mind and make something happen. She stood, intending to hunt him down. Again. He didn't seem to understand how important this was. She stood and rang the bell for her ladies maid.

Louisa

Louisa entered the hall through the servants and went toward the front entry to find Amelia. The parlor door was closed but she could hear voices inside. Louisa went to the back of the house and up to her room to change, then to Amelia's room to ready for her. Hopefully everything had gone well and Amelia was still sound. Amelia was dedicated and beautiful, but different. Her mind would spin on things, and Amelia seemed unable to stop the torrent of it without someone to anchor her. Louisa was ever wary of the next thing to set her off.

Louisa opened Amelia's wardrobe. She would need to change into a day dress from her carriage dress. She turned when she heard footsteps running toward the room. "Oh, no," Louisa said to no one. The door burst open.

"Louisa?" was all she said.

"Amelia," Louisa replied, but when she looked, she knew. Amelia was not going to come back from the edge this time. Louisa rushed forward, and Amelia fell into her arms halfway across the room.

"Louisa, I don't— I cannot— I'm so—" She was pulling at her clothes, and Louisa tried to help her from her shirtwaist so she could get to the corset and loosen the binding.

"Hush now, Amelia. Come here, let's get you changed, let's get you—"

Amelia's words were confused and incoherent, Louisa tried to keep up with the conversation but she was spinning and all Louisa could do was hold on and hope for the best at this point, until Amelia screamed in frustration and Louisa knew any minute it would all come crashing down.

"Amelia!" Her mother's screech rent the hallway, and Amelia turned.

"No," was all she said and it a whisper of a breath more than anything, but the shudder that wracked Amelia's body spoke much louder than her voice. Amelia collapsed, pulling Louisa with her to the floor in a pile of skirts.

"Amelia! Get up and get dressed. It isn't the thing to be half made at this time of day." The voice made Louisa cringe. Couldn't this ridiculous woman see? Couldn't she *see* what she did to her daughter? She steeled herself, prepared to go head to head with the woman for once, but her attention was taken by the tall, dark, brooding man who stood in the doorway behind her.

Striking, he was terrified and concerned and calm at once. It had to be Castleberry, and in that moment she doubted Lady Pembroke knew he'd followed. She wondered if he were a decent man, because right now she needed his help.

She caught his eye and pleaded with her gaze before turning her attention to Amelia's mother. "My lady, I beg you, leave her to me. I can manage," Louisa said.

"Don't speak to me in such a tone, Louisa."

Louisa glanced up to her, mere moments from letting her have her mind, but instead forced her concentration back to Amelia. "Come, Amelia, my lady. Come sit by the fire." Louisa managed to coax her from the floor, even as distant as she was. She set her in her favorite chair and loosed her fingers from her skirt. Louisa swept her favorite quilt around her shoulders, wrapping it tight.

"Do you ignore me, girl?" Lady Pembroke said.

"I beg pardon, my lady. I only meant that I could take care of Amelia for you. You needn't trouble yourself at all. She'll be right as rain soon enough." While in her head, she cursed the woman for her careless behavior.

Lady Pembroke rushed forward and grabbed Amelia's shoulder. "Amelia, Amelia, quit this act immediately and get up. Get up!"

"Lady Pembroke, this won't help. She needs quiet—"

"Do you pretend to think I do not know my own daughter?"

"Of course, my lady. I only meant—"

"You *act* as if I don't know my own daughter!" Another shriek, another cringe, and Amelia leaned into her, away from her mother. *Because you don't.* She needed to get the woman out. The man straightened, as if he'd grown several inches in standing there, as if he hadn't already been large and enough of a terror.

His countenance shifted from concern to resolve. "Lady Pembroke. A word?" The man's voice had a slight tremor to it, and he cleared his throat. "Now." The power of his carriage sent a trill of something through Louisa, and the room went still.

Silent.

The expression on her mother's face was something Louisa would carry with her for the rest of her life. A remembrance that nobody could escape a deserved comeuppance. She stood straight then turned, so smooth you'd think her a mechanical toy, as her entire demeanor shifted and she regained her composure. "Your Grace, I had no idea you—"

"If we might speak. With Pembroke as well. I have some questions."

So this man *was* the Duke, and he'd cut Lady Pembroke off without a care.

"Of course, Your Grace. I... Well, I should see to my—" Her hand fell gently open toward Amelia.

"Now would be best. I'm quite certain she'll be fine, yes? There isn't anything terribly wrong with her...is there?" She was a mouse in a trap, and he was the cat playing with her. Lady Pembroke could not admit to any sort of illness, and he knew it. Even so, her gratitude was tinged at the edge with empathy for a woman who had no power in her life either.

He smiled at Louisa as he waited for Lady Pembroke to lead him away. Louisa may come to like this man. Someday. Lady Pembroke moved from the room, and Louisa went back to Amelia and pulled her into a tight embrace. Amelia relaxed into her, then reached out of her cocoon of a quilt and took Louisa's arm. Castleberry pulled the door closed behind him, but he paused and caught her eye.

"Thank you," Louisa said, *sotto voce.*

Louisa held her for a while then as Amelia relaxed, she helped her to stand, stripped her of her clothes, and moved her to the bed. All she needed now was rest. Once she was gone, once she went that far, there was nothing to be done but to wait it out. She tucked Amelia in to rest then sat in Amelia's favorite chair to watch over her. It wasn't necessary. She wasn't watching over Amelia at all. She was keeping watch for her mother.

She stared at the door that had been filled by the man Amelia was contracted to marry. He was...large. Even if he didn't fill the doorway, his presence did. His eyes were dark and his demeanor darker, and yet he'd helped her to help Amelia. Had taken Lady Pembroke away from them so Amelia could rest. She'd thought men of his stature, men with his power, had all been the same, those upper echelons, the highest of the high, mightiest of the mighty.

She'd believed they never looked down from their broad shoulders to see what they trampled. Though Hugh had proven that thought wrong years ago when he'd rescued her. He was a mere baron, though, not a viscount or even an earl...and this man was duke, second only to the Crown.

Still.

It had taken time for her to trust Hugh as well, even though she'd known him before. Now she trusted him with everything she was. She'd had to.

She shuddered to think of where she might be if it weren't for him. She was tired of being beholden to men, but if ever she were to choose a man, Hugh would be it.

"Louisa?"

"My lady. Well, it's good to see you," Louisa replied. She'd fallen asleep in Amelia's chair and dreamt of Ellie. But she needed to put that aside.

"Have I missed supper? Tell me I've missed supper."

"Yes, quite, but not to worry. I requested a tray sent up. I'm rather surprised your mother hasn't—"

"Oh, my mother." Amelia's head fell to her hands. Then she looked up. "Castleberry?"

"He's gone, but not for long. I believe he hasn't been entirely frightened off. Not to worry." Louisa gave her a warm smile.

"Oh, Louisa, I truly thought I'd destroyed any hope of—"

"*Tsch tsch tsch*, now, don't be so cruel to yourself. You know if he were frightened off, as you say, he wasn't so worthy of you to begin with. And there's always Lord Endsleigh." Hugh. He loved Amelia and would go to the ends of the earth for her. If only he were allowed. He wasn't supposed to come around Amelia now that she'd come out and the Duke had come to claim his bride. It still hurt, because Louisa knew how good of a man Hugh was and how desperately he loved Amelia. She'd watched them the last three years and knew them to be the best of friends, and even if she held herself back from more, Louisa could see the possibility. It frightened her, as did the specter of Castleberry.

"Yes, he and I can retire as spinsters together, taking my mother and living in his modest estate on his moderate income. He would just adore that. No doubt, he'd take up knitting. Or needlepoint."

Louisa laughed, remembering their own discussion about that very thing, once upon a time in a ballroom long ago. Hugh had promised himself as her very own spinster husband, should she not find someone suitable. She supposed that was off the table at this point. Regardless, she would never relegate Hugh to such a marriage. "He would, because he loves you," Louisa said. "And you know he'd create beautiful pillows that all the ladies would be jealous of."

"But he deserves so much more than me."

"Now here we go again. Must we always go round and round like this? Must we? If Ender were to spend the balance of his days with you, not only would he be the luckiest man alive, but to have you in his life would be more than he deserves. And you as well. The two of you are well suited. Except for that one, small issue."

"That issue being that he's not good enough for me in my father's eyes? A baron only? For shame...I should only be so lucky."

"Your dear father has only your interests at heart. He wants the very best life for you. He doesn't know—"

"That I'm impaired? Oh, but he does, Louisa. He does. Don't let him make a fool of you as well. I think this to be his greatest farce—to marry his unacceptable daughter to one of the most powerful of peers. As for Castleberry, he certainly understands that I'm not well at this point."

Louisa stood before she became too frustrated. She understood the problem. She understood that Amelia was contracted to Castleberry and wasn't allowed to marry Hugh. But what she understood better than any of this was how quickly life could change and destroy everything you understood. But then, it wasn't her place to shatter Amelia, not at all. She was here to support her, and Hugh wished beyond everything else that Louisa was to be here for Amelia, solely for Amelia. She'd been disallowed from even swaying Amelia to Hugh. He would be furious if he knew she did even if she thought him suited to her. But then, the Duke...he'd managed her mother quite well, and that was quite the attribute in itself. Louisa's greatest frustration lay in the fact she was unable to speak her mind. She was a ladies maid. She was to have no opinion. A ladies maid with an opinion would find herself without said position. She wondered what Amelia would think if she knew the truth of it.

Louisa fussed about the room in her annoyance, then realized the supper tray hadn't yet been sent up, so she turned for the hallway. She'd get it herself. No doubt Amelia's mother had intercepted it or some nonsense to get her point across. And honestly, what the hell good would that do? The woman was horrid. If her mother— But she'd never had a mother, and the woman who'd taken the place of her mother had stood aside as her father had beat her senseless after finding her with Ellie. Louisa was struck by the fact that she believed mothers to be inherently good when she'd been faced with nothing but the opposite, in fact. Even Ellie's mother—

Louisa swayed on her feet and reached out to steady herself at the wall.

Ellie. Just the thought of her name made her weak. Perhaps she could send a message to Hugh, have him find out how she was. Louisa continued down the hall. All she ever wanted was for Ellie to be safe.

Louisa wondered if her father had ever come looking for her at the Magdalen Asylum...but of course he hadn't. He'd written her off. She no longer existed. He'd put her in her place and expected that she would stay there. Louisa stopped and rested her hands at her knees. Good God, she needed to stop thinking or she would never make it to the kitchens for Amelia's supper, and the girl needed to eat.

She stood tall and took a deep breath and headed for the servants' stair. Dark and steep, hidden behind a wall, as servants always should be. She and Ellie had made use of many servants' staircases that first week. Oh, that first night, when Ellie had stolen her breath. She'd no idea there would be so many staircases, so many dark corners. That first night...that night had been filled with nothing but possibility.

It was all to no avail. Hugh had yet to speak with Louisa and he was frustrated that she would search him out at his home. She understood that he wished to protect them all, but Ellie was too impatient.

She returned home and refused to attend that evening's ball. Instead, since her parents would be away, she called for a bath in the guest room. A room she hadn't entered since that night three years before. She stripped with the help of Abigail, then wrapped up in a silk robe and slippers. She followed her through the halls to the guest suite, her breath stilling when they entered.

She'd had the fire warmed and stoked in the grate to chase the chill away. It was much warmer than the cool hall behind her and yet she stood at the threshold, trying to breathe through the memories that assailed her. The dressing and undressing, the stolen kisses and private touches. She wished she had anything, *anything at all,* to remember her by. She reached to her neck, but had removed the necklace in her room to keep it safe.

She searched the wardrobe for any small thing that could have been left behind, but there was nothing. No pins, no pieces of fabric, no jewels. She stood at the window and stared down to the street below where Louisa had tossed her things, and her heart broke all over again.

She twisted her hands, thinking about the way she'd handled that night—which is to say she hadn't handled it at all. She should have been strong. Brave. She should have been the brave woman Louisa believed her to be, and perhaps that was why Louisa had left so swiftly. She'd needed more, and Ellie hadn't given it.

But it wasn't her. Louisa had said so the next day. Louisa had forgiven her failings. How naïve Ellie had been. How patient Louisa had been with Ellie's ingenue behavior—in every way.

Ellie turned and walked to the bath, the steam greeting her at the door like a hug.

Abigail stood. "It's ready, miss, though be careful. It's still a bit hot."

"Thank you, Abigail." She took the maid's hand and squeezed it, looking in her eyes and wondering for the first time if she had someone to love. Louisa was in the same position in another household. Did they care for her as a person beyond their needs of her? "Abigail, the water is clear. Do you remember the last time we were here? It wasn't like this."

"Oh yes, miss. I prepared a milk bath. Would you like one tonight as well?"

"Do you mind?" she asked, and Abigail was clearly confused. Ellie supposed she'd never asked her opinion on whether or not she could do something for her.

"Not at all, miss. I'll come straight back."

The door shut, and Ellie reached for the tray of oils and herbs, opening and smelling them until she found the rosehips she remembered. She dribbled a small amount on the surface then stirred it as Louisa had done. She ran her hands along the curl at the edge of the tub, the hard, cool weight of it such a stunning comparison to the skin of her love. So unforgiving where Louisa had been so soft and supple. Rigid where Louisa had been pliable, unmovable where Louisa had been so very moveable.

When Abigail returned with a pitcher. Ellie stood aside. "Sorry it took a bit longer. I had cook warm the milk so your bath wouldn't be cooled too quickly."

"Thank you, Abigail," Ellie said then watched as Abigail poured the contents of the pitcher into the bath and swirled the water, the scent of roses on vanilla blooming around her. "Oh this is lovely," Ellie said, and Abigail smiled and nodded.

"If you need anything more, miss, please ring the bell."

"Thank you, again, Abigail," Ellie said then watched as she closed the door behind her.

She dropped the silk robe she'd worn and sank into the forbidden bath, leaning back against the furled edge of the tub as she wished, oh how she wished, that everything could be different. That Louisa was working as a ladies maid in service to a woman like her was...inconceivable. Louisa had been the epitome of proper society. In public anyway. Her manners and behavior had been perfection. Ellie had mimicked her at times, trying so hard to be as mesmerizing as she'd been.

Ellie closed her eyes and lifted one hand out of the water, effecting that perfect hand, the soft wrist held just so, the way she could turn it and motion to others. She'd moved so gentle and seamless like a cloud on the breeze, with nary a twitch or jerk.

She watched her hand; the disconnect from her own body because of the milky water mesmerized and enchanted Ellie as she slid a bit lower, then pulled the chilled hand to her breast, gasping into the steam as she arched her back against the sudden chill. She touched herself with her fingertips at first, as though she were that window, in the dark of night.

Then she cupped her breast, bringing herself up to break the surface so she could see her hand caress her furled nipple, wrap around her breast and squeeze as Louisa had done. She teased and played, her other hand chilling on the edge of the tub, holding her in place as she touched, watched, gathered the sensations into herself and held them close.

A thread of want wove its way through her system, touching each of her fingertips, the tips of her ears, the nape of her neck, the very edges of her lips, the smooth length of her neck to the divot at the center of her collar bone.

She let go of the tub and chased all of those sensations, like the ghost of Louisa's touch. She slid her other hand from her breast to her mons, following the gooseflesh that rose despite the warmth of the water. Pushing her toes against the far edge of the bath, she anchored herself as she dreamed Louisa into being. She was wetter than wet and it had naught to do with the water.

This was all she'd ever wanted, to go back to that night, before the ball, to come back to this time and this place and remember every moment, every heavy breath, every simple touch.

Ellie sank against the edge, her head tossed back as her fingers worked through the wet folds of her vulva to find the entrance to her body, then she slid inside and found what she'd been looking for.

Her whole body tensed, sending waves of water careening against the edge of the tub, and she tried to relax into it but couldn't. She crossed her arm over her chest, her hand on her breast, holding, as she searched for that thread again but it was gone, like the weaver had tugged and the thread had respooled as fast as it had come, leaving an emptiness between her ribs.

She soothed her body, disappointed once again. Perhaps she was broken. Perhaps she would never be able to come off again. Perhaps it was just that one time, where everything had been so precarious and yet perfect...or perhaps it was what Louisa had done to her. She'd made everything possible.

Ellie needed more. And Louisa was the more she needed. She finished washing, then stood from the tub and dried herself before putting the robe back on. It was still decadent, the milk bath, the roses, the steam, the forbidden room. It wasn't what she wanted, and her heartbeat echoed in that emptiness.

The next morning, Louisa was requested to accompany Amelia with Castleberry and Hugh. Though she imagined herself a better choice than Lady Mathorpe, she wasn't comfortable with the situation. They ended up rolling the carriage top down through *the Row,* where Louisa did her level best to hide herself and Hugh surreptitiously attempted to help her hide while comforting her rattled nerves without drawing attention. Amelia, blessedly, was in her own world, her mind turning on the men who accompanied them.

Lunch was easier at Charles's home. She received a short respite from the strain while the three of them were in the gardens, then joined them for dinner, which was interrupted, of course, by Amelia's frayed nerves.

"Charles, if you don't mind, I would borrow your carriage to return home," Amelia said.

"We'll accompany—" Castleberry started.

"No, that won't be necessary. Louisa?"

Louisa stood but before she could move to Amelia, Hugh caught her arm and slid a note to her hand. Louisa looked down, then clenched her fingers around it as she caught his gaze, so many questions she wouldn't be allowed to ask, like, *Is it from her?* and *Why did you wait until now?* She turned and wrapped an arm around Amelia's waist. They walked to the mews as Castleberry instructed the footman and they left.

It was everything Louisa could do to ignore the note she'd tucked in her pocket as they sped through London toward Pembroke House. Thankfully Amelia seemed to be in her own thoughts. When they passed once again through *the Row,* she took Amelia's hands and held them, offering a bit of support in this public moment.

By the time they returned, Louisa couldn't even remember how they'd gotten here. Amelia having to nudge her to remove from the carriage. As soon as they entered Pembroke, they were called to the parlor and she was forced to hide in the doorway behind Amelia to avoid any recognition from the ladies in attendance. By the time she followed Amelia to her rooms, her nerves were fraught with tension. She helped Amelia to change, then went to her own room to hide for as long as she could manage.

She sat on the bed and pulled the note from the pocket in her skirts. There wasn't even a direction on the note. It was folded then waxed shut. She pulled it open. It was Hugh's handwriting, but her heart thumped when she saw her name. *Maitland.* It had been a long time since she'd thought of her as a person beyond her Ellie, yet here she was.

She closed her eyes. She'd been determined to put her from her mind to care for Amelia and get out of London as quickly as possible, forever, hopefully. That wasn't bound to happen. She opened her eyes and read.

Maitland wishes to meet with you.

If you wish for the same, you may use my rooms.

You know the direction. There is a key beneath the pot at the stoop.

I'll be in attendance at the Greenborough ball tonight in the hopes of seeing Amelia.

You'll have most of the night.

Should you decide to go, please be careful, as I will be otherwise engaged.

Louisa wasn't sure how she felt. She'd only just decided—though deciding to do something and doing it were different things and her heart wasn't on board with the decision, it never had been. Louisa was older, wiser. She may be frightened being back in London because her father seemed to have no morals but... she could do whatever she wanted. And what she wanted was Ellie.

Ellie

Ellie paced in Ender's library, unsure what would happen if Louisa never came. She shook her head. Louisa would come. She would. She pulled a copy of *Punch* from one of the messy shelves, sitting on the settee and flipping through the pages to distract herself.

"*Punch* is a bit low-brow for a lady, isn't it?" The voice teased like those fingertips on the glass. They crept along her skin, sinking through to her veins, then rushing her heart and sending it to beat in an unwieldy sort of manner.

She closed her eyes and concentrated on her breathing. She wished she didn't have to concentrate on it quite so much. Her ladies maid was a terror with the laces.

"Nothing to say?" She was closer, her voice heavier than she remembered. There was more in it.

She recognized the girl she knew, but also recognized that it no longer belonged to her. It was smoke where before it had been a mere breeze. "Lou—?" Her breath hitched and she couldn't finish. She reached to her chest and wrapped her fingers around the edge of her dress, pulling it away for air. "I can't—" Air shifted, light faded, and Ellie knew Louisa knelt before her. "Louisa?" she begged. She couldn't look. She couldn't be faced with an empty room and yet another shattered dream. "Please." She dropped the paper and covered her eyes with her other hand.

"Ellie," Louisa said, and the breath it came on caressed her cheek a name she longed to hear and thought she never would. "You're so beautiful. Just as I remember. If I'd known...if I'd known...if I'd known, I would have held on longer. I would have memorized every bit of you." Louisa pulled her hand away, then kissed her eyelids, swept her hands into her hair and pulled her forward. "Ellie, how I've missed you." And just like that they were kissing. And it was so much more than it ever was before. Like there hadn't been color in the world until now and Louisa painted with every brush.

Ellie took her wrists in her hands and pulled her up into her lap as she searched, and found, the body of a woman where there had been the body of a girl. Her hands were full, her flesh heavier against them, and Ellie wanted for nothing but more.

"Ellie, can't you look at me?"

She shook her head in response. She wanted only to feel, it was all she could manage. "I'm so afraid, Louisa. I'm so afraid," she cried, and Louisa kissed the tears away, her lips so soft on her own skin, the tip of her tongue hot sending sparks through her system, waking every nerve.

"I know. So am I," Louisa replied, and Ellie opened her eyes then.

This was no dream. She was here, in her arms, as she'd been the last time she'd ever seen her. She slid her hands around her waist and grabbed whatever loose fabric she could find, pulling her tight against herself as she gazed into her eyes and refused to look away because now that she held her in her sight, there was no chance she would give her up again.

"God, Louisa," she said, and then there wasn't much talking. There was breathing. There was sobbing. There were soft, swollen breasts with tight,

wanting peaks of flesh. There was the sound of fabric bunching and shifting and tearing. There was not a single care in the world for what would happen next, outside of this room.

Louisa's hands were everywhere as they shifted, trying to come together, their need to be closer still impossible to ignore. Ellie needed, so very much did she need, to feel the heat of Louisa's center, as she had in that bath. To erase every single moment that had happened since then. To do what she'd wished to that night. She wanted to forget everything that had happened between. She wanted to go back to when Louisa had been hers and there'd been nothing in the world between them. She wanted what she'd been promised that night but had never received.

She pulled Louisa's skirt up and away, and for the first time in her life declared drawers to be a blessing instead of a hindrance. They twisted together until she shifted and fell to the side, bringing Louisa on top of her, so she could explore and not have to hold on so very tight. Her body was pliable, forgiving, lissome, warm.

She reached between them, following the heat of her own body until she met the heat of hers. Then like a prayer, she reached for heaven. Louisa threw her head back and sank down on Ellie, and she cupped her mons and explored her vulva. So soft. So impossibly soft. And wet. And supple. And impossible.

"Oh God, Ellie, more. Like that. Hold me like that, then reach inside. Let me move." She glanced back down to Ellie, "Just let me…"

Ellie pushed her fingers deep through her wet folds until she found the space that gave way to her body.

"Yes, Ellie, just there. Push up into me. I want you there…just there…yes."

And Ellie pushed. And Louisa cried out as she moved on her hand, and Ellie held her tight, watching her face and all the glorious expressions she made. Then Louisa shifted, her thigh coming between them and brushing Ellie's mons, and every memory from that night returned like a wave and she arched up into her, pushing back and pulling her close, and she couldn't get close enough, she couldn't get closer, it wasn't possible, and Louisa's body tightened in her arms.

"Come off with me, Ellie. Come with me," she breathed, but Ellie shook her head.

"No, I want to watch. I want to see."

And Louisa smiled that half smile that Ellie loved so much, had missed so much, before shifting harder against her palm. "Then hold me close, Ellie, and don't look away. God, what you do to me, Ellie. There's nothing—"

Her expressions shifted like she was hunting something, then fear and shock and finally something like wonder bloomed across her face and she froze. She grabbed Ellie, held on tight, her hips pushing as the rest of her went rigid and Ellie watched, blessed by the act of it. Louisa reached up to her chest and tugged at her corset, freeing one dusky nipple, then she pinched it and Ellie leaned up and took it into her mouth, playing with the tight bud, as Louisa wove her hand into Ellie's hair and held on.

"Ellie," she called out in a desperate whisper. "Ellie, don't let go. Ellie, oh God."

Ellie tightened her hold on her waist, slipped her fingers farther into her wetness as Louisa pushed into the heel of her hand and came off with her name on her lips, a graceful breath that Ellie would never forget.

It was so vulgar, the mashing of bodies, but the result was so beautiful, so striking, and Ellie loved everything about it. She couldn't get enough. She held Louisa tight through all the little aftershocks of it until Louisa pushed Ellie's hand away, unable to handle any more.

How beautiful she was, her face so pink and glowing, her breasts full and tight, her body vibrating like a honey bee covered in pollen.

"I want to taste you," Louisa said, and Ellie shifted. She hadn't realized Louisa had collapsed against her, and they'd lain there for long enough for her breath to steady and her body to calm. It had been too long since Ellie had felt such peace.

"You what?" Ellie asked, but then Louisa kissed her and Ellie sank into it, tasting so much more than the sweetened lemon and spice. She kissed her again, reaching for the answer, to know what it was. Salt and scent, the very air of her arousal on her lips. They were saturated with it, the smell of heat, and warmth, and sex. Perfectly lurid. She giggled; she couldn't help it.

"What?" Louisa said, leaning back.

"Just... What would Hugh think to walk in here after this?"

"That he's the luckiest man alive to be in the presence of such passion?"

"What—" Ellie drew a breath and let Louisa lick and kiss her face and her neck and chest. Then her own breasts were free, and Louisa took them in her mouth together, and hummed in pleasure as Ellie melted into the settee, her body warm and open and waiting for more, whatever that more would be.

Louisa slid, pushing aside fabric until a cool air hit Ellie's skin, her vulva so hot the air was brilliantly delicious. Then Louisa slid to the floor and was between her legs as Ellie was sprawled before her, unabashed, waiting for whatever came next. Louisa smiled, and Ellie ran a hand down her cheek to her chin.

"You're so beautiful, my Ellie. You know that, right? I'm sure you've heard it from countless suitors in my absence."

"I've heard it from no one, because I haven't been listening for anyone but you, Louisa. My Louisa. There can be no one. There's no one, there never will be. I'm quite decidedly in love with you," Ellie said.

"But Ellie—"

"No, Louisa, you don't seem to understand. I'm lost to this world, to society, to my family. I cannot marry I cannot go before God and lie and promise myself to a man I cannot in good conscience love and care for. It's an impossibility."

Louisa leaned up on her knees and took Ellie's lips once more, this kiss gentler than before. Dedicated. Then Louisa searched again with her mouth, exploring all of Ellie's skin, until she came between her thighs and before Ellie knew what she was about, Louisa licked her full, then placed a gentle kiss on the burgeoning bud at the crest of her slit.

She amused herself there with generous tongue and gentle teeth, willing the small bit of flesh to grow and thrust toward her, and Ellie...Ellie hadn't felt the likes of it since that night and the rest washed away on Louisa's tongue as she tasted, tempted, and took Ellie to that special place Ellie could only ever go with Louisa. Her Louisa. This was it. There was nothing else for her; she didn't care what came next as long as Louisa was by her side, holding her hand.

Ellie lifted her head to see all those perfectly placed dark curls wound in a tight chignon in such contrast to the pale white of her skin. It was stunning and beautiful and Louisa's eyes opened to catch her gaze and when she smiled, Ellie felt it first against her slick skin, then in her belly where it rested, pulsed and pushed. Growing and building.

"Louisa?" She let her head fall back as she pushed against her mouth, her tongue swirling around her clitoris, then sliding into her body before retreating behind a gentle kiss.

"Yes, my love? What feels good? What do you want me to do?"

She looked up again. "It all feels good, Lou, I don't know what else I— Can you just— I don't know. Whatever you want, Louisa,

whatever you want. It all feels so good," Ellie said then she sank against the pillows once more, concentrating on Louisa's mouth, her tongue, her fingers...touching...tentative... searching. Louisa spread her tongue against Ellie's vulva before sucking her clitoris into her mouth, and her finger replaced the tongue on her opening, the hardness of it in stark contrast to the softness. Ellie shifted, and Louisa lifted up to look at her.

"Ellie?" she asked, and Ellie nodded, at a loss for words. Louisa slid one delicate finger inside Ellie, pushing up toward her belly as Ellie curled up around it, the sensation new and beyond anything she'd yet to experience tonight.

Louisa moved forward then and took Ellie's mouth, kissing her back to the settee as she scrambled over her, her finger still working inside her, her thumb stroking her clitoris as Louisa moved again this time sucking Ellie's nipple into the wet warmth of her mouth and Ellie cried out, and this time Louisa allowed it, and Ellie realized it was because, for whatever reason, here they were safe and Louisa knew it.

The cries of a woman were acceptable in a single man's home. *Here we are safe.* It was a ridiculous notion, yet true. People would look askance but they would shrug it off as though nothing had happened. Men, you know, would do their man things, in their man spaces. And without Ender, they had no space safe enough to be together.

Ellie sobbed at the sudden thought of it and Louisa brought her other hand up, enjoying her rosy nipples in tandem as Louisa kissed her once more and Ellie paid attention again, tasting herself on Louisa, tasting herself *instead of* Louisa and the very thought of it, the stroke of a second finger, the pinch of her hand on her nipple, brought that growing feeling in her belly to break open, crashing around her, spilling from her fire as her back bowed up off the settee, carrying Louisa with her as she flung her arms out to hold on to anything and Louisa helped her over the cliff and down into a sweeping, soaring mess of feminine flesh and fabrics.

Louisa

Louisa wrapped Ellie up against her, grinning like a child with candy. To see that fire back in her eyes that had been hers and now was again. Ellie was glorious. Louisa had an idea that Ellie didn't understand her own body; she hadn't understood her own for a long time, after all. Protected as she was in preparation for her husband. Ellie would be the same.

But a ladies maid, you see, they weren't so protected. They were open to all the crude, brash comments of the stable boys and footmen and butlers below stairs. Louisa had learned quite a bit in the past three years. How to play her own body the loveliest part of it, though she'd already managed to figure out how to get herself off. Just not like this, and not with someone else. The drawings and writings she'd been exposed to had given her so many ideas for what she wanted to do with Ellie, to Ellie, someday...but she'd never believed someday would come.

As long as they were in London, there would be no harm in them meeting here, hiding from the world. She'd have to get Hugh to cooperate, because she could only meet with Ellie when Amelia was busy with something. She imagined he wouldn't complain too much.

Louisa heard the long case clock chime in the entry and shifted, bringing them to sitting on the settee. She smoothed the loose curls from Ellie's cheeks, tried to straighten the pins in her hair somewhat, but Ellie looked well and truly fucked sitting here on this settee, and Louisa took all the joy from that thought.

"You're gorgeous," she said. "Ellie, you're stunning, all pink and rosy from my hands."

Ellie blushed further, unable to hide anything from Louisa, and Louisa chased the flush with kisses on her cheeks, her neck, across her collar bone, sucking the salt tinge from the hollow of her neck before teasing her nipples once again.

"I want to sleep with the softness of your breasts against my cheek. God, Ellie your skin. You're everything."

"Louisa, you say such...things."

"I apologize. I... Well. I'm no lady," she said with a smile, and a small wrinkle creased Ellie's brow. "Oh, I'm sorry, am I offending you?"

"No! No, not that. It's just, I wish I had the vocabulary to match you, because I want to know everything you did. I want to learn how to do that...for you. To you," Ellie said and Louisa smiled so broadly she thought her cheeks would split.

"I'll teach you everything I know," she said.

"In our cottage?"

Louisa smiled, but knew it was tinged with sadness. "Ellie, I can't leave Amelia—"

"Louisa!" The front door slammed rather unnecessarily loud or, she supposed, very necessarily. They stood, Louisa and her helpful ladies maid training replacing Ellie's bosom and her own in brilliant fashion. She turned Ellie, inspecting her then herself.

"Hugh," Louisa called out. Then she kissed Ellie on the cheek, finishing her ministrations as they waited for him to find them.

Louisa hadn't thought Ellie could get any ruddier but when he walked into the library and stopped, his eyes catching on their dishabille, she did. Louisa wrapped her up in her arms as best she could. Whispered in her ear, "It's alright, my love, my darling, my Ellie. Hugh is always a safe place for us."

Ellie nodded but remained tense as he approached.

"I see you have—er...found each other," he said, casting his gaze about the library as though he'd walked into a den of iniquity and expected to see the fodder.

Louisa let go of Ellie, taking her hand and squeezing it. She pulled her behind her to Hugh, who she wrapped in a hug. "Thank you," she said. Then she stepped away.

"Listen, I hate to—" He waved a hand at them as though he couldn't bring himself to say what he meant, and Louisa watched as he blushed about as dark as Ellie had. He cleared his throat, and she dropped her gaze to lend him the strength he needed to say whatever it was he had to say. "Amelia, she's quite upset with us—Castleberry and myself. I couldn't calm her before she left Greensborough. I knew you would want—"

Louisa released Ellie and searched for her slippers and her wrap. "She's already on her way home?"

"Yes."

"I need to get to her. Was her mother at the ball? How fast do I need to go?"

"I think her mother is already home."

"Damn."

"Yes. Damn me. Thrice."

Louisa huffed, slipping her shoes on and handing Ellie hers.

"I kept the cab. I'll see you both home. I refuse to allow you to leave here without accompaniment," he said, then pulled a cape from the back of the chair and held it out, not knowing which of them it belonged to.

Louisa took it with a smile. "This is quite clearly the cape of a lady, Hugh. Let's not forget, I am no longer of that set. A simple wrap is all I have need of."

Ellie swallowed and something in her eyes pierced Louisa's soul, so she gazed at her hands as she placed the cape on Ellie, brushing it over her shoulders and fastening the catch at her neck before kissing both of her cheeks and then her mouth. Coaxing her tongue once again to play. Ellie remained silent through all of it, but Louisa didn't have time to stop and assess. She would see Ellie again, wouldn't she?

Hugh placed the wrap on Louisa, dragging her from the thought, and they followed him out to the cab, heads down and faces well hidden—but not obviously so. Hugh helped them both up, then gave the driver directions and followed.

"Ellie, I—" Louisa took a deep breath. "I'm sorry to have to rush off, but I must see to Amelia. There's not enough time to explain well enough. Just know that there's nowhere I would rather be than with you, and for as long as we're in London, I will meet you whenever I can, with Hugh's permission and assistance."

Ellie nodded, then cast her gaze out the window, the street lamps sending occasional bars of light across her features. "I have money, Louisa. We could disappear. I have enough to buy us a life," she said, and Hugh coughed.

Louisa turned to Hugh, seeing that he'd already been informed of this, but she hadn't. She could also see how it upset him that she now knew this. "You're afraid I'll leave her, aren't you? That I'll abandon Amelia to her mother to chase my own dreams?"

"No, Louisa. In fact, I'm afraid that...you won't."

Louisa reached up and brushed the tear from her cheek then. "I'm blessed with such friendship, Hugh. And it's a mistake to not fight for her, and you know it."

"I thought we'd found a common ground but—"

"But you're up against a duke with a contract, and he's not keen to share his property," Louisa said. She thought about Castleberry and how he'd seemed decent at least. Shook her head. "I'm missing something. As usual."

"I doubt it," Hugh said.

"Louisa?"

"Oh Ellie, I'm…" Louisa brushed another tear away and stared down at her hands in her lap. Ellie reached out and took them. "I'm sorry, I cannot abandon Amelia. Not now. I want to be with you. I want the cottage and the goat and the garden. I do. But I cannot leave her. She needs me." The cab pulled to a stop in front of Pembroke House, and Louisa gazed out the window to the massive door. "I have to go." She turned back and took Ellie's face in her hands, her skin warming Louisa's cold fingertips. "I want to see you as much as possible while I'm here, if you'll allow for it."

"Of course," Ellie said. "I'll take as much of you as I can, I'll never turn you away. Don't you see, Louisa? I've only just gotten you back. I won't let you go."

Louisa ducked out the wrong door into the street then shuffled around the side of the house. She stopped in the shadows there, her heart racing, staring after the carriage as it pulled away. "*Don't you see, Louisa? I've only just got you back. I won't let you go.*" What was she to do now? She needed Ellie to understand how important Amelia was to her, that she could not in good conscience disappear from her life. The whole situation wasn't that straightforward.

Louisa wanted Ellie, and Ellie wanted Louisa, but there was the simple matter of Amelia, and Hugh, that Louisa couldn't reconcile. She loved Amelia, though she was certain Amelia saw her as no more than a helpmate. That was the dichotomy of the upper classes, those beneath them invisible until they were missed. In that truth, Louisa knew she would be truly missed, and leaving Amelia to her mother and a man who knew nothing of her episodes was something she could never do.

It would be akin to relegating Amelia to Bedlam.

Ellie

Ellie watched Louisa walk to the side entrance of the house meant for the servants. Her Louisa, no longer a lady. She'd lost all of her power, and hearing it and seeing it were two different things. It hurt her heart to think that Louisa had been cast so low by what they'd done.

"Maitland."

She closed her eyes. She was Maitland. Louisa was gone, and with her went Ellie. She nodded as the carriage pulled back to the street.

"I'm sorry. This isn't what you wished for," he said.

"To see Louisa is what I wished for, nothing more."

"Amelia—"

"Her mistress. The one you love."

"Yes."

"I've heard the rumors, Ender. I just hadn't considered that Louisa was part of it."

"A big part of it. She cares for Amelia in ways I'm unable to. I don't know what I would do without her."

"So this all worked out in your favour then?"

"No, that's not…" He shook his head, and Ellie could see the exhaustion and sadness in his features and was repentant for her snippery.

"It's alright, Ender. We'll have time to talk about all this, won't we? You can explain, tell me more? If you're willing."

"Yes, I certainly hope so. Though if Amelia does marry Castleberry, I imagine she'll retreat to his estate post haste, and Louisa will go with them. And we… Well. We will not."

It hit Ellie then that this situation had she and Ender both in the worst possible way. "There has to be a way. There has to be something," she whispered, but the words floated between them, neither of them able to allow them to gain traction or possibility.

"If only," Ender replied.

"So what next?"

"You and Louisa are welcome to meet at my home, whether I'm there or not. My people have the utmost discretion. You and Louisa…you don't need me meddling in this. Just—please be cautious. Don't put anything in writing you don't want her father or your mother reading, and for God's sake, do not leave my house together like this again. If I can help, I will, but there's only so much I can do."

Ellie nodded. "I appreciate what you have done. I know it was not willingly."

"Maitland," he said and he leaned in and took her hand, "I'm sorry if I led you to believe that I am not a friend. My behavior certainly belies that. But I am, and I will help. It would be wonderful if it all wasn't happening at the same time as Amelia and— Well, when it rains, it pours, I suppose. I've only ever wanted to keep Louisa safe. No more, no less."

"Thank you."

The carriage turned on to her street, and she knocked on the roof. The driver pulled up in front of a neighboring house. She turned back to Ender. "Thank you," she repeated. She wished there was more but she wasn't sure how she felt at the moment about any of this. It was a lot to take in. To have Louisa back but...not.

She stepped down from the carriage, pulling her cape tight as she walked to her house and slipped through the front door. She ran across the foyer and up to her room, never once drawing attention. She slipped inside and dropped her cape, then lay on her bed, pulling the pins from her hair and dropping them to the floor.

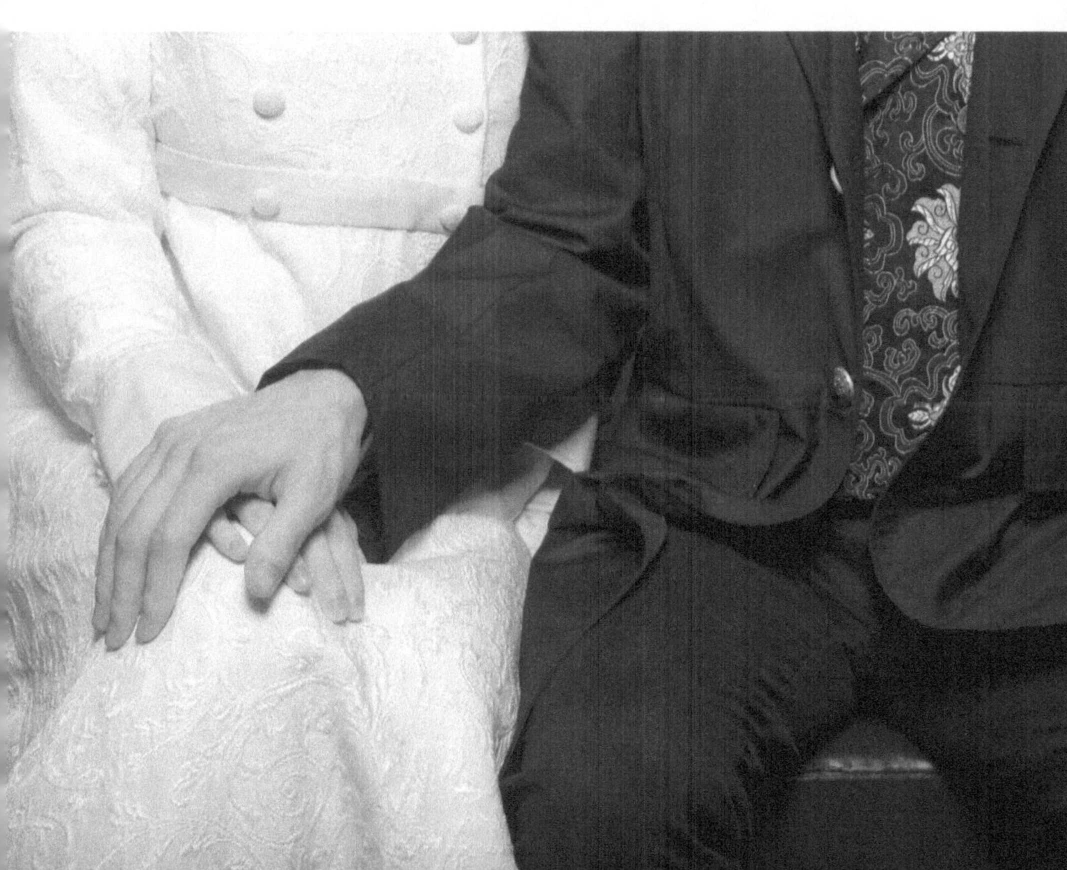

"Everything, Louisa, everything. I'm not returning. I've had quite enough of London to last me a lifetime. Pack it all."

Louisa's jaw dropped. She'd walked in the door and rushed to find Amelia packing her things. "Milady, I cannot see as how this is good. You should speak with His Grace. I'm sure he would understand."

"Understand what? That I said Hugh's name while he was having his way?" She sat at the edge of the bed. "I said Hugh's name while in his arms, and I didn't even know I'd done it. Oh, Louisa, I believe I'm lost. I thought I knew what love was, and then he touched me, and I realized I'd no idea. None at all."

Louisa sat next to her, taking her hands. She hadn't even removed her wrap. They couldn't possibly leave London now. "My lady, please, he'll understand."

"No. I cannot spend my life breaking his heart. It's better this way. I'm the only one who's broken. I was always broken. It seems it's to be my destiny."

Louisa wrapped her arms around her, and as Amelia melted into her, she let go of Ellie once more. It was impossible to carry on as they had. Impossible. She went where Amelia went, and if Amelia went back to Pembroke-By-The-Sea, then so did Louisa.

"Louisa, I do love him. I love them both. But the difference between them is night and day. I cannot have the one for the other, but I cannot dare to damage either. It's best if I go. It's best for everyone. I cannot imagine the pain I would have should either of them be injured by my choice."

"You cannot give up. You cannot run away," Louisa said.

"It's done. Please help me finish with the cases. I'd like to be off as soon as possible."

"Amelia!" The door swung wide, and Louisa released her and stood, then went the wardrobe to busy herself.

"Mother," Amelia said much more calmly than Louisa expected.

"What are you about? The duke said you weren't feeling well, then I come here to find the traveling carriage being loaded. Where are you off to?"

"Home. I'm leaving."

"Quitting London?" she squealed.

"Yes. Please make my apologies. I shall not return."

"But...but...but the duke said he would be by in the morning to check on you and finalize the arrangements."

"Please make my apologies."

"Amelia!"

"Mother, enough. I'm old enough to make my own decisions."

Louisa stilled, she put her hands against the sides of the wardrobe to steady herself. This was a nightmare.

"I'll work if need be to support us once Father has passed. Until then, we'll be happy at Pembroke."

Amelia had no idea what she was saying. Louisa hoped if they left, she could talk some sense into her. She heard Amelia packing her oils and powders, the glass clinking as she placed the bottles in a case. Her mother left the room, and the door shut behind her. Louisa poked her head out of the wardrobe.

"Carry on, Louisa. Time is wasting."

What the hell was she supposed to do now? She'd only just... She needed to send word to Ellie.

They arrived at the town station the next morning. Louisa watched as all the furniture and trunks were unloaded from the rear car of the train and strapped to the Pembroke-By-The-Sea carriage. She would never see Ellie again if she couldn't return to London. Everything hurt. She supposed some of that could be contributed to what had happened in Hugh's library the night before. Then there was the sleep in the train car that was quite unsatisfying. Though sleep was a bit of a stretch.

Amelia turned to her. "Are you well?"

"I wasn't expecting to quit London so quickly this time." She attempted a smile. She was certain it failed.

"Oh, Louisa, I'm sorry, I... should have considered you—"

"Oh, no, milady, that's not your responsibility. The responsibility is mine. You're mine, not the other way round. It's true I'm a bit...sad at leaving London, I just... It gets more and more difficult to say goodbye."

Amelia nodded. "I understand that feeling. I wish I could help you with it. Can you tell me of him? Could he come work for us at Pembroke?" Louisa cringed. "I apologize. I assumed—"

"No, milady, it's all right." Louisa tried to think of any possible way that Ellie could visit. But there was none. She would have to visit Amelia, which meant Amelia would have to be aware of— She shook her head. "There isn't a position suitable. I appreciate your thoughts, but there really isn't a position that would work in this matter."

Amelia wrapped her arms around Louisa, and she thought it was perhaps the first time. It had always been Louisa comforting Amelia, and the switch brought a tear to her eye. "You could return. I would give you the very best references, as well as settle a fair amount on you for your service."

Louisa turned. There was a reason she was so dedicated to Amelia, and this was it. She was one of the sweetest, loveliest people she'd ever met and perhaps she did return her affection, in some fashion. She had such a hard time letting that sweet part of her out in society because her mind wouldn't allow for it. Not under those circumstances. "Absolutely not, my lady. I'll not leave you. Not for all the money at Pembroke. I trust everything will work out as it should. For now, my place is with you. I hold no grudge against that. Never you think it."

"Know that should you change your mind, Louisa, the offer stands. Both for you to quit my father's employ, or for your gentleman to take a position with our household. You just need say the word."

Louisa would have cried but the whistle of the departing train startled her and she stood instead. It was too much. It was impossible. Her life was impossible. She needed to settle into this reality and let go of everything she yearned for. Because there was no possible way.

Writing the letter to Ellie had been the second most difficult thing she'd ever done. The first letter she'd written Ellie, breaking with her, had been the worst. Twice now she'd had to tell Ellie she wouldn't be able to see her again. Twice now she'd had to bleed across the parchment and hope that Ellie understood.

She wanted nothing more than to leave and go to Ellie and never return, but leaving Amelia wasn't possible. Not a full day after they'd arrived, Hugh and Charles had arrived in a carriage to find Amelia, and Louisa had sent them to the cliff house—a small, ancient building out on the far meadow of the estate overlooking the sea. It was somewhere Amelia went for days at a time, a sort of hermitage of her very own. She was happy there.

Louisa would deliver supplies in the morning before the sun rose. Peeking in the windows to be sure it wasn't some sort of massacre. She'd count breathing chests. Shifting limbs. It was scandalous, but who was she to judge? She had no leg to stand on. Those were three titles wound together. Nobody could touch them except scandal, and last she checked, Castleberry wasn't one to care about what was said of him in society.

Louisa walked back across the rolling hills to Pembroke Hall. What if...what if they were legitimate in the world's eye? What if she could make them leave them all alone, once and for all? Every day she walked the distance to the house and her mind churned on the possibility. She would remain a ladies maid, and that was fine— she'd been out of society's petty grasp for years and she'd become comfortable in that. But if she could have Ellie on top of that?

If Castleberry were to marry Amelia as planned, that was half the battle. Then Hugh would be free to marry and... She dared not hope it much less think it or say it until she had a chance to speak with Ellie. If the past three years had taught her anything it was that she needed to hold her hopes close and wish for the best.

Louisa had watched the three of them from afar and thought for sure that they'd come to an arrangement and that her idea would work.

Louisa was preparing another basket to haul out to Cliff House when the butler came to her in the kitchens.

"Lord Endsleigh wishes to speak with you. In the blue parlor," he said with a twitch of discomfort.

"My apologies, Mr. Bragant. I'll see to him." She left her work and rushed through the passages to the blue parlor, which was the largest of the receiving parlors at the front of the hall, far from the kitchens.

She thought perhaps she should share this idea of hers. Why was he here? Perhaps they were prepared to return to London? Perhaps it was time for the wedding? He couldn't have news of Ellie, for he'd been at the Cliff House all this time and she'd been checking all the packages and letters in case anything needed to be delivered to them. There'd been nothing.

She ran through the grand entry, her feet slapping against the stone floor as she rushed to Hugh. When she got to the parlor she stopped, cast a glance about the entry and straightened herself. She opened the door and walked in. "Hugh." And stopped.

"I'm quitting the estate. I thought you should know so you wouldn't waste time with preparing an additional meal."

"What? Why? I thought..."

"You thought what?"

"I thought all was well. I thought—" She shook her head. She shouldn't have been spying on them. "I'd hoped, I guess." She twisted her fingers together in her apron and tried to catch her racing heart.

"Whatever it was you thought...they're to be wed. I'm to return to London and... I don't know—"

"But I had a thought about all of this. I—"

"If it doesn't end with me marrying Amelia, Louisa, I'm uninterested in it. I cannot be part of any scenario in which she... It's already too late then, isn't it? They consider themselves husband and wife and I'm already lost."

Louisa's heart sank and she walked to him, wrapping her hands around his chin. "Hugh, she would never abandon you. What are you doing?"

His eyes were bloodshot, his hands shaking. "Seeing clearly for the first time, Louisa. I did as was expected of me. I managed Amelia and Charles and now...with your help he'll be capable of managing her from here on out. I am not needed. I suppose I never was." He turned, and she grabbed his arm.

"Hugh, don't leave her. No good will come of this."

"I'm afraid I've overstayed my welcome as it is, Louisa. I'm sorry." He walked out of the parlor, and she heard the heavy slam of the latch on the massive entry doors.

You'd think she would have learned by now. She knew better than to hope. She always had.

Ellie

The letter arrived from Pembroke-By-The-Sea nearly a week after their night together. Nearly a week of Ellie an inconsolable mess after receiving a note that said *I must leave* and nothing more.

She'd known they'd been living on borrowed time but had no idea how borrowed it had been. Nobody had bothered to explain why they'd left, not Louisa and not Ender. She wasn't the important piece to their puzzle. She was the afterthought, and that alone hurt. Burned. Like a cinder in her belly. She wanted nothing more than to belong with someone, anyone, somewhere, and she didn't.

Then another letter arrived.

Maitland,

My apologies for leaving so quickly. It was beyond my control. I'm not sure when I shall be able to return to London, but I wish for you to know how lovely it was having your friendship. It meant the world to me in the moment and I will treasure our time together for the rest of my days.

Please know I will forever think of you fondly.

It was never my intent to hurt you.

It is my dearest wish to return.

Amelia

She read the note three times. She knew it to be Louisa's handwriting, as shaky as that first letter from so long ago. She knew it was from Louisa and not Amelia. She wanted to go to her; she didn't much care about the consequences.

"Who is the letter from, Maitland?"

"Lady Amelia Pembroke," Ellie responded. "She had to quit London and return to her father's seat."

"Lady Amelia? When did you make her acquaintance?"

"At the first ball, when she came out. I was sure Aunt Rigsby had mentioned—"

"No, she hadn't. Why didn't you?" She reached for the letter, but Ellie pulled it away, folding it and tucking it in her pocket. "Let me read it?"

"No, Mother, she's but a friend. She wanted to thank me for her friendship. It's that simple." And Ellie wasn't going to share those words with anyone.

Her mother pouted as the maid pushed the tea service into the parlor. "We haven't seen much of you for three days, then you receive this letter and... Whatever happened with Endsleigh?"

"I'm not sure. I believe he had to quit London as well."

"Castleberry left. Why have they all left? It's the height of the season."

"Lady Amelia and Castleberry have a contract. There's not much point in them parading around London if they aren't of a mind to, is there?"

"Do you suppose they'll be married in secret?" her mother said as she took her tea, ridiculously excited by the prospect of gossip.

"I suppose nothing of the sort, but I'm not privy to their relationship. I was naught but a friend to Lady Amelia." She paused to consider the entirety of the situation when the butler came into the parlor.

"Baron Endsleigh for Miss Eliot Rigsby," he said and Ellie stood, almost tipping her teacup on her skirts as she fumbled with it.

Her mother looked up at her. "Well, then. Go see to him. Or, no. Take the parlor. Serve him tea. Show him how domestic you are." She put her own teacup on the service and stood. She fussed with Ellie's skirts and her hair, tucking strands away. "You should have dressed for company today."

"I had no idea—" she started but her mother cut her off.

"A lady is always ready for company."

"But I'm no lady," Maitland said, and it brought a smile to her face.

"You just might be though." Her mother turned and picked up the knitting basket that was next to the settee, handing it to Ellie.

"What am I to do with this?"

"Convince him that you're talented. Titled men need talented wives. Do whatever you must, Maitland. Do whatever you must," she angry-whispered, and Ellie cringed. Her mother seemed desperate at this point.

"Ladies," Ender said, and he looked like Ellie felt. She dropped the knitting to the floor as her mother gave him her hand and a small curtsey then left the room.

Ellie motioned to the tea service, for she wasn't about to serve him, then she sat. He declined the tea and sat next to her, which... Ellie cut a glance to the entry, unsure her mother would approve. But seeing the basket he had to kick aside once he sat and being reminded of her mother's words, she thought perhaps she might be thrilled by it.

"I must apologize," he said.

"For?"

"You know what for. For abandoning you without a word. I'm sure Louisa sent a note but I should have as well to be certain. I just—"

"She did. It didn't explain much of anything."

"She couldn't possibly," he said and his expression was so bereft she wanted to comfort him.

"Well," she said, cutting a glance to the entry then standing and shutting the door. Propriety be damned at this point. "She wrote it as though it were from Amelia, so I guess Amelia and I should meet at some point if this is to be the farce under which we continue."

"I don't know that you'll have need for that."

"They won't be returning?" Ellie asked, and something twisted in her gut. Pinched. She pushed a hand against her belly to quell it.

"I don't know. I imagine not."

"I feel quite like an afterthought at the moment. I'm hurt, Ender. I'm hurt that I wasn't told. Why have you come here?"

"I'm not sure. You're the only person who knows and... I shouldn't have come. Your mother—"

"My mother already has us married and me knitting baby shoes, so yes, you coming here looks a certain way to her. Perhaps you should go. I'm... I'm exhausted. I don't know what to say. I want nothing more than to leave London and never return, and if Louisa is trapped forever at Pembroke-By-The-Sea or Castleberry Keep, perhaps I'll start searching for a cottage in Pembrokeshire or...whatever the seat is close to Castleberry Keep. I suppose that makes more sense. If you wish to be a friend, Ender, I would appreciate your help in this, because I'm not giving up. I meant what I said. If Louisa is to play ladies maid to Amelia for the rest of her days, then I need to secure my future wherever she is."

"I'd no idea you were so determined."

"I told you I was. I meant it. I realize you don't know me well, but what you do know of me should have been enough to convince you of the level of my determination."

He laughed softly. "I suppose so. You managed to turn up in so many places, I couldn't believe my luck."

"Luck? It doesn't seem you have much of that."

"No. Not much. I should go. I wanted... I'm still not sure what I wanted."

"Commiseration?"

"Possibly."

"You know how to find me. But if you keep up with this, you'll need to deal with my mother. And I expect your help in securing my future. That's what a friend would do."

He nodded. Then smiled, albeit stiffly as he stood, and she followed him to the entry. He turned back, his hand on the door. "I will help you. I'll make inquiries, and we'll find you a home. One of us should end up the better for all this."

She reached up on her toes and kissed his cheek then stepped back. "Thank you."

Louisa

The next day, Castleberry and Amelia returned to Pembroke and they packed up and returned to London to prepare for the official wedding ceremony. Charles would meet with the Archbishop to make arrangements, Amelia would be presented to the Queen, and The Banns would be read in London and Beryshire. They would marry in a little over a month.

But Amelia wasn't the same. She was distant and wrapped up in her thoughts, more than ever before. What chilled Louisa most was that it wasn't an episode. She was...not there.

Castleberry had told her Hugh was to blame, and though she'd tried to explain differently, he refused to hear it. He'd been silent most of the return trip. His face tense with anger. He was set on destroying Hugh for abandoning them at the Cliff House.

Louisa was determined to set things back to rights. Amelia couldn't live like this. She wouldn't allow it. And Castleberry still had some things to learn; she understood his anger with Hugh—she was right put out by his departure as well—but she knew they had to get him back, not just abandon him altogether. They worked, somehow. The three of them worked.

They arrived back at Pembroke House and Louisa was helping Amelia pack her things for the move to Castleberry's townhome, as he refused to allow her to stay with her mother. She was restless and unnerved and needed to get out of the house. She'd sent a message to Hugh, but he hadn't responded. She didn't dare send a message to Ellie yet, did she? Louisa was still so frightened, but she had to get out of here. Sitting around doing nothing would get them all nowhere.

"My lady, are you sure it's all right if I leave?" Louisa asked. She was concerned with leaving Amelia alone, considering the way she was behaving.

"Go, Louisa. I'm simply packing things, so you go see your beau. I'll be fine here, working on this."

Louisa ruffled a bit at the mention of her beau. She wasn't sure how Amelia would react when she discovered the truth of it, but she knew the deception to be necessary at the moment. This secret of hers could be her lady's salvation. As well, it could be Louisa's swift end—quite literally. It terrified Louisa, but she had to take this chance for Amelia, and for Hugh after all he'd done for Louisa.

Amelia seemed happy to stay at the town house, collecting her things and readying them for their own journey to her new London residence, and Louisa was glad they were here in London so she could track down Hugh. He had to know that Amelia was not well, and Louisa knew he couldn't abandon Amelia, though by all indications that was exactly what he'd done.

Louisa considered going to Castleberry but they weren't familiar enough— she a lowly servant. She could find no situation in which that would be considered acceptable. She stopped as suddenly as the thought had occurred to her, almost tripping over the sway of her own skirts. There was one situation in which a servant could pay a visit to a duke...but she wasn't willing to chance that.

And Hugh...Hugh must be so hurt, but the only way to fix this... In truth, she wasn't sure any of her efforts could fix this if the duke was set to destroy Hugh, and that was exactly what she figured he was planning to do, no matter what Amelia said.

What a mess. Louisa straightened her back, determined to do what she must. She stopped again. She was leaving the house under the pretense of visiting her beloved, and wouldn't her acquiescence be required for this idea to work? Perhaps she should go there first. But Louisa could never go there. That would be too dangerous for both of them.

Louisa's head spun. She'd no idea where to start. Louisa drew a deep breath and headed outside and down the walk. Since one of the destinations was walking distance from where she was, she decided to let fate have it, and that was where she headed.

Ellie sat in her rooms, staring out the window. Hugh had returned. Castleberry and Amelia had returned, which meant Louisa had also returned, but she'd yet to hear from Louisa and it hurt. She was just so tired.

Someone knocked at her door.

"Come," she said, but she didn't move from her bed. She was comfortable and if someone was coming into her rooms then they got whatever it was they saw.

"Ellie?"

She sat up and turned to the entry. "It's not possible."

Louisa closed the door behind her, searching for a latch or key, but her door had none. "Ellie?" She walked to her, and Ellie could see the tension in her from across the room. She stopped walking, twisting her hands, so unsure of herself.

Ellie stood to meet her on unsteady legs. "Louisa, I don't know why— You shouldn't be here."

"I know, but I couldn't wait. I need your permission."

"You have it."

"You don't even know what I'm asking."

"It doesn't matter." Ellie ran her hands up Louisa's arms, then pulled her close, holding her tight. "I won't let you go again."

"It was beyond my control." Louisa sobbed against her.

Ellie paused. Louisa had been at the mercy of others the whole of her life, and Ellie wanted nothing more than to give her the power to do whatever she wanted. If she could. If there was any way. She

wished...she so wished she had that ability. "I know, Louisa, but never again. I can't... I won't allow for it. Look at you," she said as she leaned back, holding her steady. "You're a complete wreck."

"I *am* a complete wreck. Amelia—"

"I know you love Amelia, but I don't want to hear about her just now. I want to hear about you, Louisa." Ellie went to the door, checking the hallway and shutting it again. Then, taking a key from the ledge of the doorframe, she locked it. "How did you get in here?"

"I'm a servant, Ellie. Nobody pays any mind to me." Louisa sobbed, and Ellie gathered her tight.

"What's happened?"

"Hugh left them. I had the idea that we could all be together, but then Hugh left and—"

"What?" Ellie said then she pulled Louisa over to her bed and they slid out of their shoes and crawled up to lean on the headboard. They lay on the pillows and Louisa explained her idea, that Ellie marry Ender and they would all be able to live together somehow at the duke and the baron's far estates. It sounded perfectly outlandish...and entirely possible. Until she came to the part of the story wherein Hugh had up and left, abandoning Amelia.

"I still don't understand what you're asking of me," Ellie said.

"I'm asking you, Maitland Allison Elliot Rigsby, my precious Ellie, if you would take Baron Endsleigh as your husband and come live with me for the rest of our lives, peaceful, happy, and far from this maddening crowd, in a small cottage, or...I suppose a grand castle on the sea."

"What? Did he—"

"Not yet. I haven't spoken with him yet, or any of them, but I just... I need you my Ellie and I think this is a way for us to be together, forever. Somewhere safe where nobody could touch us. I needed your permission first, before I talk to Hugh, and Castleberry, and Amelia. Because I would never betray your trust and... Ellie, do you understand what I'm saying?"

"You wish for me to marry Ender. So I can live with him, and he can live with them, and we can all..."

"We can all be at peace, yes."

"In that case, yes, Louisa, I will marry your baron and spend the balance of my days making you happy. At the edge of England." Because of course she would. It was perfect, exactly what she wanted. To give Louisa the freedom to simply be. She felt lighter.

"You'll give up all of this?" Louisa said, waving a hand in the air.

"For you? I would give up everything, Louisa. I'd already asked Hugh to find me a cottage near the estates so I could move closer to you. I saved up money and I— I couldn't wait any longer and I didn't want to wonder, constantly, where you were."

"Ellie. You did?"

"Of course I did, Louisa. I told you, your heart is all I own. Nothing else matters. I'll follow you anywhere."

Louisa leaned in and kissed her then, like it was a first kiss, and in some ways, perhaps, it was. It was the first time—since that first time—that they'd kissed with the possibility of a future together.

"When will you ask him?" Ellie asked, and Louisa rolled her to her back, slipping between her legs, pulling the cotton nightgown up to gain access.

"As soon as I find Hugh. As soon as I know for sure it's safe to ask."

"You'll ask Hugh?"

"Yes, I'll ask Hugh first. I wouldn't dare speak with Amelia or Castleberry until Hugh agrees it's possible." Louisa pushed up, gathering Ellie's legs wide across her thighs as she pushed against her, and Ellie's back bowed, grinding her mons against Louisa, and every single bit of her body tightened then released as if her very skin took a deep breath, opening her up to take Louisa. She was hot and cold. Everywhere. Nothing was enough.

"Louisa, teach me something. You promised to teach me everything. Teach me," Ellie said.

Louisa kissed Ellie slow, sinking against her and letting her legs splay at her hips. "This is your mouth, *bouche*, comprised of lips and tongue, teeth." She ran a finger over the pointed edge of her lips, dipping it in and wetting it against Ellie's tongue before lining them with the wetness and kissing her.

"Yes?"

"Yes, and your mouth is one of your most powerful tools for making love."

"Making love?"

"Yes, Ellie. Sex, intercourse, marital relations, fucking, rutting, grinding." She pushed against her again. "But you and I, we make love, Ellie."

"I like the sound of some of those other words, though. Louisa, would you teach me those too?"

"Not until you're well and truly married, Ellie. The last thing I want to do is frighten you off."

"Frighten me? Have you gone mad? You can't frighten me."

"Then perhaps it's because right now all I want is to prove to you how much I love you before I marry you off to my friend, and words are not enough so using my body is the only option I have."

"Then show me, Louisa. Show what it means to make love and tell me about the rest after the wedding."

And so she did.

Louisa

Louisa stopped Hugh as he walked for the entry of Charles's town home. The three of them had managed to reconcile for the most part and after watching Amelia regain her footing somewhat, Louisa decided she felt safe enough to approach Hugh.

It had been a long night. Amelia was settled, and Hugh was headed for his own townhouse.

"My lord, if I may have a word."

"Is something wrong?" he asked.

"My lord, I wanted to speak with you about this predicament we find ourselves in," Louisa said.

"Which...predicament is that?" Hugh asked, and Louisa rolled her eyes. She was exhausted.

"The predicament of you, living with them as a family...for lack of a better term. You can't live with them at Castleberry and not raise some sort of suspicions. You do realize."

Hugh took her by the arm and led her into the parlor, away from any remaining servants. They walked to the settee and he sat next to her.

"I may have a solution."

Hugh's gaze narrowed on her as he froze tip to toe, his muscles tensing all the way. "Go on."

"You should marry Maitland."

"I fail to see how—" he started but then he considered. "How?"

"You marry Maitland Elliot. Castleberry marries Amelia. We all, all of us, return to your estates on the sea. Who stays in which houses is... up to us, I should say."

"You must speak with Maitland. I don't want—"

"I already have. She gave me permission to... um... She sent me to offer for your hand. As it were."

Hugh brightened, some of his old joviality returning, a spark in his eyes that had been missing for quite some time coming back. Louisa couldn't help but to smile. "Are you making me an offer, Miss Present?"

"One I would hardly think you're in any position to refuse. I suggest you take me up on it before I find myself some other—"

Hugh stood and pulled her up, then lifted her and spun.

"Dear God, put me down. I'm much too tired for this."

"Oh, but Louisa, this is me, accepting your proposal."

"Then, perhaps you should tell your bride?"

Louisa

In the end, Ellie saved them all. Louisa had thought watching Ellie marry someone, anyone, would tear her apart. But the reality was that...it was Hugh, and Hugh had saved her countless times. Castleberry had helped Hugh obtain a special license from the Archbishop of Canterbury, as they'd all decided that quitting London in an expedient manner was best and without Ellie wed, she'd be left behind.

Louisa followed Amelia and Castleberry through the nave to the front pews where they would be seated. She saw Hugh in the south transept across the aisle from them, and a shiver rushed her skin. She turned to find Ellie in the north transept behind her, waving her over. She stood and walked to her, her lungs still as a summer breeze against the chill of the cathedral. Ellie wore the dress with the stars. She hadn't even known she still owned it.

"Ellie," she said, and the first twinge of apprehension hit her belly.

"I'm nervous, Louisa."

"Why?"

Ellie took her hand and pulled her deep into the abandoned transept. "I... I know this is an arrangement of a marriage and that we will all be free to live, and—that's all well and good, and beautiful, but..." She worried her lip with her teeth, and Louisa looked about to be sure nobody had wandered close enough to hear them, then took her other hand.

"But?"

"Tonight, Louisa. It's my wedding night. With Hugh."

"And?"

"And I...I know we discussed it, and we were all in agreement that Hugh and I would—" she wiggled her fingers, "—and have children. But now that it's here, I'm nervous, and it isn't so much that it's a man. I'm thankful that it's Hugh. It's just that...well, it's not you."

"It isn't, is it," Louisa said, letting the thought sink in as Ellie had done. She played with Ellie's fingers as she considered it for the first time. Babies in theory were much different than babies in practice—the making of them much the same.

"And we will be at Hugh's townhome, so far from you. I wish..."

"What?"

"I wish you could be there. I wish you could be at his home, as awkward and strange as that sounds. I wish you could be close by."

"I wish for that as well, but it's...just not possible. I must stay with Amelia, particularly if Hugh is away. She's been recovering and we cannot take any chances."

"I understand. I only wished."

"Me too." Louisa sniffed when the processional passed through the crossing, the incense stinging her eyes as it spread. She wrapped Ellie up in a hug, kissing her cheek, below her ear, where nobody would have seen her do it, whispering, "I love you," before releasing her and walking to sit with Amelia. Hugh's one request for the wedding was that Amelia be present, that she sit behind Ellie and remain present throughout the ceremony. Louisa sat next to her, Castleberry on her other side. This wasn't easy for Amelia either, and Louisa concentrated on helping Castleberry to support Amelia.

He swept circles into her back, and Louisa watched to be sure she wasn't letting her mind have a way with her. It seemed to her then that she may soon be superfluous in Amelia's life. What a blessing that would be for Amelia to have both of these men who know her so well as to be able to care for and help her as much as she needed. Louisa knew beyond a doubt that under any other circumstances, Amelia would not have been cared for in such a manner. In any other family, at any other time, she would have been sent to a hospital for the mentally infirm.

It saddened her though that she may no longer be needed. They would retain the outward appearances, of course; they needed a position for Louisa to be relevant and explained within their household. It frightened her a bit that she was the sole person in this arrangement who wasn't bound by law.

But she trusted. She looked up to see Ellie smiling so brilliantly at Hugh that it brought tears to her eyes. She knew why. She knew it was the same happiness she felt at beginning their life together, but it was difficult to see.

"Wilt thou have this man to thy wedded husband, to live together after God's ordinance in the holy estate of matrimony? Wilt thou obey him, and serve him, love, honor, and keep him in sickness and in health and, forsaking all other, keep thee only unto him, so long as ye both shall live?"

Louisa's breath stilled and Ellie lifted her chin, closing her eyes and responding, "I will," then she tipped her face, looking over her shoulder much as she had the very first time Louisa had ever seen her, and caught her eye. "I will," she repeated. Louisa felt a warm hand at her hip, and looked to find Castleberry with a kerchief and she wasn't sure how to compose herself then. She took the soft linen and dabbed her eyes, and he rested his arm behind Amelia's back, his warm hand on her shoulder. She hadn't realized how important it would be for her to trust this man as well. But he held the balance of her life in his hands, and she wasn't sure how she felt about that. He was powerful—one word and she would be crushed, as she was nobody. She could never quite settle into the joy of the solution with her life still hanging in the balance unprotected.

She watched the rest of the ceremony without paying much attention to the words, leaning into Amelia and sharing her warmth as Castleberry comforted the both of them.

"With this ring I thee wed, with my body I thee worship, and with all my worldly goods I thee endow: In the Name of the Father, and of the Son, and of the Holy Ghost. Amen."

The full service continued after the wedding vows and after the second lesson Castleberry's hand tensed on her shoulder and she looked up.

The priest said, "I publish the Banns of Marriage between His Grace Charles Jackson, Duke of Castleberry, of Beryshire and London, and Lady Amelia Pembroke, of Pembroke-By-The-Sea and London. If any of you know cause, or just impediment, why these two persons should not be joined together in holy Matrimony, ye are to declare it. This is the first time of asking."

Amelia went stiff between them, the cathedral quiet enough the mice were frightened. But nobody declared anything, and they all took a breath as one. The first of many, she supposed. Castleberry's hand went to soothing circles in Amelia's back once again, and Louisa distracted herself from the rest of the service by concentrating on Amelia beside her.

After, Louisa waited in the narthex for the crowds to thin and the people to congratulate both Ellie and Hugh as well as Castleberry and Amelia at the front steps. Just being there had been difficult for her. She'd no intention of wandering in the after-service crowds.

"It is you."

An icicle of fear slid down the curve of her back, resting against her tailbone, melting its cold drips into her skin, sending gooseflesh back up to her shoulders, down her arms, her legs. She crossed her arms and ducked her head. If she could avoid any confrontation— *We are in public.* He wouldn't dare make a scene in full view of the church.

"Louisa, look at me," her father said, and all that cold water froze. She couldn't move. She couldn't breathe.

"Please don't, sir. You're mistaken."

"I know my own daughter," he said and took two steps toward her—much too close.

"You have no daughter, my lord. You said so yourself. You have no daughter."

"Louisa!" His voice boomed through the narthex and echoed into the nave as he grabbed her by the arm and pushed her into a corner.

"No." Louisa stopped shrinking. "No!"

"You are supposed to be at the Magdalene asylum. Why are you here?"

"Did you truly expect me to stay where you put me?" She stared into his eyes then, searching for some semblance of the father she'd occasionally wished was hers—but he wasn't there. The viscount's face was a mask of anger and hatred. She didn't know this man and she'd no purpose in knowing him in the future. She pushed against his broad chest. "Let me go before I scream."

"No, I'm returning you to where you belong. You should have learned by now to stay where I put you." He moved then, dragging her behind him down the south transept, toward south stairs that would lead to the graveyard where nobody would see them. She

fought. With all her might. This wasn't going to happen again. *This isn't going to happen again.*

She heard heavy steps behind her and screamed then stuck a hand into his ribs and pinched as hard as she could. He yowled and pushed her to the floor, releasing her, but she wasn't on the floor long. Big, warm hands lifted her, wrapped around her, squared off with the viscount.

"What is the meaning of this? You attack a member of my household?" Castleberry's voice seemed calm but it seethed with the sort of anger that could burn the world to the ground. He was a living, breathing reckoning. His expression shifted, the edges smoothing, his eyes going wide with concern. He ran his hands down her shoulders. "Are you hurt?" She shook her head, unable to respond. "Do you wish to claim him?" he whispered, and she shook her head again. It shocked her to her core to consider that Castleberry believed it to be her decision whether or not this man was her father and not the reverse. Then it shocked her to her core that she hadn't already believed it. "Do you wish to speak to him?"

"No, thank you."

He nodded once and tensed when Mayjoy spoke.

"Sir, you have no claim here. Member of your household—the very idea. This is my daughter."

Castleberry bristled. "Might I?" he asked, and she nodded once more. "As you wish." Castleberry stood tall then, placing Louisa behind him and turning back to her father. He kept one hand on her arm. "Your daughter? Sir? You must be mistaken. I am the Castleberry. This is one of the maids of work in my household. This woman serves the future Duchess of Castleberry and has for several years now."

"Castleberry?" The blood drained from his face, and he took a step back.

"Sir." He said it with such finality that her father's entire demeanor changed, shrinking before her eyes as she watched.

"I meant no offense, Your Grace, but there must be some mistake."

"Do you intend to offend me further, Mayjoy? I've made no mistake here."

"No, Your Grace, but—"

"I have no qualms with seeing to destroying everything you've built if you continue to insult me in this manner."

Louisa watched Castleberry's face as he volleyed with her father, the ferocity of his countenance somehow soothing when it was portrayed on her behalf. He was terrifying, and he was laying it all out in protection of her—a simple maid.

"Do you mind explaining to me how the daughter of a viscount ended up a simple ladies maid in the household of a duke?"

Her father sputtered in response.

"You are mistaken." Castleberry enunciated every word, each one given a pointed flinch in response from Mayjoy. Castleberry waited for a response, the silence deathly shallow.

"Your Grace, I'm mistaken. I beg pardon for this..." he waved a hand toward her, "unfortunate misunderstanding."

"There's no misunderstanding here, Mayjoy. Make no *mistake* in that simple fact. I understand everything. But you are mistaken in thinking that this woman is your property or has any obligation to you whatsoever. Is that quite clear?"

"Your Grace?"

"Is it?" And this time the Duke's voice boomed, carrying through the sanctuary and beyond even bigger than Mayjoy's had. "Explain it to me in detail."

"Yes, Your Grace. It is. I have no issue with you, this woman is not my responsibility, and I will not again cause any sort of harm to befall her, or to insult you, or any member of your household or family."

"Let it be done then. Do not cross me, Mayjoy. I will not hesitate in my retribution a second time." Then Castleberry turned to her. "Do you wish to say anything more?"

She peeked past his massive frame to the man she'd once been so frightened of. He was a paltry sum of flesh and bone at this point. Beneath her notice. She shook her head, and Castleberry took her hand and placed it on his arm, leading her away without hesitation.

He paused in the narthex. "Miss Present, a moment."

"Yes, Your Grace?" She turned to him.

"We haven't been properly introduced, which is my fault. You know who I am. However, in private you may know me as Charles. We are to be family. If not in name, in every other possible way."

Tears pricked at Louisa's eyes then at how thoughtful this man was. "Please, you may call me Louisa."

"Louisa," he said with a nod. "Thank you for trusting me. If you have need for anything, please know I am at our service."

"Your Gra— Charles, at the moment I want for nothing other than to spend the evening with my family."

He nodded and they joined the others on the church stair. Most of the congregation had already dispersed.

Ellie walked to Louisa carefully. Perfectly poised. "Is anything amiss?" she asked, running a hand up and down her arm.

"No, my Ellie," she whispered. "Everything is as it should be. Though I do have something to tell you later."

Ellie smiled, then took her hand, squeezed it and let it drop between them.

Charles was thanking the priest and confirming the reading of the Banns twice more over the next two weeks, his confirmation to be sent to the parish priest at Berryshire, so their wedding, which would be at The Keep, would be on schedule. Then he turned to Amelia, bussed her cheek and took her arm. "I've decided that the two of you are to stay with us in the guest suites at Castleberry House tonight. They're much more lavish than your townhome, Hugh, so there should be no complaint from you. If you would have your things brought over, I've already arranged for a wedding breakfast at the House."

Louisa glanced down at her toes, which peeked out from beneath her black service dress. She twisted her arms together around her waist and tried to keep herself from falling apart at the very thought of what a duke would do for a simple girl.

Then Amelia's arm came around her shoulders. "I think it a brilliant idea."

Hugh winced, then looked to Ellie, whose smile was brighter than the sun. He considered for a second then smiled to himself and nodded as well. "Thank you, Castleberry. That's quite thoughtful of you."

The door closed, and Ellie stared at Hugh. Hugh stared back at Ellie.

"Well," he said, sinking his hands into his trouser pockets.

"Well," she replied. Having nothing better to do, she walked past him to the bed and tested its buoyancy with her fingertips as he watched from the entry. After an extended silence, she heard him take a deep breath and she turned to him. Fidgeting at the door.

"We really don't—"

"Yes. We do," she replied.

"We could wait a bit—"

"No, we need to get this over with."

"Right, get it over with. Like taking your medicine or burning the garbage," he mumbled.

"Lie back and think of England and all that," she said but she felt exasperated. They didn't have a choice.

Why put off the inevitable? "Look, we've been through this. We don't need unanswerable questions from society. Besides, I want a child. Louisa and I—*we* want a child. This is the way to make that... happen."

"Yes, well. There are unwanted children we could—"

"My lord, please." They'd been through this as well, over and over. She closed her eyes for a moment to think.

"You calling my title forth isn't going to help matters. Please. *Please,* call me Hugh," he said.

She considered the difficulty for him. He was in love with Amelia, that much was patently obvious. More than that, she knew Hugh to be an honest and caring soul. This couldn't be easy for him. After all, a man had to enact certain things in order for the act itself to take place. As it were. It wasn't easy for her—the very idea—but she had very little need by way of preparation as far as she knew... She shook off the thoughts and started again. "Hugh. The simplest course from wedding to children is—"

"Sex. Yes, so we're doing this."

"Yes, we're doing this," she said, settling it once and for all— she hoped. She stood and started to unbutton her shirtwaist. Hugh looked down. Her gaze followed...to his trousers. His hands placated, but she could see that nothing, *nothing* was happening in the region of his trousers. Not a single thing. She had no idea how to...*handle* this particular issue. Her hand motioned toward him as she cut her gaze back up to his. "So...now that we're reconciled to—?"

Hugh shook his head, "It's just—not...going to happen. No fault to you, of course, but...the very idea of an unwilling—"

"I'm not unwilling—"

"'Lie back and think of England' isn't quite willing is all I'm saying."

"I won't be thinking of England. I'll be thinking of Louisa," Ellie returned with a smile.

"Won't that feel a touch like...you're cheating on her?"

"No, I'm here with her blessing. We all discussed this, Hugh. It's important and not simply because we wish for those beyond our relationship to see, but because we wish to build a family of our own. All of us. Together."

He turned at the sudden knock on the door and held his hand up to stay her. After all, they were *supposed* to be in this bedroom together. Everyone *expected* the two of them to be here. Doing what they were *supposed* to be doing as married people. It was perfectly awkward, regardless how wonderful everyone had been. And supportive. And thoughtful. They were just married and the wedding breakfast had come to an end, the afternoon waning into evening before the fire as the five of them had become more familiar with each other. And then they'd all decided to retire...to their respective suites.

Hugh took a deep, calming breath and turned the knob and the door fell into him, banging his knee as he let go of the knob and caught his true bride. "Amelia, what?" he said as he lifted her to her feet.

"I'm sorry, I'm so sorry. I just, we thought perhaps... Or, I thought— And then Charles... And Louisa mentioned—"

"Amelia."

"Yes, right." Amelia took him by the lapels and brought his attention to her with trembling hands. She smiled over his shoulder at Ellie, then back up at him with tears in her eyes. This was it— they'd planned this, Ellie and Amelia and Charles, because Hugh had been waffling. He was too thoughtful. But here was Amelia to help with her part. Ellie hurried with her trappings but couldn't manage to take her eyes from the two of them in the process.

Hugh lifted one hand, skimmed the crest of Amelia's cheek and wiped a tear aside then kissed its path. "Amelia." He sounded desolate.

"I'm simply happy. Truly, I am so..." Amelia sniffled and nodded to Ellie over Hugh's shoulder, and Ellie hurried, slipping her skirts free. When he turned to see what she was doing behind him, Amelia tightened her grip on his lapels, stealing his attention. "Hugh. Just one thing, and then the rest of our lives, remember?" She nodded then pushed his jacket off his shoulders. "Just one, small, tedious—" Ellie glanced up at her, and Amelia winced. "Not tedious...beautiful...beautiful and *important* thing, and then the rest of our lives. With all of our blessings. All of us." Amelia had managed his jacket, cravat, and waistcoat and was slipping the buttons from his shirt as Ellie was sliding between the linens with naught on but her chemise, drawers and stockings. She adjusted the fall of the bed curtains to cast shadows across her but left her breasts free for Hugh to see, as instructed, by Charles. He'd mentioned how important breasts were—as if she weren't aware.

Ellie waited. She closed her eyes and listened to the sound of clothing being removed and thought of Louisa—concentrated on her, on her mouth, her hands skating across her skin, her fingers taking her virginity. At that memory, Ellie became wet with wanting and her breath rushed her.

She heard Hugh whisper, "Have I told you today how much I love you? Because I do. I truly love you, Amelia."

Ellie watched again from behind the heavy velvet drapes. Amelia's hands stilled when his rested on top of them and she met his gaze. Ellie thought sure she should look away but she couldn't manage it.

"And I love you, Hugh. You—I married you today. You married me today." She rose up to his mouth and he took, sliding his hands down her arms and around her waist as she held on. Hugh licked, kissed, nibbled and played with her lips until she smiled against him. "I simply couldn't be happier, husband," she whispered into him.

They were so beautiful together. She'd seen them together but never this intimate, of course, never like this. This was a man and wife behind a closed door...and what was she? Technically speaking she was his wife, but here, in this room, she didn't belong. *Children,* she thought. *Children, we need children to validate this...whatever this is. For protection. But also for Louisa.* She and Louisa wanted children—they wanted a family to raise as their own, together. This was the way to make this happen because Louisa couldn't do it. Besides, as his lawfully wedded wife, it was Ellie's responsibility.

Amelia pulled Hugh's shirt from his trousers, then he bent at the waist so she could lift it from him. She skimmed her hands over his chest, and Ellie heard him hiss against her as he took her up and pushed his hips to hers. "Amelia, my love, my darling, please." And Ellie watched, waiting. "We haven't even—"

"I know, I know, but our time will come." Amelia's eyes were bright with unshed tears in the flicker of the gaslights. She slid a hand through his messy hair, then pulled him to her again and her other hand went between them, in the area of concern—his trousers, and he hissed against her once more.

"Oh God, Amelia," he groaned.

She shouldn't be watching this between them—even as she lay here practically naked. Waiting. Nervous. Terrified, truth be told. She leaned back into the shadows and listened to their heavy, breathy voices.

"Just one more thing, and then *our* wedding night. Just one more thing," Amelia said. "Be gentle. I love you."

Ellie heard the heavy click of the door opening and peeked around the curtains again when everything went silent. Amelia turned the knob for the gaslights and they dimmed around them, and she took him by the shoulders and turned him around, gave him a push. He walked toward the darkened bed, toward her, as she heard the latch on the door click shut.

The only thing he'd be able to see, above the edge of the linens on the bed, were her breasts, because Charles said men were visual creatures, and breasts were meant to arouse men, though they happened to have much the same effect on her. She smiled. She supposed she had more in common with Hugh than she'd considered.

"Maitland." He was close now, passing through the shadows closer to the bed, and she felt him pull aside the linens and the bed dipped when he put one knee and then the other on the bed. He moved between her legs, and she welcomed him.

"Shhh...I know. No more words. Let's see to this."

He stiffened. "Let's see to this?" he said as he searched the depths of the shadows.

"Hugh, come to me," she whispered. She drew her hands to her breasts and ringed her nipples with the tips of her fingers just as Louisa had done. She watched as he leaned back on his knees and released the fall of his trousers, giving her a clear view of his manhood and every muscle in her body tensed, stopping her breath as though a sudden freeze had overtaken the landscape of her flesh. His cock was large and...well kept was the best way she had to describe it. She found she wasn't averse to it, though it was larger than Louisa's fingers. It seemed smooth and somehow proud, as he stroked it base to tip.

Hugh stopped moving, yet again, "Maitland, I'm not sure I can... I care for you. I can't—"

"Hugh." She reached for him, but he avoided her hands, then grasped her thighs and pulled her down in the bed until the soft gaslight covered her face and she was below him. His cock skimmed her belly at the gap of her drawers as he leaned over her, skin to skin, and the breath left her lungs.

"Maitland." He leaned down and rested on his hips, his belly covering her most intimate parts like a security blanket, his hands skimming the flesh of her shoulders, calming, attempting to convince her muscles to relent.

It was the oddest sensation, having so much skin covering her between her thighs, and the sensations when he shifted were rather fascinating. She reached for the drapes to shadow her face once again, but he stopped her, bringing her hand to his chest, and holding it there.

"I care for you. I understand what you're trying to do, but I can't make love to a headless woman. This must be done and do it we shall, but it's me with you. I love you as family. I care for you deeply as my wife in name, as the wife of my dear friend in act. I understand what you and Amelia...and apparently Charles and Louisa attempted to do tonight and I very much appreciate it, but this is between us in this moment. Children should be created from love, and we do have that. So I will make love...with you, or not at all."

The heat of a tear streaked her face and she had the thought that he'd probably never managed to make two women cry upon taking one to bed. She calmed under his gentle ministrations and relaxed beneath him. She wrapped her arms around him, and he kissed away more tears as they came face to face in their marriage bed. His words were so powerful.

The hair on his chest crinkled against her breasts, tickling her skin through the thin chemise as he moved over her. His gaze intent as it locked on hers. "Your eyes are incredible, Maitland. I've never seen anything like them," he whispered. "I'd always thought them brown, for some reason. I'd thought you mousy. But you're beautiful. Stunning." His hand moved between them, and her muscles threatened to lock up once again. "Look at me," he said, and she opened her eyes once again. "It's just me, Hugh. This babe is ours, but she'll also be my gift to you and to Louisa."

"She?" It surprised Ellie, because men, they wanted their heirs—did they not?

Hugh shrugged and smiled down at her, and she relaxed. "May I touch you?" She nodded, and his fingers slid between her thighs, stroking her mons and her vulva. "Or he. But a little girl with your eyes? Born of nothing but love and want? She'll be the sweetest pixie. A halo of white-gold curls, those intense violet eyes, your pale skin and passionate love for those around you? She'll be a glorious child."

"What will we call her?" she asked as one of his larger, longer, fingers sank into her as Louisa's had the night before.

"She should be named for her mother."

"Alice?"

"That would be lovely. I've always loved Louisa's middle name. It sounds like it belongs to a fairy, does it not?" He rocked against her, the palm of his hand tempting her as his fingers skimmed and rocked and she became wet, so wet, just thinking about Louisa and making a child for her, a child who would bear her name.

"Hugh." His name came to her lips without effort.

"May I kiss you?" he asked so reverently it made her eyes sting with tears.

She nodded. "Yes."

He leaned toward her, and she let her eyes flutter shut as his lips met hers, so gentle it could have been nothing but a dream. But then his tongue licked her lip and she opened for him. When she did, he tasted of her and she felt cherished and loved by this man.

His muscles tensed beneath her hands, and his kiss became more insistent, his fingers leaving her body, replaced with the much-larger nudge of his penis against her. He stopped kissing her, though his lips were still caressing hers and she opened her eyes once more to see his gaze on her.

"Maitland, I love you and I love Louisa, and I will love our child with everything I am," he said against her. One of his hands came up to push the stray curls from her forehead, cupping her cheek, and she nuzzled into him as his body entered hers. She cried out silently, his penis so much bigger and more intrusive than Louisa's small delicate fingers had been. "Can you come?"

She shook her head at the thought of it. She was wet, plentiful, but the rest? "I don't think so," she whispered.

"Do you wish for me to try?" he asked as his movement stilled, and she shook her head again to say no.

He moved once more, kissing tears from her cheeks, allowing her body to adjust to him. Then she turned and kissed him. He moved into her, more than she ever thought she could be filled, and she bit down on his lip in surprise, tasting the salt of his blood as he kissed her. She released him, kissing his lip where she'd bit him. "I'm sorry," she whispered into his wound. "I'm so sorry."

His head swept back and forth against her and he kissed her again, his body moving faster, more determined, now. His hip bones were sharp against the inside of her thighs, the muscles of his arm thick and solid like brick. His chest, even, was hard and unforgiving. All of him seemed so much more hard and sharp than every part of Louisa. Right down to the part of him that pushed inside her.

She felt his big thigh come up, nudging her legs farther apart, the rough fabric covering his thighs chaffing her softer skin where it touched. Her muscles clenched against the sudden thought of the reality of him, and he came up above her.

"Maitland, stay with me. Stay with me," he said.

She nodded and tucked her face into his neck, holding on and attempting to concentrate on the emotion of him instead of the reality of his hard body, so different from Louisa. She wrapped her legs around his waist, her arms stretched about his massive shoulders. Then she felt his movements on her change, become more erratic, more unpracticed and urgent. He shifted as though searching her very depths and she thought for a moment perhaps she could come—but not tonight. She ran her hands down his back and back up, "Hugh," she said, "I love you as well."

She heard her name ground out through his teeth in a way she'd never thought to hear it, so deep and violent as he rose above her, his arms stiff and thready, his hips tight against her, his cock pulsing. Then she felt it, the sudden warm fullness of his seed. It filled her, spilled through her, before he collapsed on top of her, his arms giving out for a moment before he lifted himself on his elbows and rested his forehead against her shoulder. She ran her fingers over the big slab muscles on his back for a moment as she waited for him to compose himself.

He lifted his chin and gazed at her. "Are you well?" he asked, smoothing the errant curls from her face again.

She nodded, then took his wrists in her hands. "Is that all?"

"That's...the most of it, yes. I suppose. And hopefully, we've done this," he said with a smile.

"I hope too," she said then. "I hope." She took his face between her hands and kissed him once more. Sweetly. "Though it wouldn't be such a hardship should we need to...should it come to that."

Hugh laughed silently, his shoulders shaking under her fingers. "No, Maitland, it would be no hardship." He kissed her again though it was the sweeter, friendlier sort of kiss and much less the passionate throes of ecstasy kiss of before. "It was mostly nerves. I suppose many wedding nights are much the same."

She nodded. "I was taught that it would be uncomfortable, and painful, and frightening, but hopefully over rather quickly."

He held her gaze a pinch of concern between his eyebrows. She shied but didn't look away. "I hope it was not too uncomfortable or painful or frightening, and it was over rather more quick than I'm familiar with, if that helps."

"There was a bit in the middle...but other than that...thank you," she said, then she patted his shoulders, expecting him to move.

"I'm just— Won't you give me a moment? Amelia said to wait after, for a time until my seed would have time to make its way... you know..."

"Ahhh," she said, not knowing what to do with her legs since Hugh was still between them. She looked everywhere but at him. Reaching out and playing with the velvet curtains on the bed. "Beautiful fabric," she whispered, which sent him to laughing once more, which shifted something else inside her and the warmth of his spend leaked past his barrier and dribbled down to the bed.

He lifted, his brow crinkled in concern.

"What is it?" she asked.

"You've bled a bit. It's normal. I wasn't expecting it, as you and Louisa had said—"

"Yes, well, you're a bit bigger than all that."

He nodded, then shrugged. "I'll get you a towel. And a robe, so you won't need to dress again. Do you feel well? Beyond...beyond?" He waved a hand at her nethers, which she realized were well and truly uncovered as he moved from the bed rather expediently.

"Yes, actually, quite well."

He came back with a towel wrapped around his middle, and handed her another, laying a robe on the bed. As she managed herself and dressed he turned to give her privacy. It all seemed so odd and disconnected from what they'd just done, but Ellie appreciated it nonetheless.

When she stood, putting her hand on his shoulder, he turned and pulled her close, wrapping his big arms around her and holding her tight. "Thank you, Maitland, for being stubborn and sure of what you wanted. Thank you for being the one missing piece to our puzzle. Thank you for being my wife."

She sobbed at the unexpected words, holding his gaze. "Thank you for taking such good care of my Louisa when I was unable. I'm eternally grateful she had you in her life, and now, always will."

They kissed once more, somewhere beyond sweet but not a trespass, and Ellie turned and left him there.

Ellie opened the door to her bedroom, and Louisa jumped from their bed, rushing over and taking her in her arms. "I've missed you. Are you— How are you?" she asked, pulling back to look in Ellie's eyes.

"I'm well. You were correct in that Hugh is a perfect gentleman. He was so lovely it broke my heart a bit, but then I remembered he has Amelia. But we managed, the two of us. We managed," she whispered then smiled, nervous. They'd more than managed. What they'd done had been beautiful in a surprising way. She thought marriage to a man wouldn't have been a hardship if he'd been as wonderful as her Louisa, or Hugh.

Ellie wasn't sure how Louisa would react to her having been with another person, with a man, but she wanted to tell her everything. It was fine to discuss matters in theory, but in reality, everything could still change. In reality, either one of them could have difficulty reconciling what could be considered a cuckold in several different ways. For her part, Ellie didn't think she could love Louisa any more than she already did, but she'd been proven wrong in that thought tonight, with Hugh. Because of Hugh.

He'd been so careful, so cautious, so loving with her. He had shown her what true love is, beyond that of passion and sex. It wasn't that she didn't love Louisa, but that because she didn't love him in that way, and she still felt this incredible connection to him, that she was able to be with him intimately and not feel violated in any way...and what a gift it was. If she were to be blessed with a child from their union, she knew the babe had been borne of love, pure and simple, and that thought alone overwhelmed her— brought tears to her eyes.

Louisa took her by the hand and led her to the bed. "You should lie down," she said, "so as not to spill his seed. Remove your dressing gown, and let me care for you."

Louisa left her side and went to their bathing room. She seemed fine if a little discomfited, but Ellie hoped that any discomfort was from concern for her and not some sort of jealousy or distaste.

Ellie rested her hand against her belly. *Dear God, give us this child. Bless us with this gift.*

Louisa returned, holding a steaming basin with fresh linens draped over her arms, and Ellie sighed in the warmth it promised. Louisa sat next to her, wringing out a linen and bringing it to Ellie's face. When she leaned closer, Louisa froze, her pupils expanding. Then she took a deep breath. "You smell of Hugh," she said.

Ellie stilled. "I'm sorry, I—" Ellie shook her head and tried to move away, but Louisa stayed her with a bare hand against Ellie's now wet chest.

"No, I didn't mean... He's dear to me. He...saved me. If anything, he's the only family I've had for a long time. It was an observation." Louisa leaned over her and ran her nose up her neck, calling forth goosebumps from the depths of Ellie's body as Louisa inhaled and her voice dropped low. "I meant that the scent of him on you is intoxicating. Powerful. I feel powerful. I'm not at all upset, or disturbed, and though perhaps I should be...I'm not. I'm grateful and I'm more in love with you than I've ever been."

Ellie was shocked, but the pure erotic sight of Louisa inhaling her scent, mixed with that of her husband, made her arch off the bed. "Oh God, Lou, don't stop, don't stop." All the pent-up arousal her mind had managed to stifle when she was with Hugh flooded

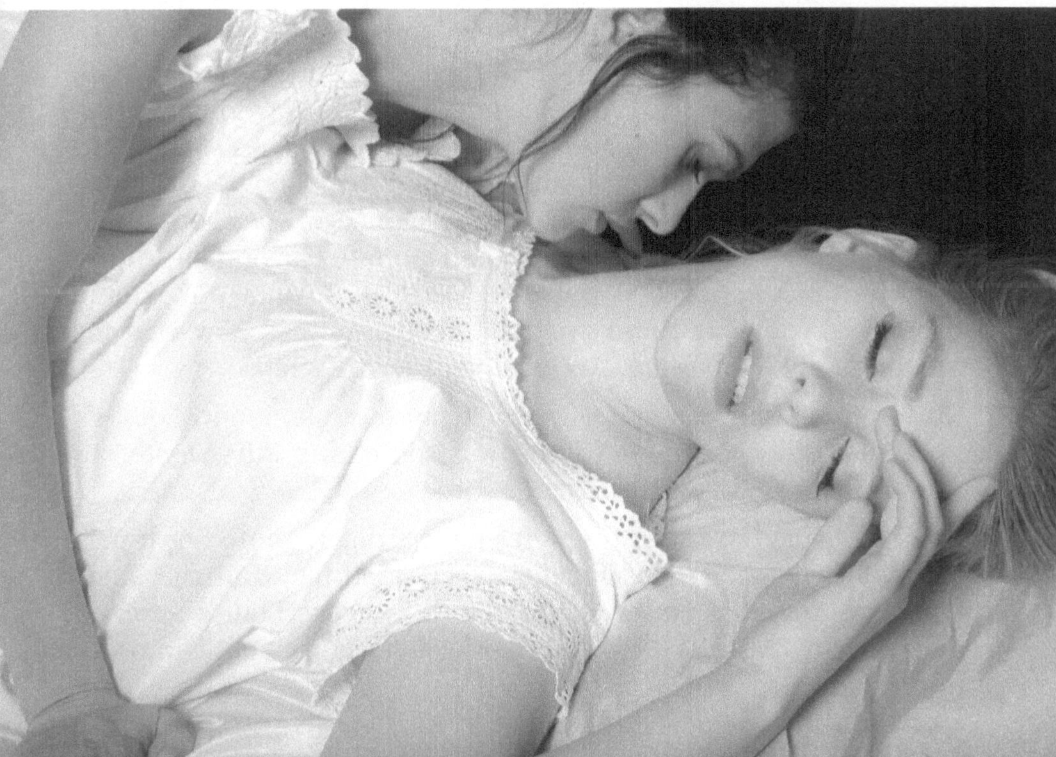

her system. Her nipples hardened, her breasts became heavy and sensitive, and that tight knot that had coiled in her belly began to unfurl. She let out the breath she'd been holding all day.

Ellie pulled Louisa to the bed as she shifted to make room next to her. Louisa kissed her way back down Ellie's neck, undoing the chemise and pushing it from her shoulders. Her hand found and tweaked one nipple, then the other, before chasing the twinge with her mouth to soothe the burn, and Maitland came off the bed once again.

"I've never been so...so... I don't have the words for this, Louisa. Oh God, I've never felt so..." Ellie stopped, furrowing her brow in concentration. "I've never— Oh God, Louisa." She took her face between her palms and pulled her up to look into her eyes. "I couldn't wait to come back to you, my love. I couldn't wait to return, to share these things with you. He spoke to my emotions, he aroused my body, but my mind—it wouldn't answer him. But now, with you touching me, everything is coming. I feel so open, so... What he brought forth, the pure love, the pure gentility of it, Louisa." Her lover dragged her name from her on a moan. Ellie took Louisa's shoulders and turned her to her back, but just as quick, Louisa tangled her legs and flipped back over Ellie.

"No. You will lay here and suffer my ministrations. You will lay here and make our babe while I pleasure you. Let me do this for you. Let *my* love carry his seed deep into your womb." Louisa covered her head to toe, her hands everywhere, then she shifted to her side, and Ellie saw Louisa's hand hover above her mons, unsure, and Ellie wondered if Louisa's concern was more about disturbing the work she and Hugh had labored for, or if she didn't want to touch her there—where he had—or... "You can make me come with your mouth on my tits and you know it. Save that for another night," Ellie said, stopping her maundering.

The look she was met with, the white-hot passion in Louisa's eyes, the thick, heaviness of love was something Ellie wanted to wade and lavish in for the rest of her days.

Lou leaned over her then, her fingers digging into her hip as she pulled her body closer before she kissed her, and she knew then that Lou could taste Hugh as well, because Louisa groaned and pushed against her tongue harder before sucking it into her own mouth.

Ellie pulled Louisa's hands to her breasts then bent one knee until it found its way between her lover's legs and she pushed into her hard. Louisa gasped against the contact and her mouth once again found Ellie's breasts. Lou's gentle touch and soft skin against hers, the sweet voice, her wet mouth, the way she would hum as she licked and teased her...Ellie was lost, so lost...so very lost.

Ellie's release came fast, as she knew it would, and wave upon wave of shudders wracked her physical form as her soul dug deeper into Louisa, the claws of it sinking in further with each pulse, the solid, complete permanence resting heavily, releasing some pent-up intensity she'd no idea existed within her.

Louisa softened upon her, caressing her skin, smoothing her hair, like Hugh had.

"I love you, my Louisa. With all my heart, I love you." They lay there breathing against one another for a while. "I'm not done with you yet, though, my love."

"No? And I'm not done with you. I'll never be done with you," Louisa said.

Ellie grabbed her chin and brought their lips together in a searing kiss as Louisa straddled her, her mouth crashing against hers in an almost violent clash of teeth as they pulled, pushed, grabbed and held onto each other as they never had before.

Ellie put her hands on Louisa's ribcage, pulling hard, moving her up her body as she slid lower in the bed, until she heard Louisa's hands slap the wall above her head hard to keep her balance and her mons skimmed over Ellie's chin before hovering over her where she wanted her. Ellie put both of her hands on Louisa's hips and pulled her down to her mouth, licking, savoring, and exploring. She hummed against her, then brought one hand up to play against her breasts as she drank of Louisa's sweet, honeyed folds, then she lifted her other hand, threading it between her legs and holding her arse, pulling her down to her face. Ellie tweaked her breasts and slid her fingers into her, searching, as Hugh had, for something she thought perhaps she found when she heard her lover scream into the night and hoped the household would believe it her own wedding night's passion.

Not long after the first wedding, they removed to Castleberry Keep in Beryshire, the seat of the Duke of Castleberry, Charles. Charles had made all the arrangements: the packing, the shipping, the travel, and Louisa had naught to do but accompany them. They were starting to leave her out of Amelia's day-to-day arrangements, even going so far as to hire a ladies maid to manage Amelia's wardrobe. But she wasn't doing a very good job of it.

Louisa fussed with Amelia's wedding gown, wanting it to be perfect for this day. It had been nearly a month since the first wedding, with the lot of them waiting for the Banns to be read both in Beryshire and London. Today Amelia was to marry Castleberry and Hugh, and Ellie would serve as witness.

It was bound to be a long day, a difficult day, what with all the family and acquaintances in attendance when all they wanted at this point was to be left alone. Charles regretted not obtaining a second special license from the Archbishop and having both ceremonies that day. But it was better this way. He'd been determined to keep this wedding small. Ceremony, tradition, and his own status determined otherwise, however.

So far the move from London had been easy and seamless, and of course nobody gave a second thought to her traveling with Amelia, with Hugh and Ellie joining them since his estate was close to Castleberry's. It was difficult for her to see Ellie so close to Hugh at times, in the public eye, but ever since the wedding night it had become easier. They'd spent their moments together early in the night then Ellie would come to her and they would make love until they passed out from exhaustion. He'd become an extension

of them as he was necessary to the family she and Ellie wanted, of course. Not to mention the alternative being never seeing her again. She would take these temporary painful moments in lieu of that forever, and she would do it happily.

Louisa turned Amelia toward the long cheval mirror and finished bustling the skirts of the soft pink gown. It was beautiful, perfect, and Amelia looked like a princess. Today she would be a duchess in truth as the wife of The Castleberry. Such a lofty position, and Louisa knew Amelia could manage it with the help of her men. How odd it seemed now, all that had happened in the last month or so. She never would have believed any of this possible. Yet here it was.

"Louisa, thank you for your help today, even though you're no longer my ladies maid."

"Oh, but I am, Amelia. I am, for all intents and purposes. To the world out there, I'm your ladies maid, and in truth I am happy to be so as well."

"You are so much more than a maid. You're family, and you're a lady once again as you once were. You know that even if you refuse to accept it. Your father can do nothing and you're my chosen sister. Louisa. Truly you're more family to me than anyone ever has been. Even before all of this."

Louisa looked up from the bustle to see Amelia wave her hand in a circle. "I can hardly believe this is happening. It's a bit terrifying," Louisa said as she stood tall, settling into the posture that had been beaten into her with a ruler as a child. A posture she'd ignored for quite some time. A posture that denoted her birth.

"Yes," Amelia agreed with her. She knew she did, and she knew why. If anyone outside their new family were to find out about them... Louisa turned for Amelia's dressing table and shook off the thought. They would be safe out here...out here at the ends of the earth, as Amelia always called it. Louisa picked up the jeweled combs Castleberry had sent for Amelia to wear, then turned back to find her staring at her.

"Louisa, I—" She let out a breath, and Louisa watched her for the signs that she was becoming overwhelmed. The little ticks and twitches that warned of a coming episode. Louisa had been well-trained to care for this beautiful, special woman, and care for her she did, and would, until the end of her days. She saw no evidence of distress, so she looked up to Amelia's warm eyes with a smile. "I'm so incredibly nervous. It seemed so simple when Hugh and Maitland did this."

Louisa took her hands and squeezed. "It will be the same for you and Castleberry."

"You know he told you to call him Charles," Amelia said.

"I know...and perhaps someday I'll be used to it."

"I understand. You'll be there with me. You'll stand with me as Maitland and Hugh will stand with us."

"Amelia, I'm not sure that's—"

"Louisa, that wasn't posed to be a question. You will stand with me. I need you next to me. My mother will have to understand that it's important and Hugh cannot stand by my side, so she'll allow it."

"I... Yes, if you think it necessary."

"I do, so we've bought you a gown to wear. You cannot stand for a wedding wearing your black house uniform."

"Amelia—"

"It's done. I gave the dress to Maitland, so if you're finished fussing with me, you should go to her."

Louisa smiled at the very thought of seeing her love. Ellie. She thought about the night they'd first met. Everyone knew her as Maitland, but she...she never had. To her she'd always been Ellie, and she always would. Her darling Ellie.

"Louisa..."

So perhaps it was to be the official end of Louisa being a servant in the house and becoming a member of the family. Of course, it was all in theory, never on paper, but they had all been insistent that she accept the fact that she was no longer a ladies maid, but once again a lady. The confrontation with her father had allowed for that, but Louisa continued to ignore it. It was so much easier to hide. She appreciated the familiar.

Louisa shook off her thoughts. "Apologies, I was..." She sighed and took Amelia's shoulders and turned her back toward the mirror, sliding the combs into her upswept hair.

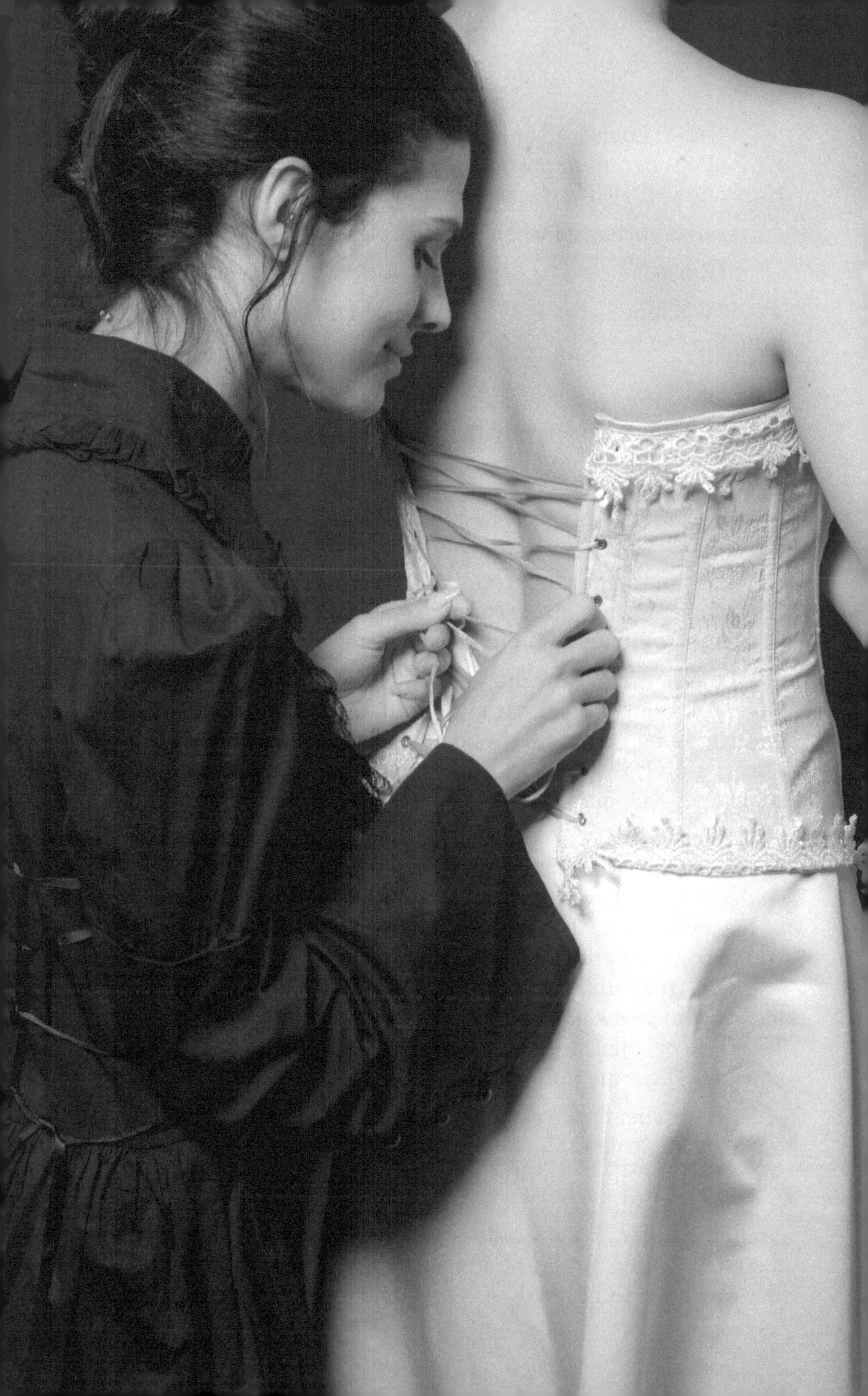

"There. Louisa, it's perfect." Amelia turned and wrapped her arms about her, then pushed her to the door. "You need to change. Hurry now, they'll be expecting us soon."

Louisa curtseyed when Amelia released her. "Yes, milady."

"Louisa."

She grinned at her. "Yes. Amelia." Louisa winked and rushed from the room.

Amelia was constantly thanking them for saving them all. As if that were even possible. A lowly miss and a ladies maid. The very idea they could save anyone—well. She opened the door to her suite, and Ellie rushed to her. "Louisa," she said, wrapping her in a warm hug. "We have a gift for you." She took her hand and pulled her through their sitting room and bedroom to the massive closet that used to be a separate room. It was now a passageway as much as a closet, with an adjoining nursery they hoped to fill.

Louisa stopped in the entry, tugging on Ellie's hand. "What have you done?" She stared at the gowns on the racks. Where once there had been Ellie's beautiful silk and satin creations and Louisa's drab work wear, there now hung nothing but clouds of color.

"We—Amelia, Charles and Hugh...and myself—we decided you needed a wardrobe suitable for a lady of your stature." Ellie smiled then cut off the complaint she saw forming in the pinch of her eyebrows. "Today is your day, Louisa. We are presenting you to society as the belle you once and always were to us. To me. As such, Hugh and I went to Madame Basire, who deconstructed one of your black gowns and created an entire wardrobe for you. They'll need final fittings, of course, but until then...this is your new life. These are your clothes."

She ran her hand over one of the dresses her fingers, skimming the myriad pleats in the bustle. The first day Louisa had worn this color had felt like the first day of her life. That had been Ellie's coming out, and today, she supposed, would be a sort of second coming for her. They would stand together, the five of them, at the altar. Louisa would no longer be the ladies maid but the lady she was born to be, and society would see her again, notice her, recognize her and realize she hadn't disappeared. She'd been here the whole time, waiting. "What have you…" But she couldn't finish the sentence. She glanced at Ellie through a watery gaze. "I never expected this much."

"We know." Louisa turned at Charles's voice behind her to find he, Hugh, and Amelia, wrapped up together in their wedding finery, their ribands and sashes and shields across their broad chests, bracketing Amelia between them like the most powerful royal triad she'd ever seen. God, they were stunning. She inspected the dress she wore, then Ellie's, and realized just how far from grace she'd fallen.

"Louisa, you're not simply a ladies maid. You're family, and I don't believe you understand the extent to which we all believe that. You continue to keep yourself separate from us, upholding some appearance we aren't aware needed upholding," Charles said, and

Louisa felt the familiar pinch of fear between her shoulder blades relax. The weight of fear lifted under his gaze as though he willed the truth into her.

"But society... If I come out, if I'm seen to be...who I am—"

"I thought it had been made clear at the wedding. When I confronted Mayjoy. He is of no concern to us. You may be whomever you wish to be and if you wish to remain as a ladies maid, I'll see to it that everyone here understands that is also your choice. But Louisa, I don't believe it's how you wish to be seen.

"In my home. In my household. On my land. Under my purview. You are no less a lady than Amelia or Maitland, and you will be acknowledged and treated as such."

Louisa tipped and Ellie caught her up, holding tight until she got her legs back. She supposed she'd remained hidden, thinking it was necessary for them in keeping up appearances. But the truth of the matter was that as a lady, she'd be welcome to do as she wished, as long as her father or husband didn't object. And considering she no longer had either of those to contend with... "I'm overwhelmed," she said. It was the headiest understatement she'd ever stated.

"We thought perhaps you could use a nudge in this direction," Hugh said. "I know you're content and happy to live out a quiet life with Ellie. But I also happen to know you missed all the trappings of being of your station. We want to be sure that at this point, it's up to you how you live your life. We are here to support you, care for you, and see to it that you are safe and well in doing it."

Louisa released Ellie then and fell in his arms. Certainly she'd heard Charles, but to hear Hugh say it... "I don't know where I'd be if it weren't for you and I'm not sure I've ever thanked you for it, Hugh. I would never have survived. I would never have—"

"Hush now, Louisa. You've thanked me quite enough without words. You've given me my deepest heart's desire and made an impossible dream possible. Without you, none of us would be here today."

Amelia wrapped around her back as she hugged Hugh, then Charles took up the space at one shoulder as Ellie did the same at the other and Charles's big arms squeezed the lot of them until Louisa needed air and pushed them all away.

"I'm blessed. Truly. Thank you." Then she placed a kiss on every cheek, and Ellie rushed them out of the room to help her dress for the wedding. "I may like to keep a couple of the older dresses, Ellie. Just because."

"Just because?"

"They are rather more comfortable when you aren't required to wear them," Louisa said with a smile. She was overwhelmed. She had everything she wanted, everything she wished for.

"I do have a final gift for you. We'll call it a wedding gift. It's from all of us, again, but I told them I needed to give this to you alone," Ellie said as she took Louisa's hand and led her into the nursery. Hanging there, on the wall where they'd planned to put two rocking chairs and a crib, was her mother's painting.

Louisa's knees wobbled and she collapsed in pile of skirts in front of it, unable to look away. "How?"

"I mentioned the painting to Hugh, and he and Charles paid a final visit your father. While there, Charles decided to also collect everything that remained in the house that was yours. Turns out they'd left your room to waste. All of that's here, in another guest room. You can do whatever you wish with it."

"Everything?"

"Everything. The clothes, the furniture, your jewelry, and possessions...everything. Hugh said they arrived with a cart and some men and asked where your things had been kept, and Charles told them to pack the room and leave it barren—and so they did. Even Hugh had been shocked. He'd assumed they intended to take the painting and nothing else."

"Charles..."

"Yes. It was all Charles, really."

"But why?"

"Because he was able. If you have power and you don't use it to help those who are unable to help themselves, no matter how small and insignificant the action... then what kind of power do you have?"

"I don't know what to do with it all." She shook her head in disbelief. It was an embarrassment of emotion, and she had nowhere to place all of it. She supposed she was lucky to be member to a house of five.

"You never have to see any of it again if you don't wish to. Charles had it all crated and placed in the room. But he was quite adamant that nobody touch any of it until you decided whether it was to stay."

"Charles."

"Yes."

"But you...you remembered." She turned then, catching Ellie's gaze.

"How could I forget that day, Louisa? It was one of the best days of my life," Ellie said breathlessly, her eyes wide as though she were shocked that Louisa didn't already know.

"Oh, Ellie." She took her hand, shaking as it was, and held it tight as she pulled her to her feet. "It was mine as well." Ellie swept a curl from her cheek, tucking it behind her ear as the worried crease between her eyes softened, and Louisa leaned up on her toes for a kiss. It was sweet, momentary, momentous.

"We have to get you ready for the ceremony. Come on, up with you," Ellie said when she leaned back, eyes of glass, and Louisa nodded.

"I have some things in a chest...baby blankets and such that we may be needing soon." Louisa leaned into Ellie, placing a hand over her belly and gazing up into her eyes.

"We don't know yet for sure."

"No...but it's been a month of trying, and you have yet to have your courses."

"This is true. Can you imagine?" Ellie said, her eyes wide as she put a hand over Louisa's and held her there.

"With you? I can imagine anything." Louisa kissed Ellie again, a bit deeper this time but still sweet so as not to muss her beautiful face before the wedding.

"I can too, Louisa. For the first time in a very long time, I can imagine us. Though this is a bit bigger than the cottage we wanted." She twirled a hand around them.

"And we still need a goat."

Everafter

Castleberry Keep

1882

STAND AND FACE ME, MY LOVE,
AND SCATTER THE GRACE
IN YOUR EYES

~Sappho

Louisa

"My darling, my darling." Louisa knelt on the floor next to the bed as she spoke to Ellie, skimming her hands around her distended belly. "My darling, my darling. This isn't the worst of it. Not by far. We'll make it through this. Trust me. Help me, just a bit."

Ellie groaned and stretched as best as she could then rolled to her side, curling her body around her giant abdomen, the babe nestled against her spine inside.

Louisa reached up to Ellie with the cool linen. "Ellie, my love, hang on to me. Listen to my voice. We'll get through this. I promise you." She smoothed her hair back from her face and watched as her eyes fluttered open for a moment.

"Louisa, I love you, but please do what you must to save the babe. Whatever you must. Save our child."

Louisa leaned up and kissed Ellie, kissed until it tasted of salt from her tears. "Ellie. Stay strong. Stay strong," she said. "Stay strong." Ellie seemed to go quiet and relax into the pillow, and Louisa turned away. "Isn't there anything we can do? Isn't there... Who else can we send for?" She twisted her hands together. What use was all the money in the world if they couldn't help Ellie through this? She could barely hold herself together. To have Ellie, to hold her and love her, only to lose her. She stopped. She couldn't. Her shoulder blades tightened and she shrank against the bed.

Hugh approached her. He showed her his hands, then laid them on Louisa's shoulders and held her as he gazed at his wife. "The doctor says the babe is turned. We have to wait and hope she gets into a better position." He moved one hand to her face, bringing her gaze to his. "Listen to me. I'll protect her with my life. I've sent for the midwife at Pembroke-by-the-Sea. She's helped to birth hundreds of babies, all of them healthy. She'll be here as soon as she's able."

Louisa stood, wrapping her arms around Hugh as best she could. "I can't lose her," she whispered.

"None of us can, Louisa. None of us can. We'll do everything—"

"I know you need her to keep up the—"

Hugh took her face in his hands again, his thumbs across her lips. "Don't, Louisa. It has nothing to do with that. Don't you believe for one minute that *that* is all Ellie is for us. We're family. All of us, and by now you should know this like you know your own heart."

Louisa nodded and melted against Hugh's chest. "I'm sorry, I know, I do… There's just been so much, Hugh. So much, and I'm so tired and this… I can't lose her. Not now." This hurt. Like nothing she'd ever felt. Louisa didn't think it was possible to feel a knife through your heart where none physically existed. She'd been hurt before when she'd first lost Ellie, when she'd been sent away, when her father had done his best to ruin her, when she'd been thoroughly and completely destroyed. At least she'd thought so at the time.

Seeing Ellie in such pain, however, was so much more.

Hugh's hands smoothed down her arms and wrapped her up in the embrace. He was her oldest friend and the only man in the world who could touch her like this, and for whatever reason, she needed it—she needed him. Even Charles didn't touch her. Couldn't, really. He was such a powerful presence his very demeanor still frightened her at her core. She knew he was safe, she knew he was gentle in his way, but she didn't have control of some of her reactions with him because he was just…so very much. But Hugh… She fell against him and let him support her. The three of them had created something special, even as he was a very permanent part of an entirely different relationship at the same time.

"Come on. Louisa. Come lay with her, talk to her. Let her hear you so she knows everything is going to work out. Because it will. We aren't going to lose your girl today."

He pulled her around to the other side of the bed, fluffed some pillows, and laid her down amongst them. When he returned to the other side of the bed, she'd already scooted herself up against Ellie until there was no space between them. Her arms wrapped around her, her mouth at her ear. Perhaps if they told stories to pass the time while they waited. To keep their minds off the work of it.

"Hugh, have I ever told you about the night I first saw her?"

He shook his head as he smoothed the cool linen across Ellie's brow then sat at the edge of the bed next to her. "No, you haven't." He placed his hand on Ellie's belly, smoothing his fingers across the little bumps that appeared, shifted, and disappeared from her skin as the babe rolled within.

Louisa watched his hand on her stomach, skin to skin. It was no longer strange to see someone else touch her Ellie. He was her husband; he had the right to touch her where Louisa didn't, and this was his baby, just as much—possibly even more—than it was hers. Louisa had no rights where Ellie was concerned, none whatsoever as far as the law went. Louisa would have no legal rights to the children they would share, children who would know her as a mother. Her body shook and her hands tightened on the sheets draped across her love. She still had fears, but they lessened with every breath she took, every step through this life with them.

"Hugh," she said and her voice broke. She swallowed when it felt as though her throat tore.

He looked up at her again, and his hand moved to her cheek, reaching across Ellie. "Tell me, Louisa. Tell me about the night you first met."

"You were there, you know. The night we met. You were there."

"I don't remember."

"There was nothing remarkable about it. It was another crush, during yet another season. One in which I continued to avoid capture, and you as well, you know, because of Amelia."

Hugh smiled at that. "We had that in common and I was ever so very hopeful."

"As you should have been, as was right, because look at you now," Louisa said with a smile.

"So tell me," he said.

Louisa took a deep breath and snuggled into Ellie. "It was my third season. I needed a husband or I would be a spinster. At that age, I was already on the shelf and though I was thrilled at the prospect, my father was not."

Hugh shook his head, then smiled at her, and she felt his warmth and love all the way to her toes. "Ellie was so beautiful, she was... I'm not sure I can even describe it."

"Try." Hugh whispered.

And so she tried.

Ellie

"Hugh don't listen to her. That's not at all how it happened. She paints me a simpering miss along with the others," Ellie said.

"Ellie, I thought you were sleeping," Louisa started, but Ellie wouldn't have it.

"No, listen here, I'm not going to lay here and labor while you tell my husband half truths," she said with a smile. "I'm doing well at the moment, so it's my turn." Ellie rocked against the mattress until she sat up on her elbows, then she scooted up toward the headboard as Hugh stood and helped her, shoving pillows behind her back. She groaned against a rather mild contraction, then patted the bed next to her, and Hugh sat with her at the headboard, taking much of her weight as Louisa lay back down on her opposite side, her head in her lap...or what was left of it at this point with their babe taking so much space. "What she said was fairly true...but I was no sweet miss, you'll see. That night was the first night I saw you as well. Do you remember?" she asked. Hugh turned to her and smiled.

"I do remember, now, from Louisa's telling. That dress was stunning. I'm not a man who considers fashion, but Louisa is correct. You were the most beautiful woman at the ball that night. I hadn't even thought about it. I didn't know that was you at the time. But I do remember you."

"Aren't you sweet?" Ellie paused and breathed as another contraction came upon her, the tightening of her abdomen stilling the babe inside, spreading tension to the whole of her body before fading away. She adjusted her position. She leaned against Hugh a bit more as Louisa moved up toward the headboard next to her and began kneading her lower back. "Oh God, that's wondrous."

Hugh adjusted the sheets over her, and Ellie smiled. She loved he knew how to make her comfortable. She loved how he paid attention in that way. Amelia was a very lucky woman, and Ellie considered herself lucky to be married to such a considerate man, even if he wasn't hers. Sharing a child with him, while the prospect in the beginning had been terrifying, was a blessing. Hugh had been a stranger to her, beyond the ballroom, until they'd been married. The prospect of having a child with him, of creating a child with him, had terrified her, but he'd made it into something beautiful. He was the true blessing in her and Louisa's life, and she thanked God every single day for him.

"What are you smiling about?" he asked.

"I was thinking about our wedding night."

Hugh grinned. "It could have been worse."

"Worse? It was lovely. You weren't merely a gentleman but a loving, caring husband. I consider myself quite lucky in that, you know."

"You've never told me of that night," Louisa said.

"I intended to tell you everything as soon as I returned to our bed," Ellie said as she shifted to see Louisa. "But you had some rather sudden plans of your own that night."

"Oh, did you now?" Hugh asked, and Louisa reached across Ellie and smacked his arm.

"As if any of this is your business, sir," she said.

"Isn't it though?" he asked, and Ellie and Louisa both glared at him. "Alright, alright, so be it," he said with a laugh. "I was teasing you both. Don't have me drawn and quartered yet."

Ellie laughed and turned back to Louisa as she sank into the pillows again. "I can't see as how it would hurt anything, Lou. I mean, he was *there*...for most of it."

Louisa leaned into Ellie and kissed her, opened her mouth with her tongue and pressed in until there was only the breath between them. "Tell me then, my darling. Tell me about that night."

"I'll start, shall I? Since the two of you are occupied," Hugh said with a smile. Louisa scooted up in the bed when he waved his hand, and Ellie shifted down to rest across her belly as Hugh took over massaging her back. "It was beautiful for a wedding night, was it not? We'd all returned to Castleberry Hall for the wedding breakfast, and then that afternoon was one of the most incredible afternoons—"

"Why?" Louisa asked.

"We didn't know each other. Not really. Maitland and I were perfect strangers—save those times she attempted to harass me in society we hadn't spoken at all."

"Oh, well, yes."

"And I wasn't so excited about the prospect of that night. So sitting about and chatting—"

"Not so very eager to ruin your stranger wife?" Ellie smiled. Neither one of them had been looking forward to the actual act of consummation.

"Not exactly...but who's telling this story?" he asked.

"I am," she said with a grin. Ellie settled in, between her husband and her wife, and she took over the telling for a while.

Hugh

"Hugh breathed through the emotion Maitland's story brought back to him. It was seemed odd to him that he should become aroused for Maitland when he felt for her in a different way than his Amelia, but he had, and they'd been successful in the endeavors. He was a man, of course. But his interactions with Maitland were much more perfunctory. Not that they were emotionless and mannered, but the purpose was different. He and Maitland loved each other, as all of them did, in some regard. But he belonged to, and with, Amelia.

He felt Maitland shift against him and he looked to find them both watching him. Maitland brought his mouth to hers with one finger under his chin, and he kissed her. Not quite like a lover, but nothing like a brother either. Then Louisa leaned over and kissed him as well, kissed the both of them.

Hugh heard a knock at the door and turned. "Enter," he said.

"Hello," came the tiny voice of his wife, Amelia. Hugh bussed Louisa and Maitland one more quick time then stood and went to her, pulling her up in an embrace and leading her to the bed where Maitland labored. "I wanted to come check on you, see if you need anything," she said as she sat on the bed at Maitland's knee, and Hugh took up his spot behind her back once more.

Maitland closed her eyes, and Hugh pressed his hands into her back, feeling the strength of another contraction coming on. He turned to Amelia, not wanting to worry her. "We were exchanging stories. Louisa told me of the first time they met, and...other such things," he said with a smile.

Maitland laughed, her muscles relaxing as the contraction eased. "And I was going to set the record straight because Louisa made me out to be a simpering miss, which is unacceptable."

"Now's your chance," Louisa said, and Ellie smiled—and that smile, from her, in this moment, lit up the room like nothing else had. It was a contagion, and both Louisa and Amelia smiled in return and Hugh felt blessed to be a mere witness to it.

"Alright, Ellie, set the record straight. No simpering miss... What happened next?" Hugh asked and he watched as these women looked into each other's lives, their very souls, and shared the most intimate moments. He wasn't sure how he'd been blessed to be witness to this, of all things. He loved them both so very much, he would hang the moon for the lot of them and burn the world to the ground should one of them hurt. It wasn't the family he'd expected, but it was the family he was given and he couldn't be more thankful for all of them. He couldn't imagine life without each of his women. Every one of them important to this life.

He took Amelia's hand and showed her how to help him ease Maitland muscles. Wondered for a moment where Charles was hiding. Probably in the study with a snifter of brandy, or more likely—scotch. The birthing of babies terrified Charles. Amelia settled in at Maitland's knees as she shifted more toward Louisa to make room for her on their massive bed.

"It was true," she said. "It was a crush. And we were situated in an inappropriate location, and my dress was magnificent. All of these things were true."

"But?" Amelia prodded.

"But...everything I'd done had been done with purpose. I was there to snare a husband as quick as possible so I could be done with it, as one does. Because I wanted to leave society as rapidly as I'd entered it. I'd no interest in the parties and the matrons and the rest of it. I wanted a quiet life, a country manor, several children to raise, and a husband to provide that who would give me the children and otherwise let me be," she said with a grand smile at Hugh.

"You're welcome," he replied, and she smacked his leg with a wink, then she turned back to Louisa. "I felt your gaze, and it was like nothing I'd ever felt. I knew you were watching, but I miscalculated my trap. Because with that sort of intense regard, I had expected to turn and catch the eye of a man."

"I'm no man," Louisa said.

"That truth is certain, my darling, and I am ever so grateful for it."

"But what about the ball?" Amelia asked. Hugh knew how she loved stories. As she'd no interest in being a part of society, it all seemed quite grand and beautiful through the experience of others. In Amelia's own reality, that kind of function, that sort of attention, terrified her to no end, and she was thankful to be done with it for the most part.

"Yes, the ball. So there I was, expecting to turn and gaze upon my future husband."

"But you didn't," Louisa finished with a smile.

"That's it? That's all?" Amelia asked when Ellie paused because of a contraction, but she watched Ellie and the understanding followed, and Amelia flushed from embarrassment.

"I'll carry on the story from here, shall I?" Louisa said, turning to Ellie, who nodded as she tried to breathe. It seemed to Hugh this contraction was a bit stronger than some of the previous and Louisa knew it, so she picked up where Ellie left off. Mostly.

"'You'll call me Ellie.' That's all she said. I'd been so frightened at first that I'd smiled without looking up. I wasn't yet ready to meet those wondrous eyes, but the assumption Ellie made in that simple phrase was the most beautiful sentence in the history of speech."

Ellie smiled and squeezed Louisa's hand, her breathing stilted and short, a sheen of perspiration across her lip and forehead. Louisa gazed up at Hugh, and he winked then squeezed the excess water from a cool rag from the basin next to the bed and dabbed Ellie's face.

"Ellie had followed me to the retiring room when I fled the ballroom, or so I'd thought, but perhaps it was an accident. However, it had happened I'd been found, and in that moment when Ellie said those words, I..." Louisa leaned closer to Ellie and placed a kiss on her forehead, and in any other household it would feel an intrusion to watch, but not here. "I never wanted to flee again," she said. "I'd been terrified to meet her eyes because this thing that I felt, it wasn't like anything I'd ever felt in all my life. It was how I expected to feel when I met a husband…it was the feeling that had been explained time and again by happy wives everywhere before they bid their goodbyes and disappeared from my life." Louisa paused, closed her eyes and rested her head on the pillow next to Ellie for a moment. Hugh squeezed her shoulder and motioned to Amelia that they should leave them for a moment.

"I finally felt composed enough to be able to look up into her eyes and not give away how flustered I was. And so I did. But I'd been wrong, so wrong, so very, very wrong. It felt like forever before I could speak. I was trying so hard to find words, anything with which I could greet this angel before me." She faced Ellie, their eyes locked together. "For you were an angel, haloed in the blondest hair, the only depth of color those eyes, those deep, mesmerizing lavender eyes. How is that even possible?" She blinked. "I opened my mouth and willed myself to speak. But 'Lou—' was all that came out. I was horrified. But Ellie took my hand and said—"

"'Lou is a beautiful name,'" Ellie interrupted, and Louisa smiled and he watched as Louisa sank into the words. Letting the feeling embrace her once again.

"I feared she'd abandon me, but I decided right then that it would be better to have had this small moment than to lose her after many more. I held my breath, hoping I still had a friend."

"And you did, of course you did. You had much more than that." When Ellie said that, Louisa glanced up, catching his gaze as he blew a kiss from the entry. Amelia had already left the room, giving them a little privacy as they reminisced.

"Tell me more about that day, my darling Ellie," she said, then Hugh pulled the door closed behind him.

Hugh heard Maitland cry out and ran for the stairs, Amelia and Charles following behind. When they reached the door to her suite, Charles took his shoulder, and he turned.

"Let us know. We'll be right here," Charles said.

Hugh thought a moment about how different Charles was now than when they'd first met. He was somehow softer, yet still stiff and sharp around the edges. Hugh nodded and as he turned back to the entry, Amelia ducked into the safety Charles's arms. That was something else that had taken time to change, Hugh appreciating Charles and what he was for Amelia, what they were together, the three of them.

He entered the room and pulled the door shut behind him to find Louisa rubbing Maitland's back, whispering, while Maitland appeared to be tense but sleeping, and Louisa asked him the question with her eyes, to which he shook his head. No news yet.

He turned back toward the door and let Charles and Amelia know she was well enough, so they could return to the study for the time being, instead of pacing the hall. Then he closed the door once more and went to the bed, lying down behind Maitland. He wrapped his arm over her body and took Louisa's hand in his own, squeezing it to reassure her. "Tell me more about when you first met," he said, hoping that keeping her talking would alleviate some of the concern for Maitland. He knew Louisa, knew what she'd endured more than anyone else. He carried her secrets and her horrible past with her, so she would never be alone with it. Because of that knowledge, he wanted to help alleviate any difficulties for her as best he could, as he always had.

It seemed odd, the two of them tossed together the way they'd been. But her first season her mother had put her in his path, and though they hadn't suited in that way, because Louisa was a sapphist and he was in love with Amelia, they did suit as friends. They'd searched each other out at balls and societal functions, because it had kept the attention from them, and that first year, they'd become close.

"Hugh," Ellie said. "It's your turn. You tell me about Louisa, something I don't know."

"How will I know what to say?" Hugh asked. "Louisa has told you everything about her past."

"Not everything," Louisa said then and caught his gaze.

A shudder slid down his spine as he realized to what she referred. "I'm not of a mind to speak on certain things," he said, and Maitland struggled to sit up a bit, Louisa helping her.

"I know what happened," she said. "I know how he saved you. I didn't mean that part, unless you need to speak of it, and perhaps you do," Ellie said, her hand tightening on Louisa's.

Hugh shook his head. "Perhaps later," he said. He would like to speak about it, sometime, with someone, but it seemed a cruel thing to speak with Louisa about that night and the days that had followed, and at the same time he would never discuss it with anyone but her, because it was her story, not his. Even as painful as it was for him to live, to remember, for her it was much more so.

"I would like to speak of it, once and for all," Louisa said.

He searched Louisa's gaze. He didn't know what he was looking for but whatever it was, he didn't see it. He nodded.

"I don't have all the pieces. I would like to have them filled in," she said.

Hugh nodded again as if she needed his permission to do this. She didn't...but he was here for her, as he had been that night.

They waited, letting Louisa consider. "It's only that...I don't understand where you came from. One minute I was alone with him and the next...there was you."

Hugh nodded when she paused long enough. "Perry and I were in the study that overlooks the side garden. We heard something and he went to look out the window, and the next thing I knew he'd gone out of it and I followed. I didn't know it was you until after he'd run off." They sat in silence for a moment as Hugh considered. "I would have married you," he said. "I meant what I said. I would have married you and taken you away from all of it, but I never had that chance. It was taken from me, as you were." He closed his eyes as he remembered, attempting to forget, his throat tight against the emotion. "But I would have married you."

Louisa took his hands then. "I would have let you, had I known, but then—"

"How could you? Hepplewort is dead now. He crossed the wrong man not long after that, and he suffered for what he did." Hepplewort had crossed Perry, in fact, as well as Perry's brother, the Duke of Roxleigh. But that night, they hadn't even known who he was because once they'd pulled him off Louisa, he taken off, and Hugh had been caring for Louisa, then Perry had been managing the situation and…Hugh wasn't sure. He only knew that *that* night, he'd managed to slip away. "Perry," Hugh said. "Perry was with me that night. He helped me. It was his wife…" Hugh let that statement hang in the air.

"You saved my life, Hugh. Twice."

"You would have done the same for me, Louisa, and in the end you saved us all."

Ellie groaned, and Hugh stood to try to get her into another more comfortable position, when a knock came at the door. He went to open it.

"My man has returned with the midwife. She'll be up in a moment," Charles said, and Hugh nearly collapsed from the relief of it. Charles wrapped one hand around his arm, as though to lend a bit of support.

"Thank you," he said. He felt his body shaking from head to toe and knew he needed to calm his nerves before returning to Ellie and Louisa. He turned back from the door. "The midwife has arrived. I'll go greet her, shall I?" Then he nodded and pulled the door behind him. He leaned a bit too heavy on Charles, realized he'd slumped a bit against his shoulder.

"I'll go greet her, shall I?" Charles repeated in the same jovial tone Hugh had used, and he straightened.

"Fuck's sake, Charles, I had to get out of there before I caused a panic."

Charles squeezed his arm. "It's fine, Hugh. I was jesting."

"Why would you attempt a new form of communication at this particular juncture?" Hugh asked.

"No time better than now," he said with a shrug. Hugh laughed. "See?" Charles pointed at Hugh. "It worked. Come, let's go greet the midwife. Amelia is asking all sorts of questions about childbearing, and I need to get her away before my line is jeopardized by knowledge."

"Please tell me you're still jesting, Charles," Hugh said. "If Amelia's afraid to have children, she shouldn't be forced into it."

"I am, Hugh," Charles replied. "But we should cross that bridge when we are approaching it, perhaps not right this moment."

"That I can agree with," Hugh replied. Their Amelia was a special woman. So brilliant and strong. Her brain so beautiful in the way she saw the world.

They came down the main stairs together, Charles attempting more lighthearted jesting before they found Amelia speaking with a small stout woman in the entry. She turned to them as they approached. Her eyes narrowed.

"Oh, no," Charles said.

A spear of fear worked its way down his throat to his gut.

"Husbands," Amelia said. Hugh glanced to the midwife, who happened to be looking off in another direction. "This is Margarethe. She's brilliant with birthing babies."

Hugh nodded when she turned and gave him a very thorough once over. "This is the father?" she asked.

"Yes, ma'am. Lord Endsleigh. I'm certain you can call him Ender," Amelia said with a smile.

"Lord Endsleigh, take me to the woman."

"Margarethe is quite perfunctory," Amelia said, and Hugh motioned to the stairs.

"Right this way." She followed.

"Hugh, we'll stay down here until you have need, shall we?" Charles said, and Hugh glanced back over his shoulder in time to see Amelia look at Charles in disbelief.

Hugh laughed nervously but continued on.

"Childbirth is no laughing matter, sir," Margarethe said.

"No, ma'am, apologies. It was something Castleberry said."

"Are your friends always here?"

"This is his seat, so yes. We're the visitors at the moment."

"Did you not plan for this birth? She shouldn't be traveling if she's laboring."

"We planned for her to labor here, as a safety measure. It's closer to Pembroke, and Amelia said you're the absolute best if we had need," Hugh said, and the woman harrumphed in response.

"I delivered that child into this world and I'll deliver her children as well, I imagine. Might as well deliver this one too. I'm told the babe is turned."

"That's what the town physician said. Maitland, my wife, wanted to labor quietly but when the physician refused to deliver the babe, we sent for you."

Another humph from Margarethe. "I never understood men who deliver children. Men are only good at putting things into women, not taking them out."

Hugh stopped and looked back at her, but she just returned his gaze without a flinch. He nodded to the door, then opened it. "Maitland, the midwife is here," he said.

He was met with a loud groan from Ellie and *"Hugh?"* from Louisa, so he flew the door wide and rushed to Ellie's side, taking her hand and giving her something to crush if she chose to. And crush she did. He feared his bones would crack.

"You should leave. This is women's work," Margarethe said.

The resounding, "No!" came from all three of them at once, and Hugh looked up to find the woman with a smile on her face as she approached the bed.

"So be it, but you'll do as you're asked, no questions," she said.

"Whatever you say," Hugh replied.

Maitland collapsed back to the bed in a heap of fabric and sweat, and Hugh reached over to the basin, pulling a fresh linen through the cool water then bringing it to her forehead.

"Good, good," Margarethe said. She came up next to Ellie, rubbed her hands together, then placed them on Ellie's big belly, feeling her way around. "Oh, she's a feisty one, this babe. Yep, yep, she's right side up the tot. You're doing well though. Carry on." She proceeded to push and prod at Maitland's distended belly for a minute, and Hugh watched as the little bumps that made up his child's arms and legs seemed to fight back. Then the woman nodded. "I need a cup of tea. I'll return." And she disappeared out the door.

Maitland groaned, bringing Hugh's attention back to the room. "She woke the baby," she complained as she wrapped her arms around her belly and sank into the pillows.

Hugh smiled. "I believe it's your turn to regale us, Louisa. Take us back to the beginning. Not the first night, but after. When everything was fresh and new."

"Oh, I don't know," she started, but then Ellie pleaded with her and Hugh saw all their love and passion in that look.

Louisa

"I still dream of that blue-eyed girl," Ellie said before crying out from the onset of what seemed to be a rather powerful contraction.

"I know you do. So do I," Louisa said, and she wrapped an arm around Ellie and rubbed the tight muscles of her lower back. "So do I."

The woman returned, a team of maids with linens and buckets of steaming water behind her. She closed the door after they left and rolled her sleeves. "Right, it's time to get this babe out of you, I think."

She walked to the bed, giving Louisa and Hugh instructions for how to arrange Ellie on the pillows, bringing her all the way to the end of the bed and standing there with her feet on her shoulders as she checked her, and Hugh cast his gaze anywhere he could but there, and Louisa felt light-headed as Ellie screamed and latched on to both of them with all her might.

"The two of you can hold her legs here, like this. It isn't going to be comfortable, or easy, but now the faster we get this babe out, the better."

Louisa and Hugh held Ellie's legs and spoke as the woman fussed. She brought a bucket to her feet and started drying off silver tools and laying them out. Louisa was thankful Ellie didn't have a view over her massive belly of what she did.

"Right then," she said. Ellie tensed at the onset of another contraction. "You two support her, help her, concentrate on her. I'll do the rest. Maitland, you push."

It was minutes later—though it felt like hours— when the midwife pulled a small, screaming, bloody mess from Ellie's body. She held the babe upside down against herself for a moment, wiping and clearing and using the tools to suck out her nose and such. Then she lifted her, still attached to Ellie, and laid her across her chest.

Ellie lifted one hand and placed it on their daughter's head. "You were right, Hugh, and she's beautiful."

Louisa had tears streaming her face as she leaned in and kissed Ellie on the cheek, still holding Ellie's leg as instructed. She looked up to see tears streaming Hugh's cheeks as well. "She's beautiful, Hugh."

He nodded but couldn't seem to speak.

"Pay attention, people. We're far from done here. Apparently your doctor is more a dolt than I assumed. Maitland, hold on to that baby. You're going to feel a—"

Ellie cried out, holding the babe and lifting from the bed. "I thought it was over!" she said through the scream, quite clearly pushing again.

"Not as much as we'd like, my dear. Seems your babe has a sibling."

Hugh looked at Ellie, then at Louisa. "Another babe?" He went pale, and Louisa narrowed her gaze on him.

"Come on, Hugh. Keep it together. Just a few more."

"Push Maitland, push with all your... There," the midwife said, and Ellie collapsed to the bed once more, the midwife cleaning yet another babe, this one a son.

"Hugh?" Louisa said.

"Louisa," he replied.

They looked at each other for a moment, then they both looked to Ellie, who was the happiest she'd ever seen her. "I knew there was something special going on in there," she said. She kissed the top of her daughter's head with a smile and reached for her son. Ellie lay there, between her husband and her wife, holding the first of their children, while Louisa cried and Hugh was panicked.

Louisa reached over and squeezed his hand. "It's not so bad, is it?"

"Oh, no, God no!" he exclaimed. "I'm just...trying to wrap my head around how we've all come so far in such short a time. A year ago..."

"Yes, well. Go tell Charles and Amelia before Charles needs medical attention. Poor man."

Hugh straightened. "Yes, quite." He put some pillows under Ellie's leg, and with a nod to the midwife, ran to the door.

"That's it then," the midwife said, and she tied off both babies' umbilical cords and held them to be snipped. "You'll have to do it as my hands are full."

Louisa took the scissors from the small tray and clipped both cords as Margarethe held them steady. She helped to scoot Ellie up in the bed, surrounding her with pillows before she gathered her things.

"I'll be back in a bit. I need to take this to the kitchens and check them." Then she turned and walked from the room, a towel-covered bucket in her hand.

Louisa crawled up in the massive bed next to Ellie, dragging blankets and clean towels with her to be sure the babies were warm. Babies. Ellie handed one to her, then pulled aside the shift she wore, helping the little boy to one of her nipples. She let out a breath, closing her eyes.

"Okay. I can manage this. Perhaps," she said. They hadn't yet decided whether or not to use a wet nurse. Ellie had been against it, but now with two babies, Louisa wasn't sure.

"Hand me Alice," she said, and Louisa gazed down into the tiny baby's face, her little fists shaking as her tiny bird mouth rooted in the blankets.

"Alice?" Her voice broke and she cleared her throat.

"Yes, Alice. Hugh thought she should be named for her mother."

Tears welled in Louisa's eyes as she helped Ellie adjust the tiny babe against her other breast. "Of course he did," she said. Then she snuggled next to Ellie and watched the babies, checking often to be sure everyone was good and pink and warm.

"And what did he think if the babe were a boy?"

"We hadn't discussed it, actually. Only that we wished for you—" Ellie groaned against another contraction, her back bowing as she held the babies and Louisa smoothed the tension in her forehead with her palm.

"I had an idea..." Louisa said when it passed.

"Tell me," Ellie said, gazing up at her.

"I've always liked the name Gabriel. One of the angels, who brings messages from God... like his mother."

Ellie closed her eyes and turned her face into Louisa's palm, kissing her there as she had once before, and Louisa closed her palm and held the kiss to her breast.

"Gabriel. I like it," the words were dry. Louisa smiled, leaning forward and kissing her so sweetly.

"Oh my Ellie. Look at what you've done," she said as she leaned in. "I always told you you were brave."

Ellie let out an exhausted laugh, leaning her head against Louisa's chest. "Could you have ever imagined such a thing, watching that girl in the ballroom?"

"Not in my wildest dreams, Ellie. Not in my wildest dreams."

NO HONEY FOR ME
IF IT COMES
WITH A BEE

~Sappho

Ellie
&
Lou

"And what is the use of a book," thought Alice,
"without pictures or conversation?"

Lewis Carroll
Alice's Adventures in Wonderland

Thank you!

JennLeBlanc.com
JennLeBlanc.com/newsletter
Instagram @JennLeBlanc
Twitter @JennLeBlanc
Facebook.com/illustratedromance